THE OCTOBER BOYS

BY ADAM MILLARD

Cover Design © 2019 by Don Noble
https://roosterrepublicpress.com

ISBN-13: 978-1-947522-02-2
ISBN-10: 1-947522-02-7

BLOODSHOT BOOKS

READ UNTIL YOU BLEED!

THE OCTOBER BOYS

ADAM MILLARD

"First of all, it was October, a rare month for boys." –
Ray Bradbury, *Something Wicked This Way Comes*

"Man is the cruellest animal." – Friedrich Nietzsche

ONE

OCTOBER 31ST, 1988
HAVERING, LONDON

The werewolf reared up, its thick brown fur buffeted by the outside wind, its howl guttural and authentic. Standing in the hallway behind the lamenting wolf, a short vampire watched nervously through the eyeholes of its plastic mask. The miniature bloodsucker clutched a large cauldron of treats—some good stuff, too, the quartet of boy-callers noted as the werewolf did its thing—and waited for the trick-or-treaters to legitimately announce themselves.

"Trick or Treat?" the four boys on the step called in unison. It came out all as one word: *Trickertreeeeeeeat?*

The werewolf stopped howling and ferally pawing at the air long enough to usher the small vampire forwards, and the vampire held out the treat cauldron as if it were a ticking time-bomb. Clearly the wearer of the Bela Lugosi mask was not a fan of Halloween, unlike the werewolf—perhaps the Lugosi boy's father—who had, judging by the decorations inside and out, gone to a lot of trouble. The boys had ventured through machine-created fog, past cemetery gates and foam headstones, to reach the house. This was a family which took its Halloween celebrations very seriously indeed.

"Offer them the cauldron, Jake," said the werewolf, the fur-and-rubber mask muffling his voice. "They're not real monsters, are you boys?"

The boys laughed; two of them—Luke Davis, zombified to

within an inch of his life, and Ryan Fielding, a decent Pugsley Addams—shook their heads. Despite their assurances, the Lugosi boy still appeared reluctant to draw closer. The werewolf clicked his tongue and snatched the large cauldron out of the Lugosi boy's hand.

"You'll have to forgive him," said the werewolf. "It's the first Halloween we've dressed up for, and it's really freaking him out." He crouched down next to the Lugosi boy. "Go and help your mother with the vol-au-vents. I'll make sure the trick-or-treaters get what they deserve."

The Lugosi boy pulled the plastic mask from his face and disappeared through a door at the end of the hallway. Once he was gone, the werewolf straightened up and held out the cauldron. "Go on then," he said, now sounding a little disappointed, as if the romance had been stripped from the night by his son's apparent reticence.

The boys exchanged glances, each one waiting for the next to dip into the cauldron first. Ryan Fielding shrugged, took a dainty step forward, and grabbed a handful of treats. "Love your decorations," he said, as if the moment required something— some little observation—to fill the awkward silence which seemed to have descended.

"Yeah, no-one else in this street's bothered," Tom Craven said, adjusting his neck-bolts and wiping green face-paint from the back of his hand. "Apart from the old bloke at the end. He's put a pumpkin out. It's not a very good one, though. Hasn't even carved it. It still has the supermarket sticker on it."

"Well that's not very good, is it?" said the werewolf, dishing out treats to the three boys yet to help themselves.

"My mom says Halloween's just a stupid American holiday," said Marcus Berry as he struggled to remove his boxing gloves so that he could make a start on the snack-size chocolate bar the werewolf had just dropped into his bucket.

"Mark my words," said the werewolf, "ten years from now, this whole street, the whole *borough*, will have spooky decorations up. Halloween's going to take off big time."

Marcus smiled slightly. He had never been comforted by a werewolf before. Brightening even more, he said, "Guess who I am?"

The werewolf took a step back, appraising the black kid's costume. Boxing gloves, a stars-and-stripes robe, a black eye which the werewolf hoped was simply a make-up effect, and not something the boy had received for believing in the magic of Halloween. "I'm going to take a guess and say you're a boxer."

The boys all erupted in laughter, all except Marcus, who didn't see anything funny about being the only one of them in an ostensibly ambiguous costume. "Of course I'm a *boxer*," he said, trying not to sound hurt. "But which one?"

Sensing the boy's chagrin—and not wanting to give the poor kid's friends any further ammunition—the werewolf said the first thing which came to mind. "Ali!" he said. "You're Muhammad Ali!"

The boxer visibly deflated. "I'm Apollo Creed," he sighed. "You know, from the four Rocky films?"

"That was going to be my next guess," said the werewolf. Lying to children was easy; doing it convincingly was not. "I *love* those movies. Especially the one with Mr T."

"I don't like the one with the big Russian," said Marcus. "Apollo dies in that one."

"Marcus is going to be a boxer when he grows up," said the little zombie, Luke. "Isn't that right, Marcus?"

The werewolf didn't think it possible, but the little boxer shrank even more, as if ashamed that the subject had even arisen. He looked as if he might cry, which was the last thing the werewolf wanted: a teary-eyed boy standing on his doorstep with a black eye. He did the only thing he could in that situation and thrust the large cauldron in the general direction of the boxer. "Here you go," he said. "Go on, take it."

Marcus frowned, as if unsure whether this was some sort of elaborate prank, one which would result in disappointment. He could not read the werewolf's face, could not see whether there was a malicious grin beneath the fur and rubber.

"Please," said the werewolf, and Marcus had to admit, the man sounded genuine. "I doubt I'll have any more trick-or-treaters tonight. It's already pushing eight, and apart from you boys and a couple of Disney princesses, it's been a bit of a washout."

The four boys exchanged tentative glances, and then Tom Craven stepped forward to accept the cauldron and its myriad goodies. "That's really kind of you," he said, taking the cauldron by its handle. It was heavy, filled with enough sweets to last them a week, if they rationed—which they wouldn't. "We really appreciate it."

"Yeah, and it's good to see that at least someone in the area is getting in the spirit of things," Luke said, motioning to the cemetery comprising the front garden.

"It'll be even better next year," said the werewolf. "I'm going to build a crypt, and it'll be filled with all manner of nasty shit."

The boys giggled. Swear words were funny.

But as they walked away, with a full cauldron of treats and a spring in their step, they had no idea that next year—by the time the nice werewolf had erected his crypt and filled it with all manner of nasty shit—things would be very different indeed.

The sound of an ice cream truck off in the distance, incongruous for late October, was how it all began.

TWO

Tom heard it first; the faint jingling of some off-key melody dopplering through the night. For a while Tom just stood there listening, trying to figure out the tune. And then he got it; it was Pop Goes the Weasel, only not the way he had ever heard it before. Not a single note was in key, and so the tune meandered up and down, one note three octaves too low, the next an octave high. It resulted in something nightmarish, the kind of thing one might hear on the soundtrack to some bad horror movie. Tom wasn't allowed to watch horror movies, but that didn't mean he hadn't.

"What's the matter with you, Frankenstein?" Ryan had stopped stuffing penny chews into his mouth long enough to notice Tom had stopped walking behind them.

"I'm not Frankenstein," Tom said, turning his head this way and that in order to gauge just where the tinkling melody was coming from. "Frankenstein was the name of the creator, not the monster."

"So, what was the monster's name?" Ryan said, a confused expression upon his face.

"Do you guys hear that?" Tom said, holding a finger up as if testing for wind direction.

"Hear what?" Marcus said. "I can hear Ryan chewing blackjacks."

"The old man with the shitty pumpkin at the end of the street can hear Ryan chewing blackjacks," added Luke, slapping Ryan playfully on the shoulder.

"Just listen," Tom said. "There it is... I think it's coming from over there." He watched as his friends tried to figure out just what it was they were meant to be hearing, and for a moment Tom wondered whether he was hearing things. Perhaps it was tinnitus. But tinnitus didn't usually sound like Pop Goes the Weasel; at least, he didn't *think* it did.

"Is that a... is that an ice cream truck?" Luke said,

incredulous.

"Thank God for that," Tom said, heaving a massive sigh of relief. "I thought I was going mental."

"What's an ice cream truck doing out on Halloween?" Marcus said. The boxing gloves were now draped over his shoulders, the laces wrapped loosely around his neck.

Tom followed the atonal music as it moved around them— and that was the strange thing. It seemed to be circling them, had gone from left to right in less than thirty seconds.

"Whatever it is," Ryan said, "it needs tuning. Sounds bloody awful."

"It's *Pop Goes the Weasel*," Tom said, for now he was certain he was right.

"That's not *Pop Goes the Weasel*," Marcus opined. "That's Pop Goes the Chime Cassette. I think it's been chewed up by the deck."

It was only then that Tom realised it had begun to rain. October rain was not uncommon; October ice cream trucks were. "He can't be doing much business tonight," Tom said. For some reason his mouth had dried up. He licked furtively at his lips in an attempt to moisten them.

"I don't know," Marcus said. "I think it's a smart move. Think about how many kids are out tonight, trick or treating, some with their parents. All that guy has to do is pull up right next to a throng of ghouls and, wham! Easy money."

"How many trick-or-treaters have you seen tonight?" Tom asked. "According to the guy at the last house it's just us, Belle, Snow White, and Cinderella."

Marcus shrugged. He was just as clueless as his friends, it seemed.

"Are we going to knock any more doors, or what?" Luke said, pulling the hood of his coat up to cover his hair, which was already painted to his forehead in thick slices. "Getting a little bit wet just standing here."

Tom sighed. Something about that ice cream truck really bothered him, and yet there was nothing *really* strange about it, not *really*. Times were tough, people were struggling for cash, that bitch Thatcher had put more people out of work than the

Black Death. Was it so weird that some guy had chosen to make a couple of extra quid while the getting was good? "We can do a couple more," he said. "But if I'm being honest, I don't think this rain's going to stop. The green's already dripping from me, and Marcus's black eye is washed off. I'm thinking we do three more doors, then head back to Luke's. Does your dad still keep his dirty magazines in the shed?"

Luke nodded. "Behind the lawnmower. He knows Mom doesn't like gardening. Safest place to stash his filth."

Tom straightened his neck-bolts, perhaps for the final time. "We can eat some sweets, look at some ladies for a while, then I'd better get home. Mom finishes her shift at eleven. If I'm not in bed by the time she gets back, she'll have a conniption." And she would. As far as she was concerned, Tom was home watching kid-friendly horror movies with Luke. He knew he was pushing his luck already; his mother didn't often finish her shift early, but it wasn't beyond the realms of possibility. If tonight was one of those rare nights, then Tom would be in for a good hiding. He wouldn't see daylight until January, for his mother was strict. *When I say jump, you say how high* was one of her favourites. Tom thought the saying was odd, as she had never had reason to ask him to jump.

The next door they knocked went unanswered. There were people in there—Tom could see them moving around, could hear the TV blaring—but apparently trick-or-treaters were just as unwelcome as Jehovah's Witnesses or insurance salesmen. *It's not like we're trying to sell you double-glazing*, Tom thought as he knocked for the final time. They were just kids, having a little fun on Halloween. Whatever happened to spirit?

In the distance, the ice cream truck played its cacophonous chimes.

Half a pound of tuppeny rice...
Half a pound of treacle...

Tom, half-soaked from the rain, shivered. He still couldn't shake the fact that there was something odd about that truck, something... *wrong*. Every now and then it would fall silent, and Tom would forget about it, concentrate on the job at hand:

extracting treats from unwilling residents. But then it would reappear—one moment from the north, then from the south, sometimes near, others far—and Tom's blood would turn to mercury once again. It was childish, he knew, the ridiculous imagination of a twelve-year-old boy working overtime. He could see, however, that his friends were just as perturbed by those discordant bells. None of them voiced it, but each of them felt it.

Tom just wanted to go home, wash off what was left of the green face-paint, and wait for his mom to return from the hospital. She would chastise him for waiting up for her—she always did, but nine times out of ten she would settle on the sofa next to him and attempt to engage herself in whatever Tom was watching on the TV—but Tom didn't care. The whole night had been a washout, and not just because of the inclement weather.

That's the way the money goes.
Pop goes the weasel.

"I think we should call it a night," Luke said, surreptitiously checking the darkness all around them, as if searching for some hidden predator, some wild animal hiding in the shadows. Tom knew it was the chimes that had pushed them all over the edge, and now they were just children, out after dark, scared of the night the way they had been when they were six- or seven-years-old.

Every night when I go out.
The weasel's on the table.

"It is getting pretty late," Marcus said, checking his watch. It was a *Thundercats* wristwatch. Marcus had made no secret of the fact that, if he failed as a boxer, he wanted to be Lion-O when he grew up.

Take a stick and knock it off.
Pop goes the weasel.

"I'm not going to argue," Ryan said, peeling the wrapper off a blackjack and pushing the chew into his mouth. "I don't think we did too badly, considering we're surrounded by cynics." His tongue and teeth had already turned black; he looked like a demon. A fat demon wearing a stripy tee-shirt and a bad haircut.

Up and down the city road.
In and out of the eagle.

Tom suddenly realised that the chimes were drawing near again. The ice cream truck was on its way. *And it shouldn't be,* Tom thought. *It shouldn't be.* "You want to walk back to mine?" Tom asked Luke, trying to hide the fear from his voice and failing miserably. If his friends noticed, though, they didn't show it. They were probably just as frightened as he was. Four little boys, all in a row, terrified of the jaunty song. "I've got *Gremlins* on VHS. We could watch that—"

"*Gremlins* is a Christmas film," Luke said, laughing nervously.

"Not really," Tom said, annoyed that Luke was trying to wriggle out of it. Tom didn't want to walk home alone, not tonight, not with that thing out there. If he could just convince Luke that—

That's the way the money goes.
Pop goes the weasel.

Tom saw it first. It appeared at the end of the road like a phantom, its white and yellow paintwork—even from this distance—scratched and rotten. The chimes had stopped, but its engine continued to chunter away, a sonorous grumbling which was more animal than mechanical.

There it sat, at the end of the road. Watching.

"Okay, is anyone else creeped out by the spooky ice cream truck?" Black chew-juice dripped from the corners of Ryan's mouth.

Although he was scared, Tom knew they were probably just letting the night get to them. It was Halloween, after all. They were seeing monsters in everything—even a beat-up old ice cream truck. Still, he had been wrong before. Heart in mouth, he said, "We start walking. It's probably nothing, but I say we get to Marcus's house, and then—"

"Wait, *my* house?" Marcus said.

"Your house is the closest," Tom said. And it was, although

at four streets away it was still a fair walk.

Marcus thought about it for a moment, shrugged, and said, "So we're going to run away from an ice cream truck? Is that what's happening?" He shook his head, tried to force a smile, behind which the fear remained. Tom could see it; no matter how tough Marcus was trying to act.

"Do you think he sees us?" Luke asked, motioning toward the idling truck at the end of the street. "Maybe he's just waiting to make a sale. Maybe Marcus is right; tonight's a great night to earn a little extra selling cones to trick-or-treaters."

Tom shook his head, doubtful. "Let's just get to Marcus's. We can discuss the guy's strange business practices there."

They started to walk. Slowly at first, no-one quite ready to admit they were absolutely terrified of the rumbling vehicle behind them. Tom almost preferred the chimes; at least you knew where the truck was when the chimes were spilling from its speaker like

Half a pound of treacle—

something from a bad horror movie.

"Is it following?" Luke, like the rest of them, was loath to look back. What if it was right there, sneaking up on them, waiting for the right time to strike. What if its driver peered out through the windscreen, teeth blacker than Ryan's, only the whites of his eyes visible, a demonic grin upon his face? *Come and get your ice cream, little ones. Pop goes the weasel!*

"It's just sitting there," Tom said, glancing back along the street. And since it was just sitting there, didn't it prove that they were just being silly, that Halloween had burrowed under their collective skins and nothing more? But they kept on walking, nonetheless, putting as much distance between themselves and the ice cream truck as possible.

With each step Ryan took, the cauldron, heavy with treats, thumped against his bare knee. It was like a drumbeat—a death march—and Tom didn't like it one bit. He snatched the cauldron from Ryan's hand, and just before Ryan could contest, Tom said, "I'll give it you back when we get to Marcus's. Don't worry, I'm not going to eat it all on the way."

Half a pound of tuppeny rice.
Half a pound of treacle.

The chimes started up a second before the truck's engine roared, and then it was coming toward them. Speeding. Careening across the lanes as if out of control, almost barrelling into the parked cars lining the street. The lunatic behind the wheel nothing more than a shadow, a silhouette.

Tom turned to see his friends were already running. Ryan was making a strange noise, a keening, as he fled.

That's the way the money goes—
POP GOES THE WEASEL!

Tom ran, too, too afraid to turn back, to see how close the truck was. Its engine was loud, its chimes even more tuneless than they had been earlier. It was as if the sudden acceleration had taken something out of the truck, leaving it sapped of power.

At the end of the street, Marcus and Luke went one way, but for some reason Ryan took a left. Tom knew where Ryan was heading; he was making a run for his own house. But that was seven, no, eight streets away. He would never make it.

"Ryan!" Tom called, arriving at the junction already breathless, unsure which way he himself was going to run. He didn't have time to stop—the chimes grew louder to his rear and that engine! It sounded like a jetfighter, something from a war movie—and before he knew what was happening he was rushing after Marcus and Luke.

I should be at home! Tom thought as he sprinted after his friends. *I should be at home waiting for Mom, and she'll kill me! If the ice cream truck doesn't, she will!* He didn't realise it immediately, but tears were streaming down his cheeks, tracking clean lines through his faded green face-paint.

Every night when I go out.
The weasel's on the table.

"Come on, Tom!" Marcus called from the pavement. He had stopped, stood at the entrance to a thin alleyway. Luke had carried on and was halfway down the dark passage by the time Tom arrived.

Take a stick and knock it off.
Pop goes the weasel.

Tom stopped at the mouth of the alley, turned back just in time to see the ice cream truck turn left so fast that the wheels on its right side left the tarmac. A screech of brakes, and then the roar of acceleration, and off it went, its chimes dipping and rising.

Breathless and nursing a stitch in his side, Tom watched the truck as it meandered along the street, moving away from them.

Moving toward Ryan.

"It's going after Ryan," Tom said. "That's what it wanted. It wanted to split us up, and now it's going to get Ryan."

Marcus started to jog down the alleyway. "We'll call the police from my house," he said. He looked, Tom thought, so ridiculous, those boxing gloves dangling from his shoulders, that rain-drenched stars-and-stripes robe fluttering behind him as he went. It was almost surreal, and Tom felt guilty as maniacal laughter threatened to erupt from his throat.

It was shock. He was in shock, and that's why he had no control over his emotions.

Tom took one last look along the street, but the ice cream truck was gone, its jangling bells fading, and Tom knew, just knew, that he would never see Ryan Fielding alive again.

He ran down the alleyway after his friends, tired and scared and feeling guilty as hell.

THREE

OCTOBER 21ST, 2016
REDBRIDGE, LONDON

"**A**re you even listening to me, Tom?" The way she said it suggested it wasn't the first time she'd asked, but Tom had spotted the hotdog truck parked at the entrance to Valentines Park and, as was always the case when he saw one, he froze up. Memories of that night all those years ago came flooding back to him, paralysing him with fear and remorse and a sense of shame. Even though it wasn't a hotdog truck which pursued them through the streets, even though it wasn't a hotdog truck which took Ryan, even though there was nothing incongruous about seeing hotdog trucks in the middle of October, the low thrum of an idling engine always set his teeth on edge and brought gooseflesh to his skin.

"I'm sorry," Tom said, turning to Danielle, turning his back on the hotdog truck and its long line of patient customers; parents appeasing their hungry children with greasy burgers so that, if only for a few minutes while they ate, they would have complete silence; lovers almost kissing but not quite—not appropriate with so many children about—and staring dreamily into one another's eyes, oblivious to anything going on around them. "I was miles away."

"You're always miles away." There was more than a hint of frustration in his wife's tone, and was that a tear threatening at the corner of her eye? Tom didn't know what he had done, but whatever it was, Danielle was upset about it. "You haven't been listening to a damn word I've said, have you?"

Tom shrugged. The smell of charring burgers drifted under his nose, and for a moment he thought he might be sick. He hadn't felt right all day, but that damn hotdog truck, combined with Danielle's apparent anger toward him for Lord knows what reason, might be the thing to push him over the edge. "I couldn't hear you properly over the sound of that bloody truck." It was an awful excuse, and he regretted it as soon as it passed his lips. Danielle looked mortally offended; that he thought he might lie his way out of it beyond her comprehension. He knew he had to try again. Start from the beginning and try to find out what was wrong. What was wrong and how he could make it right. "I'm listening now. I'm sorry, but that damn truck—"

"I'm going to stay with my sister for a couple of weeks." Pinched lips, wide eyes, she looked like a caricature of herself. Her dark brown hair whipped across her face as the wind blustered through the square, and she cursed, spitting it out. How angry did you have to be to reproach your own hair?

Tom was, for a few seconds, lost for words. What had brought this on? What could he possibly have done that had pissed his wife off so much that 'a couple of weeks' at her sister's was the only possible answer? When he did finally manage to speak again, his voice was cracked. "I... I don't understand. What have I done—"

"Oh, come on!" Danielle said. In the queue for the hotdog truck, people turned, wanting to get a look at the domestic dispute unfolding next to the park gates. Children sniggered, as they were wont to do when such things happened in broad daylight. Danielle lowered her voice. "Things haven't been right between us for some time, Tom. You know as well as I do that we're failing. I just need a little time to recharge, time to think..."

Angrily, Tom interrupted. "It's because of the kid thing, isn't it?" It wasn't a question; it was always because of the kid thing, because he had just turned forty and she was only thirty-two, because all of her friends had children, because her sister—the one she was about to go and live with for fuck knows how many weeks, even though they despised one another at the best of times—had a whole litter of boys, and because Tom had no desire for such things. In his mind he was too old now to start raising a child. By the time the kid was ten, he'd be fifty, and far too old to kick a ball around the park. By the time the kid had left university, he'd be about to draw his pension. But that was just making excuses, trying to ignore the real reason why he didn't—

had never—wanted a child.

The ice cream truck.

He feared that sonofabitch would come back, only Tom was far too old now for that evil prick, and so it would take the next best thing. His offspring.

"It's not just that," Danielle said, though judging by the trepidation in her voice even she wasn't sure that was true. "You've been drinking a helluva lot lately, and I want you to get some help." She sighed; Tom tasted the coffee on her breath a second before the wind whipped it away. "I know things are always hard for you at this time of year but drinking yourself into a stupor most nights isn't going to help. Do you have any idea what it's like? I'm scared to talk to you, in case you fly off the handle at me—"

Tom thought about protesting, but he knew she was right. He had been a little edgy recently, but didn't he have a right to be? Wasn't that his prerogative?

"—and I just think some time apart, just to figure out how best to approach this, would do us both the world of good."

It would do you the world of good, he thought caustically. *It would probably be the end of me.* Now was not the time to be alone; it was October. Halloween was fast approaching, and with that all the memories of what had happened back in '88. The only way he would get through it was ensuring he was drunk for the duration, something he could do more freely if Danielle, judgmental bitch, wasn't there to chastise him every time he refilled his glass. Now that he knew she resented it, he knew he would have no choice but to tone it down a notch. But if she wasn't there, the world was his oyster and to hell with the hangovers. *Oblivion here I come.*

"Maybe you're right," Tom said. "I have been drinking a bit too much recently, but that doesn't have anything to do with..." He trailed off there, too terrified to even finish the sentence. Staring into his wife's eyes, he could see she knew how that one was supposed to end, and he could also see that she didn't believe a word of it. It always came back to that ice cream truck, that fucking demon barrelling toward them in the night.

"I just want you to get some help," Danielle said. "This has been going on for too long now, Tom. You've spent half your life looking over your shoulder. That's no way to live. That's not fair on you and it's not fair on me." And now there was a tear; Tom could see that she was trying so hard not to completely break down. A quick glance toward the queue off to their left revealed the hotdog truck's potential customers were no longer interested in the arguing couple. They were far too busy drooling over the prospect of a heart attack wrapped in bread.

"I can get help," Tom conceded. "I can make an appointment, see the doc, get some medication." God this was hard. Had he already been aware that he had issues? Hearing the words coming from his mouth, admitting it for the very first time, was like a stab to the heart. He winced, not with pain but with shame. That he had put Danielle through this was inconceivable.

She deserved better.

He would do everything in his power to make sure she got it, even if that meant a couple of leather couch sessions with some head shrink.

"I love you, Tom," Danielle said. "We can get through this, I know we can. I just want us to be happy. I just want *you* to be happy... with me."

Tom nodded. He wanted to be happy, too. He wanted it so badly.

Pop goes the weasel, he thought.

It was going to be a tough few weeks.

* * *

OCTOBER 24TH, 2016
REDBRIDGE, LONDON

The waiting-room was just about as typical as it could be, bordering on cliché. Upon coffee tables, well-read celebrity-scandal infused magazines were stacked in piles. Pan pipes—was there anything *less* relaxing? —were pumped into the room via concealed speakers. A vending machine offered a plethora of unhealthy snacks, the thought of which turned Tom's stomach. Behind the reception-desk, a pair of ageing women wearing far too much make-up and unbelievably fake smiles discussed their events from the previous weekend: *Oh, it was lovely, June! We had the pool to ourselves, and on Sunday morning we had strawberries for breakfast!* Tom felt sick just listening.

Other than him, Doctor Kurian's morning appointments seemingly consisted of an elderly male who had chewed his fingernails to the quick and was now sucking on his thumb, a woman whose face was contorted into a perpetual frown and whose legs danced nervously as she sat waiting, and a young boy whose mother kept assuring him 'Everything's going to be okay, Simon. It's for the best... it's for the best." Simon didn't believe her, and Tom wanted to intervene, tell the poor kid the truth, that it wasn't going to be okay, that the nasty head doctor was going to extract all sorts of information from him—stuff he'd wanted to keep a lid on—and then use it against him.

The pan-pipe melody suddenly cut out, and a too-loud male voice, no doubt belonging to the shrink Kurian, filtered into the room. "Alex Wise to room one, please. Alex Wise to room one."

The nail-chewer stood up, took a deep breath, and marched toward the doors at the end of the waiting room.

Room one? How many rooms were there in this place? How many doctors, other than Kurian? Not that it truly mattered; one shrink was as good as another. Besides, Tom didn't really believe he could be helped by words and emotional confessions alone. He had agreed to see Kurian for one reason. To get back his wife. Danielle had insisted he get help, and so here he was, doing everything he could to placate her, to make her come home, to prove that he was willing.

It was all nonsense, of course.

As was the drink problem Danielle insisted he had. Tom could stop any time he wanted, but that was the thing: he didn't want to. He needed the release, needed that extra help to sleep without dreams, needed booze to steady his nerves so he could get through the day in one piece.

Just yesterday at work—a small Ford dealership, at which he talked people into buying the latest models on shitty credit terms—his boss had taken him aside and voiced some concern of his own. Martin Cook wasn't a bad boss (he always bought the sandwiches on a Saturday morning, and for three Christmases in a row had taken the entire team out for drinks) but yesterday, when he began prattling on about how the devil's whiskey had destroyed his brother-in-law, and how it would do the same to Tom if he wasn't careful, Tom wanted to punch him in the head so hard.

This wasn't about drink.

It was about doing what he could to avoid October.

Pop goes the weasel.

Twenty minutes after the nail-chewer was called into room one, he emerged looking none the better for it and, after making another appointment with the ersatz-chirpy ladies at reception, he slunk out of the building like a broken man, a part of him left behind in room one.

"Tom Craven to room one," said the voice as the panpipes were interrupted once again. Tom stood, nodded at the nervous-looking Simon for no particular reason, then made his way toward the doors leading to Kurian's office.

Kurian was an amiable-looking man. He reminded Tom of Mark Ruffalo, the guy who had played The Hulk in the Avengers movies, before he changed into a giant green monster, of course.

If the reception area had been a cliché, then Kurian's office was about as formulaic as it could be. Upon the walls, Kurian's accreditations hung in expensive-looking frames. An off-white ceramic phrenology head sat front and centre on Kurian's desk, surrounded by flyers and support leaflets. A single filing cabinet sat against the wall to Tom's right.

That's where he keeps us all, Tom thought. *That's where he stores all our fucked-up stories.* That filing cabinet probably contained more horror than Stephen King's out tray. Sitting on top of the cabinet, a stack of mind-related books stretched up toward the ceiling. Their spines—*Prescribing Guidelines: 3rd Edition, Draw on your Emotions, The Compassionate Mind*— suggested some heavy reading. E.L. James must have been shitting herself.

Tom settled himself down on a leather armchair across

from Kurian. He wasn't quite ready for the couch yet; that was reserved for people with real problems. The guys who had been molested as children by their perverted uncles; the ladies who had survived sexual encounters and yet continued to live the nightmare; the children—like Simon out in the waiting room—who secretly harboured murderous thoughts and were just one step away from becoming the next Dahmer or Gacy.

Kurian cleared his throat, glanced down at the paperwork attached to a clipboard in his lap, and said, "Mister Craven." His smile revealed two rows of perfect white teeth. "I'm just going to run through a few things with you before we start. I apologise in advance for how tedious this part it, but it's essential that I make some notes to get a better idea of your life up to now."

"I wasn't molested," Tom said, a little too defensively. Where the hell had that come from? This was a head-doctor he was dealing with; surely such a statement, spat out before proceedings were even underway, could mean only thing: he was molested. Lots.

Kurian's smile widened; Tom could now see the inside of the man's cheeks. "I'm very pleased to hear it," he said, and then he began to scribble frantically upon the page attached to the clipboard.

Tom shrank into the armchair, wishing he hadn't spoken at all.

Kurian ran through the confidentiality agreement—that he had a duty to inform the proper authorities if he believed Tom, or a member of the general public, was in danger. He quickly ran through a few basics: ethnicity, smoker/non-smoker, married/single, the kind of thing Tom had come to expect from such sessions. His GP must have worked off the same checklist.

Finally, Kurian settled back into his own chair. The leather creaked beneath his weight. He glanced once toward the clock, and then asked Tom to begin.

For the longest time, Tom sat motionless and silent in his chair. He had come all this way, had made it through the initial barrage of info-extraction, only to freeze up when it really mattered. *Way to go, Tom.*

The clock ticked steadily and inexorably on.

Tom fought to get the first word out, but when it came, and then another, and a third, he relaxed a little. It wasn't going to be a wasted journey, after all.

As he proceeded to tell the good doctor about the events of that terrible night back in '88, Kurian made plentiful notes. The frantic scratching of pen on paper was off-putting at first, but Tom quickly learned to ignore it.

When Tom explained how the ice cream truck—wraith? — barrelled toward them, intent on running them all into the ground, Kurian *uhhm*ed and *ahh*ed, nodded his head a little, as if, in his own mind, he had arrived at the crux of Tom's problem. Surviving an attempted murder had to have a negative effect on a guy's life, didn't it? Or did it? Perhaps it should work the other way, with the survivor feeling almost reborn, lucky as hell, and ready to take on the world content in the knowledge that if he could outdo death, he could pretty much do anything.

Tom paused momentarily as he recalled the moment the ice cream truck, with its clanging chimes, decided to pursue Ryan— little fat Ryan, dressed as Pugsley Addams for no other reason than he already looked like him, and it would be a shame not to capitalise on such good fortune by dressing as a generic ghoul. Little fat Ryan who would never make it to his house. Tom realised that he wasn't talking, simply running the images through his own mind like some grisly video nasty. Kurian waited patiently and Tom cleared his throat.

"It went after Ryan," Tom said with a shake of the head. "I don't know whether it was because he was the weakest of us all, or the slowest, or just that he was alone, running the wrong way when he should have been right next to us..." He trailed off there, for he knew what came next.

"Take your time," Kurian said in that relaxed monotone he had ostensibly perfected over the years.

Tom took his time.

FOUR

Marcus's house was a terraced affair, wedged between a pair of identical residences, and as the three of them bowled through the door, breathless and yelling at anyone near enough to hear them, Marcus's father appeared in the hallway, gripping a cricket-bat in one hand and a half-eaten sandwich in the other.

Clive Berry cut an intimidating figure, having been a semi-professional boxer himself, and then, according to Marcus, a collector for one of the most feared gangsters in East London. But standing there, seemingly unsure whether to thwack the kids who had just piled into his hallway with the cricket-bat or offer them the remains of what looked like a cheese-and-pickle wedge, he didn't look so tough.

"What the hell is going on!?" he said, his accent neither Jamaican nor Cockney, but something in-between. He lowered the cricket-bat, rested it against the doorframe to his right. "You boys scared yourselves something silly?"

Tom wanted to scream at the man, tell him to call the police before it was too late, but he knew it was already too late. Deep inside, he knew.

"Dad, there's a guy out there trying to run people over!" Marcus was doubled over trying to catch his breath; the boxing gloves around his neck almost touched the hallway carpet.

Clive Berry frowned, and in that moment, Tom could see why the man had been an enforcer for powerful people. He had that look about him, one which said there would be no second chances if you failed to stick to an agreement. According to Marcus, his father had broken more legs than osteogenesis imperfecta, whatever the hell that was.

"He try to run you over?" Clive was addressing only his son now. Of course he was. Tom and Luke were just his son's friends. If they were mangled beneath the wheels of a demonic ice cream truck, Marcus would find new friends. So it goes.

Marcus nodded and straightened up, his breath regulated enough to explain what had just happened. "It's an ice cream truck, Dad. Can you believe that? In October? But I don't think he's got ice cream to sell. We have to call the police, Dad. The sonofabitch—"

"Watch your language, boy," Clive said, lifting his hand as a warning. The threat didn't seem real with that half-eaten sandwich still clenched there.

"—he went after Ryan. Chased him down the street, Dad, and Ryan's not like us. He can't run, Dad."

"Ryan the fat one?" Clive asked, as if it mattered somehow. *Yeah, Ryan's the fat one. Make a hell of a speedbump someday, that Ryan.*

"Mister Berry, please," Tom said, not liking the sound of his own voice. Whiny, small, terrified. "If you could just call the police. I think something terrible might have happened to Ryan." He knew something terrible had happened to Ryan Fielding; there was no way on God's green earth he had outrun that truck.

Clive Berry motioned toward the living-room. "This better not be some sort of... foolish Halloween prank, boys, 'cos I ain't in the mood."

"It's not a prank, Dad," Marcus said, rushing into the living-room and snatching up the telephone from its cradle. He dialled 999 and waited a couple of seconds before speaking. Tom mouthed the words as they came out of his friend, spilled forth from his lips, a torrent of madness. When he was finished, he replaced the telephone and turned to his father, who had now finished his sandwich and simply stood there in the middle of the room, staring at the television encased in a wooden cabinet three feet to his left. Crude rubber puppets were belting out a musical number and dancing. Here was the Queen, rubberised and thumping Prince Phillip with a hammer. Tom didn't know what the show was, but it looked absolutely terrifying.

"How long did they say they'd be?" Luke asked. He looked

more like a zombie now than he had all night.

"I'll getcha some towels," Clive said, and with that he left the living-room.

After a few seconds, Marcus whispered surreptitiously, "He's gone to hide his marijuana plants."

They sat down, all three, nervous as hell and waiting for the police to arrive. On the television screen, some spitting latex politician used a combination of big and curse words to comedic effect. Just when Tom didn't think any of them were going to say anything, Luke did.

"Do you think he made it?"

Ryan. Did Ryan make it all the way home? Was he there now, damp and breathless and crying into his Mom's fat bosom, whining about the nasty ice cream truck?

Pop goes the weasel.

Tom shook his head. "That thing was doing some speed," he said. He felt guilty almost immediately.

What was he saying?

That Ryan, their best friend since they were little kids, was now nothing more than a piece of roadkill? All squashed and bloody against the kerb, with one eye in and one eye out, just like the cat they had found last summer? Is that what he was saying?

"He might have made it into someone's yard," Marcus said, unravelling the boxing gloves from his neck and draping them over the arm of the chair. "He can't run, but maybe he got behind a wall. That lunatic wouldn't drive at a brick wall, would he?" He sounded dubious.

When the police arrived ten minutes later, Clive answered the door to let them in. "I don't have a clue what's gone on out there tonight, officers." As if they were going to blame him and it was best to get his protestation out of the way first, before they got the cuffs on and dragged him toward the Panda outside. Tom wondered how many times Clive Berry had been arrested. Marcus always said his father was too smart to get caught, but that was what they all said... just before getting caught.

As yet more police officers piled into the tiny living-room, wet from the rain and stern-looking, Tom, Luke, and Marcus exchanged nervous glances. They had never seen so many uniforms in one place. There must have been three cars sitting out front, four to each car. Tom was just pleased they were taking this very seriously.

Five of the policemen stood at one end of the living-room, pretending to be involved when it was quite clear they were more occupied by the rubber puppets now dancing again on the screen.

"Turn that off, Constable Brownlee," a severe looking officer said, motioning to the TV. Constable Brownlee, looking more than a little disappointed, reached down and pushed the button on the front of the set. The puppets continued to dance for a moment before the screen went dark and they were reduced to a tiny white dot, which faded to nothing over the course of three seconds.

The severe-looking officer, a man they would come to know over the impending weeks as Sergeant Wood, ushered aside two constables and arrived at a vacant armchair. Clive Berry's armchair. If Marcus sat in that chair, he would be on the receiving end of a whooping, but Tom didn't think that same punishment would extend to the sergeant getting comfy in it now, not unless Clive Berry was feeling brave and stupid all at the same time.

"Okay, lads," Sergeant Wood said. "What's been going on?"

At first it was a competition to see who could talk the loudest and without taking enough breaths, but then Tom took over at the request of Sergeant Wood, and only then did it start to make sense.

"Did any of you get a good look at the driver?" Sergeant Wood asked. "Was he white, black, old, young—"

With a shake of the head, Tom said, "Just a shadow." What did that even mean? Just a shadow? But that was all Tom saw of the driver; a dark outline where there should have been a person. It didn't make sense, but then nothing of what had happened in the last hour did, really.

Sergeant Wood nodded and pushed himself up from the armchair. He removed his cap and wiped a bead of sweat from his balding head. Turning to one of his colleagues, he said, "I want you to head on over to the Fielding residence, make sure the son made it back okay." He turned back to Tom, Luke, and Marcus. "If what you're saying is true, I'd be surprised if we didn't have at least one decent witness. Pop Goes the Weasel, you say?"

Tom nodded.

"There can't be too many ice cream trucks out on the roads tonight," said Wood, sighing heavily. "In fact, I've never heard of something so ridiculous. It's Halloween, not Summer Solstice, for Christ's sake."

The constables began to file out of the room, thanking Clive Berry for his hospitality as they went. If only, Tom thought, they checked the spare bedroom. He was certain they would find something of interest up there, something Marcus liked to call 'Wacky Backy'.

"I suggest you boys get yourselves home," Sergeant Wood said, regarding each of them in turn. "You all live local?"

"I don't want to walk back on my own," Luke said. He looked genuinely scared; Tom had never seen his friend so frightened. Luke was one of the toughest guys at their school. He liked to brawl, and he was in all the sports teams. Luke was the kind of kid who would grow up, join the army, serve twenty years and spend the next twenty manning the door of some boisterous nightclub. And yet here he was looking as if a sudden change in wind direction would push him over the edge.

"What about you?" Sergeant Wood said. "Got far to walk?"

Tom shook his head. "Not really." He was trying to sound brave, and yet he didn't know why.

"And you?" Wood asked Marcus.

Marcus stopped chewing his nails long enough to muster a reply. "I'm already home."

Sergeant Wood turned to one of the few remaining constables—Brownlee—and said something indistinct before marching from the room.

"Come on then," Brownlee said, smiling. "Let's get you two home."

* * *

It was half-past-ten when Constable Brownlee pulled the Panda away from Tom's house. Tom raced across the driveway, gravel crunching underfoot, and arrived at the front door, out of breath and looking across both shoulders, half-expecting the ice cream truck to be there, sitting, idling, its shadowy driver standing at the hatch with a blood-drenched cone in his hand. After fumbling with his key for ten seconds or so, he managed to slip it into the chamber and turn.

The house was quiet, dark, and most importantly empty. His mother hadn't finished her shift yet, would probably be another hour or so if there was no traffic on the ring-road. Tom locked the door behind him—his mother would ask why, and he would tell her there were some kids out there being dicks, that's why—and quickly rushed upstairs to wash the faded green paint off and change into his night clothes.

He made his way downstairs just five minutes later, rushed into the living-room and over to the phone table, upon which sat the telephone, a pen, and a flowery address book filled with the names and numbers of all his mother's friends and associates.

Tom didn't need the book. He knew his friend's number off by heart. He picked up the handset, dialled, and then waited. He didn't have to wait long, however, as there came a sudden click and then a female voice said, "Hello?"

Tom didn't know what to say. He wasn't used to speaking with adults that weren't his own mother. Mrs Fielding was a nice lady, but Tom didn't really have a lot to do with her. "Erm, Mrs Fielding? It's Tom. Tom Craven…"

"Oh, Tom, is he with you!?" Mrs Fielding said. She sounded frantic all of a sudden. "The… the police are here… they're saying… I don't know what they're saying. Just tell Ryan to come home. Tell him he's not in any trouble, Tom. Just come home now…"

Tom's heart was in his mouth. Ryan had not made it back, as Tom had known he wouldn't. "Ryan's not with me, Mrs Fielding," he said, feeling like one of those doctors whose job it was to tell desperate family members that they had better set one less place at the dinner table from now on.

"Then where the fuck is he, Tom?" She was screeching now;

Tom imagined a roomful of police turning to the distraught woman. Was Sergeant Wood there? Tom wondered. "Why are *you* safe at home and he's not? Why do you kids have to go fucking around in the dark, huh? What did you think was going to happen!?"

Not this, Tom thought. Being chased by an ice cream truck with a madman behind the wheel in the middle of October was the *last* thing he'd expected as he'd pulled on his socks and shoes earlier that night.

Just then, a male voice replaced Mrs Fielding's. "Is that you, Tom Craven?"

Sergeant Wood.

So, he was there after all.

"It's me, Sergeant Wood," Tom said. Part of him had wanted to hang up instead of speaking, but to what end? He had done nothing wrong, was just ringing to check up on a dear friend.

Dear Ryan, who had not made it home and was probably all churned up as if he'd been run through a wood-chipper by now. Dear, dear, Ryan.

"I want you to hang up the phone, Tom," Wood said, calmly. "We're doing everything we can to find your friend, but you're going to have to let us to our job, okay?" Then a little lower, not much more than a whisper. "Mrs Fielding is very agitated right now, as is to be expected. Go to bed, Tom. Try to get some sleep. We'll be in touch if there is any news."

Click.

Tom stood there for a few minutes, phone in hand and a tremendous feeling of loss coursing through him. Rain hammered at the living-room window, a thousand tiny skeletal fingers.

To the police and his own mother, Ryan Fielding was missing, but Tom knew better. That sonofabitch had got him. Had mowed him down before disappearing into the night.

Finally, Tom cried, and he was still crying when his mother returned home forty-five minutes later.

FIVE

OCTOBER 24ᵀᴴ, 2016
REDBRIDGE, LONDON

Kurian paused momentarily from his note-taking and regarded Tom with a certain amount of sadness. Tom couldn't believe how much he had just told the psychiatrist; he had surprised even himself.

Could I tell him all of it? Tom wondered. There was so much more to come... so much terror yet to reveal... so much—

"Thank you for that," Kurian said. "I can't begin to imagine how difficult that was for you, but I truly think we're getting somewhere." He put down his clipboard and leaned forward. "I have a couple of questions, if you're feeling up to it? I really want to try to find out more."

Tom shrugged. It wasn't as if he had anything better to do. Danielle wasn't waiting for him back at home, ready to massage his shoulders and tell him everything was going to be okay. He had no real plans for the rest of the day. A movie marathon, perhaps, followed by a joyless five minutes of masturbation, culminating in yet another sleepless night in which the Ice Cream Man would most certainly make an appearance, in some form or other. "Go ahead," Tom said. "I really didn't... I didn't think I'd be able to tell you any of it. Might as well strike while the iron's hot."

This seemed to please Kurian. Those perfect white teeth, a brand-new cemetery of ivory tombstones, appeared once again. Tom wondered, not for the first time, how much all that fine dentistry had cost Kurian. Was psychiatry a well-paid profession? Tom had learned everything he knew about shrinks from early morning Channel Four reruns of *Frasier*. The Crane brothers always seemed to do okay for themselves. "Do you feel at all guilty for what happened that night?"

Just like that; no foreplay, no dancing around the question trying to find the right words. Straight to the point with a heated needle; Tom felt it penetrate his heart. "I feel... I feel..." What did he feel? It wasn't *his* fault, after all, that Ryan Fielding had been about sixty-pound overweight, almost a whole other twelve-year-old. It wasn't *his* fault Ryan's mother fed him all the beige stuff when she should have heeded the paediatrician's advice and served the boy up some salad once in a while. It wasn't *his* fault that the bastard behind the wheel of that ice cream truck had turned left instead of right, gone after the weakest link with his chimes a-chiming and, more than likely, a dirty hard-on in his pants.

And yet Tom *did* feel guilty. As if he had abandoned Ryan out there on that rain-soaked road; as if there was something more he could have done. "I feel like a piece of shit most days," Tom finally managed. "And not a day goes by that I don't think of Ryan Fielding trying to put some distance between himself and that fucking truck." The way his back-fat wobbled as he ran. *Faster, Pugsley, faster!* Of course, Tom kept that part to himself.

Kurian nodded along, as if he understood, but how could he? How could anyone? "And how long afterwards was it until they discovered the body? The police, I mean?"

Tom was taken somewhat aback. Had he failed to include that most important segment in his confession (and it was a confession, no matter which way you looked at it). "They *never* found a body," Tom said. "Ryan just disappeared, as if he'd never existed to begin with."

Kurian frowned, and Tom knew exactly what the psychiatrist was thinking. He was thinking People don't just vanish. They have to go somewhere. They have to exist, and continue to exist, in some form. But that was where Kurian was wrong. Ryan disappeared that night in '88 leaving nothing at all behind but an empty bedroom and a grieving mother.

"But if he was run over," Kurian said, "then surely there was some sort of evidence. If not a body, then the remains—"

"The police didn't find a *damn* thing, and still haven't to this day," Tom explained. "When Ryan's mom died just a couple of months later, she was fat too, you see, I think the police stopped looking at all. Can you believe that? It was as if they had been given permission to brush the whole thing under the rug and pretend none of it had happened. I'm still convinced that prick Wood didn't believe our account of what transpired there that night. A runaway ice cream truck in the middle of October? I mean, that's just fucking crazy, right?"

Kurian shook his head. "Nothing surprises me these days."

"Yeah, but this was thirty years ago. Kids were safe on the streets back then. At least, we thought we were." *You could leave your doors unlocked*, Tom thought. Back then there weren't paedophiles; there were just perverts. Perverts and maniac ice cream demons.

Demon.

That's what it was. Tom had made the mistake, in the beginning, of believing the thing responsible for Ryan's abduction was a man. But it wasn't a man. It was something else, something much darker, much eviller than any man could ever be.

"Tom. You don't mind if I call you Tom, do you?"

Tom shook his head; it was his name, after all. He wasn't one for formalities.

"Am I right in assuming this childhood trauma has followed you into adulthood? Always there, niggling at the back of your mind like a sore tooth?"

"I'd say that's a good assumption," Tom said. He really needed a drink. Something strong, something to numb every ounce of him. "Danielle thinks this is going to help, but I have to be honest with you, doc, I don't think anything is going to make a blind bit of difference." No negativity, Danielle had warned him just before leaving the house with a suitcase trailing behind her on squeaky castors and a taxi idling on the driveway. But it was hard not to feel anything but pessimistic. His wife was leaving him for an indeterminate amount of time, and he was about to embark on a course of treatment he neither believed in nor wanted. It was purely placatory, a way of getting Danielle to come home sooner rather than later.

Kurian didn't seem discouraged by Tom's candour; if anything, his smile grew wider. "You would be surprised how many times I've heard that in this office, Tom. Most people are sceptical about what we do here. I guarantee, maybe not now but after a couple of sessions, you'll start to feel better. It's a long process, and some people never do get to the bottom of their problems. But you already have a head-start. You know what your problem is, what made you feel this way. And that can only work in your favour."

"Lucky me," Tom murmured.

"Our time today is coming to an end," Kurian said, glancing up toward the clock for a final time, "but I would like for you to make a follow-up appointment on your way out. And try to stay positive, okay? You can't allow your childhood demons to dictate what happens to you in your adult life. You must stay—"

Just then, there came a muted tinkling. A mobile phone ringing. Doctor Kurian, seemingly embarrassed, began fumbling for it in his trouser pocket.

Fear froze Tom, paralysed him to the point that he couldn't breathe, couldn't swallow.

Kurian's ringtone...

Half a pound of tuppeny rice.

Half a pound of treacle.

It was some kind of sick joke. Someone had got to Kurian first—Danielle?—and told him all about the silly fucker who feared an old Nursery Rhyme. And Kurian must have set his ringtone accordingly. Maybe he had even arranged for this call to happen now, while Tom sat before him, spilling his guts. To what end? What was he playing at?

Maybe that was Danielle on the other end of the line, waiting for Kurian to answer so they could have a jolly good laugh about it. *You should see his fucking face!* Kurian would say. *Oh! It's amazing. He looks like he's going to cry!*

Tom tried to speak, but nothing came out. He could only watch as Kurian answered the phone, only it wasn't Kurian now. It was *him*.

The Ice Cream Man.

Where Kurian had sat only a moment ago, the Ice Cream Man now perched, feet up on the chair, knees tucked into his chest, like a bird-of-prey about to swoop. A pair of crimson eyes watched Tom as he squirmed in his chair, wriggling this way and that and moaning deep within. The rest of the Ice Cream Man was impossibly black. Vantablack, scientists would call it. The darkest black known to man, and liable to send you crazy if you stared at it for too long. His crimson eyes, set into an otherwise featureless face, didn't blink. His fingers and toes were long, spiderlike, possessed of razor-sharp nails.

This isn't happening, Tom told himself. Then what? Had he fallen asleep talking to Kurian? Was this a nightmare, or one of those terrors people talked about. Not quite asleep, not quite awake, but something in-between, where the brain—sick sonofabitch—could play tricks on you.

When the Ice Cream Man spoke, Tom prayed he would wake up before he died there in that chair, a coronary whilst sleeping. "It won't help." Deep, sonorous, something between a hiss and a grunt. "None of this will help you."

Tom had never felt so helpless in his life. At least back in '88 he had had an entire road to run along. Here, pinned to the chair and without a voice, he was vulnerable.

The Ice Cream Man rapidly twitched as he repositioned himself on Kurian's chair, his claws tearing into the black leather. "I remember you," he said. "And you will never forget me." That last part wasn't a question. "No matter how hard you try I will always be there. I'm always there. I'm coming back, Tom Craven. I'm coming back for more."

Tom screamed. He didn't think anything would come out, but it did. Finally. "You're not real!" he yelled, the movement returning to his limbs, to his shoulders and neck. Slowly, as if learning what each muscle does for the first time, it was all coming back. "No, no, no, no, no! Not real! Not real! Not—"

"Tom!"

"—real! Not! Real!"

Tom stared wide-eyed at the man sitting across from him, Kurian, and for the longest time he drew a blank. It was as if his brain had completely shut down, couldn't comprehend what had just happened, if anything.

The mobile phone in Kurian's hand was now silent. Had he answered it? Was there someone there on the other end of the line, listening to his crazed outburst?

The Ice Cream Man was gone, if he had ever been there to begin with. Now there was just Kurian, whose countenance was one of absolute bewilderment. "What just happened, Tom?"

Shaking his head, Tom tried to explain. "He was here!" he said. "Your... your phone... what's your ringtone?"

Kurian frowned. "My ringtone?"

"Your fucking ringtone, doc!"

"I don't know," he said. "It came with the phone. I haven't got around to changing it just yet. Hate technology. Wouldn't know where to start."

"It was Pop Goes the Weasel!" Tom said.

"No," said Kurian. "It wasn't." He seemed so sure of it, too.

Taking out his own phone, Tom said, "What's your number?" He was determined to prove it.

Kurian reluctantly recited his personal number, then held his phone up in the air, waiting for it to start ringing, the lines in his forehead growing deeper.

Tom finished dialling the number. "Now we'll see," he said. Could it be that Kurian's ringtone was something else entirely, a tune reminiscent of that haunting Nursery Rhyme—The Ice Cream Man's entrance music?

When the phone in Kurian's hand started ringing a second later, Tom's question was answered. The sound emitted was an automaton chime, a near-perfect rendition of Greensleeves, and it sounded nothing like Pop Goes the Weasel.

"Catchy," said Kurian, allowing the ringtone to play on as if to satisfy Tom's craving for self-humiliation. "But as you can see, it's not what you thought it was." After a few more seconds, Kurian cancelled the call and slipped the phone back into his trouser pocket.

Pushing himself to his feet—his backside was drenched with sweat, and his legs felt sore, as if he had just finished a long run—Tom apologised to the doctor and made his way toward the door.

He didn't stop, even when Kurian's concerned mollifications became a bellow. He didn't stop when the receptionists stopped discussing the previous night's soap operas and clambered to their feet to see what all the fuss was about. He didn't stop when the boy—little Simon, who would probably go on to massacre his entire family with a hatchet—began to weep, overwhelmed by the whole thing.

He didn't stop until he was half a mile away, and then he doubled over and vomited, splashing his recently polished shoes with upchuck.

I'm coming back, the Ice Cream Man had said.

Wiping stinking drool from his chin, Tom found himself making the sign of the cross, despite not setting foot in a church for over twenty-nine years.

SIX

OCTOBER 24TH, 2016
REDBRIDGE, LONDON

The house was cold when Tom returned. Was Danielle's absence having a strange effect on the thermostat? Tom didn't know, but he shivered as he entered the living-room and dropped his keys on the coffee-table with a loud clunk.

The refrigerator held a fresh six-pack of beers, and Tom downed the first one as if it were water. He set a second down on a coaster next to his car keys and took out his phone.

Would Danielle be pleased to hear from him? Probably not, but since today had been her idea it seemed only right to fill her in on what had happened. He would keep the Ice Cream Man's sudden reappearance to himself, though. That wasn't what she wanted to hear. Something like that would keep her away even longer, and that simply wouldn't do. He was scarcely surviving as it was.

After three rings, Danielle answered, not with a 'hello' but with her usual, "Tom?" It was how she answered the phone to everyone, by speaking the caller's name as a question, as if they were about to divulge some terrible news and this would somehow move things along a little more swiftly.

"Hey, babe," Tom said, trying to sound upbeat. "How's your day been so far?" She liked it when he talked about her; she liked it even more when *she* talked about her.

"Oh, not awful," she sighed. "Jayden took a pretty nasty knock to the head at school, and so we spent most of the morning at the hospital."

Jayden was Rebecca Lebbon's oldest, and Aunty Danielle's favourite—even though she wouldn't admit that to her sister. "Shit, is he okay?" Tom hoped he sounded sincere; he couldn't care less about the boy, who was always getting into scrapes. All he cared about was getting his wife back so they could draw a line underneath all this and move on. Together.

"Three stitches, but he'll be okay. Don't think there's any breaking that boy."

I'd like to prove you wrong about that, Tom thought but didn't say. "Yeah, tough as nails, that one," he said, taking the easy option.

"How did it go?" She was referring to his meeting with Doctor Kurian, but she might as well have been asking him what he'd had for breakfast, such was her coldness.

"It went well," he said. Lies had never been a problem for him. "He's a nice guy. Looks a lot like Mark Ruffalo." He picked up his beer can, took a long swig before placing it back down on the coaster. He wasn't really enjoying it. Something more burning was required to soothe his anxiety.

"Did you tell him everything?" In the background, a whole menagerie of children was bickering. Tom could hear them cursing at one another in language you'd expect to hear on a football field.

"I told him a lot," he said, which was the truth. Kurian had managed to extract more from him than even his wife, which might have had something to do with the fact he was being paid to do so. Danielle often nodded along, but deep down she wasn't taking it in. "I've got another session in a fortnight, and Kurian thinks we've laid some good foundations." *His words, not mine,* Tom thought. If it were up to Tom, he would never set foot in that office again. He still hadn't decided whether he was going to make the follow-up appointment. Not after what had happened there today.

"That's good," Danielle said. Tom could tell she wasn't really listening. She was probably too busy watching Jayden, Joel, Justice and Oscar tearing seven shades of shit out of one another. Tom would be surprised if those four kids made it to twenty without at least a stint in the slammer.

"So, when are you coming home?" He wanted to add something about the house being so terribly cold without her, but he didn't get a chance. Danielle's reply was swift and severe.

"Not for a while."

Brutal.

Tom's heart sank. Was she not missing him the way he was missing her? She couldn't be, otherwise she would do everything in her power to see him again. "Well that sucks," Tom said, trying not to sound too dejected and failing miserably. "I went to the doctor, just like you wanted me to, and—"

"You've had one session, Tom," Danielle interjected. "These things take time, and we're lucky we have that going for us. The last thing we want to do is rush this. If I come home now, nothing will be different. You'll still be drinking every night, waking up in pools of your own sweat, terrified of something that happened thirty years ago."

"Twenty-eight years ago," Tom corrected, although it wasn't important. It felt as if it were just yesterday. "So, you're saying this silliness is going to continue? You're staying away indefinitely?"

"It's not silliness, Tom," Danielle said. For the first time since their conversation began, Tom knew he had her full attention. "This is how our marriage is going to survive. You need some sort of... some sort of closure, and I'm hoping your psychiatrist will figure out way of giving it to you." She paused, and for a few seconds Tom could only listen as the sound of four boys fighting reached a crescendo. Rebecca—seemingly at the end of her tether—reproached them with a barrage of foul language, which explained where the boys had picked it up from.

And you want one of those little fuckers, Tom thought, remembering how much Danielle liked to go on about being a mother. She couldn't even cope with him, had run away at the first opportunity, how was she going to fare with a petulant little human? At least Tom could wipe his own arse.

"Look, Tom, I've got to go." She sounded distracted once again. "If you want me to come to your next appointment with you, just let me know. I'm here to support you, despite what you think of me. We're going to get through this, Tom. I know we are. We have to."

Tom sighed. He didn't want Danielle with him the next time he visited Kurian and he told her as much.

"Well, if you change your mind you just have to say. I'll call you in a couple of days, make sure you haven't burned the house down."

There would be no burning down of houses, for that suggested Tom would at least attempt to cook something, and the last thing he wanted right now was hot food, or any food for that matter.

When she hung up less than thirty seconds later, Tom sat with the phone in his lap, staring down at the screensaver. It was a selfie picture of them sitting on a boat in the middle of a lake; Tom had taken it when they'd camped at Brecon Beacons last year. In the picture, Danielle was smiling, but Tom was not. Had it always been that way? Was his wife right, that he needed to get help to save their marriage? That picture had been taken during one of the happiest moments of Tom's summer, and yet he looked as if he might cry spontaneously at any given moment.

The picture eventually faded, and then there was only a black screen.

Story of my life, Tom thought.

SEVEN

OCTOBER 24TH, 2016
BIRMINGHAM, WEST MIDLANDS

Tired, battered, and breathless, Marcus Berry moved sluggishly around the ring. He could no longer hear the crowd—chanting his name, or at least his moniker 'The Banger' as loudly as they could—but he knew they were growing restless. This fight should have been over three rounds ago, and yet his opponent was still up, still fighting, and looking a lot better than Marcus felt.

Maybe his father had been right; forty was too old to come out of retirement.

Dodging a barrage of body-shots, Marcus unleashed a powerful right jab which snapped Samuels Jr.'s head back but did nothing to take the wind out of his sails. The sonofabitch had an iron jaw, and no matter how many times Marcus connected sweetly, it was never the *coup de grâce*.

The bell put an end to the ninth, and Marcus listlessly made his way over to his corner, where his father stood waiting, a water-bottle in one hand and a towel in the other.

"You hear that?" Clive Berry said as Marcus slumped onto his stool. "They're booing. They came to see a champ, and they got a chump instead. I told you this was a stupid move, son, but you wouldn't listen—"

"Just give me the damn water," Marcus said, snatching the bottle out of his father's hand and replacing it with a bloody gum-shield.

"You're too old to fight," his father went on. "You're ruining your legacy with this shit. People would have remembered you for being Marcus 'The Banger' Berry, three times heavyweight champion of the midlands, and now what? They're going to remember you for the time you lost your fucking mind and decided to have one last fight."

"You're supposed to be encouraging me," Marcus said.

"I didn't want to be any part of this, son," Clive said. "You're making a damn fool of yourself out there. The only thing keeping me here is the fact someone's got to drive your busted-up ass home afterward."

Marcus swilled water around his mouth and spat it into the bucket at his father's feet. Saliva, pink with blood, now covered the base of the bucket. "You're getting paid for this," he reminded his father, whose addiction to buying expensive boxing memorabilia would be sated for the next month or two. "I'd appreciate a little respect."

"Respect is earned, son, and I don't respect any of this." He handed Marcus the gum-shield back and dropped onto his haunches so that they were eye to eye. "Just do me a favour, yeah, and finish this guy so we can get the hell out of here and put this all behind us."

Nodding, Marcus thought about telling his father that he planned to fight on after this, that the organisation had already lined up his next opponent, Frankie McMahon. That tonight was merely a warm-up bout, and that the real fight was going to come six months from now in London. He thought about telling his father all those things, then saw the concern etched into the old man's face and decided against it.

He climbed to his feet and jabbed the air three times. His father removed the stool and climbed from the ring, shaking his head.

Samuels Jr. was ready to go across the ring. He looked fresh, as if he could manage another twelve rounds. Marcus knew he had to knock the sonofabitch out in this one, or at least give him something to think about. On points, Samuels Jr. was winning. Marcus knew that, and so did his opponent. If this went the distance, there would only be one outcome, and that simply wouldn't do.

The bell rang, the referee stepped aside, and Marcus charged forward. The crowd—a half-filled arena of fight fans—were chanting his name again, but when Samuels Jr. connected with a heavy right hook, everything went silent once again.

Marcus was momentarily rattled; his head buzzed as his skull returned to its proper place. He threw his guard up and blocked one, two, three body-shots before swinging wildly, hoping to meet his opponent's jaw and put an end to the round, and the fight, but he missed, went over the top of Samuels Jr.'s head. From the corner, he heard his father bellowing to *Get a fucking grip, son!*

Marcus grabbed onto Samuels Jr., held him in place. The referee was already trying to break them up, and that was when Samuels Jr. whispered something into his ear which turned his legs to jelly and his blood to mercury.

"I'm coming back, Marcus."

Marcus pushed his opponent off and took three steps back. Samuels Jr. was no longer standing there. In his place, a jet-black shadow of a man. Dark red eyes—as if they had been taken out and marinated in blood before being popped back in—bore into Marcus, into his soul.

The Ice Cream Man.

Time froze, and Marcus struggled to stay up. His knees threatened to buckle. His heart raced so quickly that he feared he was in the early stages of a coronary. *This isn't real*, he told himself. He had taken one too many punches to the head and now he was hallucinating, seeing their childhood aggressor in place of Samuels Jr. Almost thirty years had passed since he'd seen that infernal face for the first time, and although it haunted his dreams—and often his waking hours—this was the most real it had ever been.

"Ah, you remember me!" said the Ice Cream Man. "This pleases me."

"You're not real," Marcus mumbled through his gum-shield, then swallowed a mouthful of bitter blood. All around the ring the crowd had fallen still, as if someone had paused real life. Marcus turned to find his father, rendered motionless in mid-shout. When he turned back, the Ice Cream Man was right in front of him, his hellish face an inch from Marcus's own. Marcus could smell the evil; sulphurous and wicked.

"I'm coming back, Marcus, for the ones who got away." A thick black tongue—split into tendrils at its tip—darted out of

The Ice Cream Man's mouth and lapped at Marcus's sweaty cheek. "I'm the dark in the corner of your room, the stench you can't quite put your finger on, the feeling you get when you're home alone."

"You're a fucking *figment*," Marcus said, but if that was the case what was happening in reality? Had he been knocked out by Samuels Jr.? Was he currently lying on the canvas, his father looming over him with the smelling-salts and a 'told you so' on his lips? Time had ceased to move forward, and that just didn't happen in real life.

"A figment?" the Ice Cream Man hissed. "I like that one. I might keep that one, if you don't mind." Then, before Marcus had time to realise what was happening, a cold black hand reached out and snatched him by the throat. His feet lifted off the canvas—all two-hundred-and-twenty-seven pounds of him, hoisted into the air as if he weighed nothing—and all Marcus could do was stare down at the monster, a monster which grew realer with each passing second. "I should have taken you twenty-eight years ago. You *and* your friends." His eyes blazed with fury now. Crimson flames danced around his eyeballs, reminding Marcus of a NASA video he had watched not too long back about sunspots. "I got one of you, though, didn't I?" he said, somehow sibilant without the required consonant. "Little fat bastard didn't know which way to run, did he?"

Marcus kicked out, but the Ice Cream Man didn't even flinch.

"You cost me dearly that year," said the demon. "But I'm coming back, Marcus, for you and your friends."

Marcus's feet were back on the canvas, and there, in front of him, stood Samuels Jr., his face contorted with rage, his fist already making its way toward Marcus's jaw. He didn't have time to throw up his guard or sidestep the imminent blow.

He didn't have time for *anything*.

Darkness came less than a second later, but, even though he was unconscious, Marcus felt every ounce of pain as his body thumped to the canvas.

* * *

OCTOBER 31ST, 1988
HAVERING, LONDON

Marcus felt a little lost once his friends and the policemen left. It was just him and his father, and his father wasn't in the best of moods; it was as if the presence of the law—in his living-room, no less, where he weighed and bagged up his weed and counted the illegal profits he made from it—had only served to fuel his rage, and Clive Berry was not what anyone would call 'chirpy and approachable' at the best of times.

"You'd better get your arse up to bed," his father said, settling down in front of the television and switching it back on. He didn't look at Marcus as he spoke, just continued flicking through the channels, looking for something to watch. He came across a boxing match; the red graphic in the corner—a large 'R'—suggested the fight had already been won by one of the fighters, and his father was simply watching the highlights.

"We almost *died* out there, Dad!" Marcus said, exasperated. Didn't his father care? Would he even have mourned if, instead of Ryan, *he* had been the one the ice cream truck mowed down?

Still focussing on the television set, which flickered intermittently as a gale blew through the street and the rain drum-rolled at the windows, his father said, "You kids sure do like to exaggerate. There wasn't no ice cream truck out tonight. I would have heard it. You and your retarded boyfriends just shit each other up real good, that's all. And if you really want to get into it, shall we talk about that fuckwit mate of yours, *Tom Craven*, and inviting every pig on the beat over for a good look around the place. Shall we talk about that?"

Marcus shrugged, though he wasn't sure why. His father was too engrossed in the fight, was already dodging left and right, throwing out weak jabs as if it were him standing there in that ring. "If Mom were here, she'd—"

That did it. Clive Berry snapped his head around, an angry owl, and bore into Marcus's eyes with unreserved fury. "You'd better apologise now, boy, or so help me God, you'll be going to bed with a sore arse and a black eye."

There were many things which pushed Clive Berry's buttons, but Marcus had learned quickly that mentioning his mother, or the night she'd been hit by a speeding Volvo and thrown twenty-five feet across the street, was undoubtedly the quickest way. Marcus seldom brought her up, but when he did, you could guarantee it was during an argument, to unceremoniously hurt his father.

To elicit *some* kind of response from him.

It never failed, and Marcus never felt guilty about it afterwards.

"I'm sorry," Marcus said, though he really wasn't. His mother would have believed him about the ice cream truck; she would have believed anything he said.

For the longest time his father just sat there, head on a swivel, anger in his bloodshot eyes. In the background, the two featherweight boxers continued to pummel one another. Marcus concentrated on the screen rather than his vexed father.

"I want you to go upstairs," his father said, "and I want you to take off that ridiculous outfit. Put the gloves back in my memorabilia room and brush your teeth. I don't want to see you again until morning." He turned his attention to the television and relaxed back into his armchair as Marcus mouthed a curse-word and left the room.

Upstairs, Marcus changed out of his Muhammad Ali costume and returned the boxing gloves—worn once by Michael Spinks, according to his father—to their case. The memorabilia room was nothing more than a spare bedroom filled to the brim with boxing ephemera: a pair of trunks once worn by Larry Holmes hung on the wall, a fading signature at the corner of the accompanying poster; a gum-shield which had once protected the teeth of Gerrie Coetzee sat encased in glass upon a waist-high shelf; a stack of *The Ring* magazine, whose earliest issue was printed in 1922 (that particular one sat behind glass) and costed only twenty US cents, according to its cover. *What would twenty cents buy you these days?* Marcus thought. A ten-pence mix? If that.

Downstairs, his father was laughing maniacally at something or other. One of the boxers must have gone down;

that never ceased to cheer the cantankerous fucker up.

Marcus left his father's memorabilia room and headed across the landing to his own room. Closing the door behind him, he found himself wondering if everyone had made it home okay; if Ryan had somehow managed to evade that careening ice cream truck. Death, for a twelve-year-old boy, was inconceivable, especially when the person doing the dying was of the same age. Would Ryan be at school tomorrow, excitedly explaining how he'd managed to outrun a maniac on four wheels?

Marcus hoped so.

The alternative didn't bear thinking about.

Intentionally not brushing his teeth—in an act of betrayal that made him feel as if he had somehow got one over on his father—Marcus readied for bed.

His sheets were cold, scratchy, and unwashed. He couldn't remember the last time his father had put them through the wash. "Mom wouldn't let them get in this state," Marcus mumbled, pulling the itchy coverlet up so that only his nose, and the features north of it, were exposed to the cold bedroom air.

He lay there awhile, listening to his father cackle and curse at the television set, watching the lights come and go beyond his *He-Man* curtains, an eerie effect resultant of passing cars. Somewhere off in the distance, the sound of sirens penetrated the night, and Marcus wondered whether they belonged to the same policemen who had, up until a half-hour ago, stood in his living-room, shaking their heads doubtfully and taking three very scared boys at their word.

No matter how hard he tried, he couldn't sleep. There were a million things he should have been doing in that moment; like trekking over to Ryan's house to see if he had returned safely. Ryan and he were not as close as Ryan and Tom, or even Ryan and Luke, but they were four corners of the same square. Take one away and the whole thing collapses.

Marcus listened as his father's laughter turned into a cough and splutter. What could be so damn funny down there? Funny enough for his father to almost choke on his own merriment?

When he was absolutely certain that sleep was not

forthcoming—and that he was wasting his time just lying there, staring at the cracks in the ceiling—Marcus threw off the covers and climbed out of bed.

It was going to be a long night.

Seating himself at his desk, which took up an entire wall of his room, Marcus flicked on the table-lamp and picked up a pencil.

When he grew up, he wanted to be a comic-book artist. He wanted to draw superheroes for a living, people like Captain America, and Judge Dredd, and Green Lantern. And though he wasn't very good now—human anatomy was awkward, and no matter how much he practiced he just couldn't get the knack of hands or feet—he knew that if he applied himself properly, he could do whatever he wanted to.

His father didn't know about his aspirations; it wasn't the kind of thing you could tell a man whose entire life revolved around boxing and drugs and making easy money, no matter how illegal it all was. Marcus had often wondered how that might go. "Hey, Dad, I'm going to be a comic-book artist when I grow up." To which is father would undoubtedly reply, "Over my dead body." The only way he would ever make his father proud was by becoming a fighter, by doing the very thing his father could not, due to a bleed on the brain he had suffered during birth. His father wanted to live vicariously through him, and how the fuck could he do that if Marcus was creating superheroes and villains all day long?

Marcus was currently working on a new character: The Sphynx. She was a little like Catwoman, and a little like Wonder Woman, but that didn't matter to Marcus. She looked great in spandex, and once he'd figured out how to do her hands and feet, she would be amazing.

He was just about to start working on a side-profile of The Sphynx when a tinkling of bells froze him stiff.

Half a pound of tuppeny rice.

Half a pound of treacle.

Leaping to his feet, Marcus rushed across to the window. Peering through a crack in the curtains, he saw the ice cream truck slowly moving down the street toward his house, but it made no sense.

Where were the cops?

It wasn't as if the sonofabitch was inconspicuous, driving around with his chimes at full volume in the middle of the night. All they had to do was follow the sound of the creepy Nursery Rhyme and they'd catch him.

That's the way the money goes.

Pop goes the weasel.

The truck pulled up to the kerb just beyond Marcus's minute front garden, and it was then that Marcus realised it was here for him.

"Dad! Dad! The ice cream truck! It's right outside!" He ran for his bedroom door, almost tripping over an untidy mess of dirty clothes he was hoping to get around to washing this week. He yanked the bedroom door open, but then something very strange happened. The door slammed shut again. Marcus pulled it open, just an inch this time before it crashed back into its frame. Downstairs, his father cursed and bellowed for him to 'Shut the fuck up and get into bed, or so help me God...'.

Marcus could no longer open the door. It was stuck fast; something was keeping it shut, keeping him trapped in his room.

Making his way over to the drawing desk he had just abandoned, Marcus picked up his sketchpad and pencil and moved back to the window. The chimes were quieter now, but that didn't make them less terrifying. Marcus was about to draw the driver, if only he could get a good look at the man, when he saw a dark shape, almost liquid, move from the front of the truck to the open hatch on the side.

"What the..." Marcus didn't get to finish his sentence as the shadowy figure spilled out onto the street via the hatch, ostensibly breaking up and coming back together in front of Marcus's disbelieving eyes.

Either he was mistaken—and he had fallen asleep after all, and this was the resulting nightmare—or he had inhaled too much of his father's wacky backy, the scent of which had begun to permeate his bedroom, which explained why his father was laughing so heartily. There was no third option as far as Marcus was concerned, because people didn't just come apart and then mesh again like that. He was not great at physics or biology, but he knew what was possible and what was science-fiction.

The figure, jet-black and ominous, stood motionless for a moment or two. It wasn't until a minute had passed that Marcus realised the fucker was trying to sniff him out. Every now and then it would throw its head back, inhaling the air all around it, trying to locate the boy who had escaped.

And then its head snapped upwards, and its eyes settled upon Marcus, partially concealed by the curtains and wishing he would wake up already.

A voice, wet—as if its speaker was talking through its owns bile—suddenly filled Marcus's bedroom. Startled, he turned to face the semi-darkness, expecting to find the figure standing there. But the room was empty; the thing, whatever the hell it was, was still down at street level. "No essssscape," it said. "Now or later, your choice."

It wasn't much of a choice. It wasn't *any* kind of choice. It wasn't fucking *happening*! It couldn't be.

"No," Marcus said, his voice tiny and frightened.

"Yessss," replied the voice.

How could this be? The figure was down on the street, staring up at him with glowing red eyes and its body writhing and drifting away from it like oily tendrils. How could its voice be so near, so distinct, as if it were coming from just behind him, a breathy and sibilant whisper which caused every individual hair upon his body to stand on end?

Marcus, for reasons unbeknownst to him—although he thought the police might be interested in what the truck and its driver looked like—began to sketch the apparition and the vehicle behind it. The truck was absent a number-plate; that was one of the first things Marcus thought to take down as he started drawing, but it just wasn't there.

The pencil suddenly became impossible to control; the dark figure's maw fell open to reveal several rows of impossibly sharp teeth. A grin. The pencil moved across the page, scribbling out the sketch Marcus had drawn, replacing it with thick, dark lines. Marcus gasped, fought for control of the pencil, but it was as if an invisible hand was holding it in place, making Marcus draw what *it* wanted.

And still Marcus couldn't scream for help; his voice was stifled before any noise came out.

Downstairs his father cackled obliviously away.

BEH—

Marcus watched as the letters formed on the page beneath his now-censored image, drawn by his own hand and yet not.

—IND

The temperature in the room had dropped substantially in the last minute; Marcus shivered. His breath crystalized in front of his face.

—YOU

Suddenly the pencil flew from his hand and shot across the room, so quickly that it pierced the poster .there—a large cinematic print of Will Smith as Ali—and penetrated the wall beneath.

BEHIND YOU...

Marcus, the paralysis which had rendered him unable to move for the past few minutes suddenly removed, turned around, and standing there, in the darkness at the corner of his room, was the Ice Cream Man. His incorporeal form seemed to writhe and squirm as he stepped from the shadows; thin tendrils of black lapped at the air, obsidian flames that were cold instead of hot. His eyes were burning orbs of rage, and yet the grin stretching across his face, revealing a thick black tongue and those razor-sharp fangs, was so wide it might very well have met at the back of his head.

Before Marcus could scream, before he could stamp on the floor so that his father might hear and come to his rescue, the Ice Cream Man's perpetually altering hand snapped out and latched onto his arm.

And then they were outside. Wind and rain pelted Marcus's cheeks as the Ice Cream Man dragged him unceremoniously across the ground toward the truck parked at the kerb. Digging his heels into the muddy grass, Marcus struggled to break free of the Ice Cream Man, whose grip was vice-like and staunch.

Managing a guttural appeal for help, Marcus hoped someone had heard him. He could see, through the living-room window of his quickly fading house, a figure moving around, and then his father's face appeared between the curtains.

Marcus yelled again.

Shock washed over his father's face, and then he was no longer peering through the living-room curtains. He was rushing down the path—a black knight ready to fuck the Ice Cream Man up—and calling Marcus's name.

Almost at the truck now, Marcus glanced up at the thing dragging him through the street, tried to peel the tarry fingers from his arm with his free hand.

"Marcus!"

His father was going to reach him in time; there was no way the Ice Cream Man would make it to the truck, load Marcus in, make his way around to the driving seat, and drive that thing out of there before Clive Berry got to him.

"Marcus!"

It was at that point that Marcus realised he was no longer being dragged through mud and puddles. He was lying on his back, staring up toward the darkness and the rain falling from seemingly nowhere. The ice-cold hand was no longer wrapped around his forearm; a slight stinging sensation was the only intimation that it had been there at all. Then he was being pulled up by his sodden pyjamas into a sitting position.

"What the fuck are you *playing* at, boy?" His father looked angry. He shook Marcus violently, punctuating each word with a shake of its own.

Grabbing onto his father, he pulled him in for a tight embrace. It had been so long since he had hugged his father—at least a year—and although it felt foreign, it also felt good, for he was safe now. Safe from the Ice Cream Man.

"Did you see him, Dad!" Marcus said, peeling away from his father and turning to the road. But there was no ice cream truck sitting there; no dark, ethereal man-thing making a run for it. There was only a car-lined street, tarmac peppered here and there with ever-increasing puddles, and the houses of their neighbours. "I don't... I don't understand—"

"I don't know what the hell is going on, Marcus, but I'm getting sick of your silly games—"

"You had to have seen him, Dad!" Marcus said, incredulous. "He was dragging me toward the truck!"

"What truck?"

"The ice cream truck!" Of course, now that there *was* no ice cream truck it was almost impossible to convince his father that there ever had been.

"Boy, I'm getting sick of all this talk about some phantom ice cream truck." His father pulled him to his feet and began marching him back to the house. Now Marcus knew how those guys on Death Row felt.

* * *

OCTOBER 24TH, 2016
BIRMINGHAM, ENGLAND

Marcus came to on the table in his dressing-room. Standing over him, a concerned expression deepening the myriad lines in his face, was his father. He looked older, somehow, as if Marcus's comeback fight, and subsequent loss, had aged him considerably. Behind those worried eyes was the same man, though. The man who had dragged him back to their house back in '88; the man who hadn't believed his story about the shape in his bedroom, about how he had been standing there one moment—upstairs, shivering and terrified—and then how he was outside, being yanked toward the idling ice cream truck at the kerb.

"Feeling better about yourself now, champ?" His father sounded annoyed; the question was rhetorical.

Marcus pushed himself up into a sitting position, his legs dangling over the end of the table. "What happened out there?" He couldn't remember, and although the last thing he wanted was Clive Berry's 'I told you so', he had to know how he had ended up on a table back in his dressing-room.

His father cleared his throat and began to limp slowly around the table as he spoke. "You got your ass handed to you, that's what happened." He shook his head. "You thought it would be a great idea to come out of retirement, fight without the proper training, and then step into the ring with Samuels Jr., a man who might well have been able to beat you when you were in your prime, let alone in your forties."

Marcus pawed at the bruising on the left side of his face; his right eye was almost entirely closed up, swollen. "He knocked me out?" It was a stupid question. Of course, Samuels Jr. had knocked him out.

"You weren't even defending, Marcus," his father said. "Just standing there like a wet fish. You might as well have painted a target on your damn face—"

"I saw something, Dad," Marcus said, for he had, hadn't he? He had seen that demon from all those years ago; the bastard who took Ryan.

I'm coming back...

"Did it look like a big-ass fist?" said his father, still pacing angrily around the table. "I'll bet it looked just like a big-ass fist, 'cos that's the only thing—"

"Shut up, old man!" It came out of nowhere, but it did what it was intended to; it shut the old man up. His father stood there, mouth opening and shutting like a beached fish, and it would have been comical if Marcus wasn't sore and bruised and terrified about what had just happened out there in that ring. "The fight doesn't matter. I'm... something *bad* is about to happen..."

His father smacked his mouth shut. After a few seconds he said, "I don't know what's got into you, Marcus—"

"You remember the night Ryan Fielding went missing?" Marcus cut his father's diatribe off before it even got started.

"I remember you boys came a-screaming into the house on Halloween," his father said. "Almost broke down the door. I remember your dumb friend, Craven, inviting a boatload of cops over."

"Do you remember what happened after that?" Marcus asked. "Later that night?"

Clive Berry nodded; his lips began to curl up, as if remembering the events of that night were humorous to him. "I remember whipping you good with my belt," he said, "after you tried to crawl out the house after lights-out."

Marcus remembered that, too. He hadn't been able to walk properly for a week. His father's mastery of 'the belt' was endless.

"You were babbling on and on about some bogeyman. Even as I whooped you, you kept insisting there was some... some evil shadow trying to get you." His faint smile dissipated. "I came so close to hauling you to the doc's, get your head tested. Losing that friend of yours, that Fielding boy, really fucked with your brain, you know?"

"We didn't just *lose* him, Dad," Marcus said angrily. "He was taken. Whoever was driving that truck took him, and..."

And what?

And now he's coming back for me? For Tom Craven, for Luke Davis, and for me?

The ones that got away.

The October Boys.

"Well, I hate to be the bearer of bad news, son," his father said, "but that friend of yours, the one that went missing? He's been dead for nearly thirty years by now. Probably died the same night you and your friends came barrelling through our front door. And the guy that did it? He's probably dead, too. And if he's not, then he's just an old man now, a helpless old man, still sick and twisted, but can't do anything about it."

Marcus knew that his father was wrong. That sonofabitch was no man; it was evil incarnate, an infinite malevolence that would simply exist until the end of time, or until it was stopped.

Pop goes the weasel...

"He was there tonight, Dad," Marcus said. "In the ring... that bogeyman I told you about all those years ago was in the ring with me tonight. That's why I froze up. It was like I was paralysed, and no matter how hard I tried I couldn't shake free..."

"You got knocked out by Samuels Jr.," his father interjected. "That's all that happened tonight, son. Ain't no such thing as bogeymen, or ghosts, or phantom ice cream trucks, and if you keep talking like that, I'm gonna have no choice but to drag you to the nearest asylum, you hear me?"

Marcus was half-tempted to tell his father that asylums were no longer as prevalent as they once were but thought better of it. He was wasting his time here, having this discussion with the man who hadn't believed him back then—when it was going on all around—and so was it such a surprise he still didn't believe him now, almost thirty years after the incident.

Stepping down off the table, Marcus walked slowly across to the corner, to where his clothes lay in an untidy pile. As he began to dress, his father continued to speak. Something about being too old for the ring, something else about coaching someone different for a while, Marcus wasn't really paying attention.

What he had seen tonight was real, of that he was certain. But why now? After all these years, why was the sonofabitch coming back?

Marcus knew what he had to do. He would be prepared this time, for things were different now. He was older, stronger, wiser.

This time he would fight back.

EIGHT

OCTOBER 25TH, 2016, LUTON, BEDFORDSHIRE

"Daddy! Daddy!" The quilt peeled back from Luke's face to reveal his daughter, Lydia, standing there with teddy in hand. Blinking the sleep from his eyes, Luke sighed deeply and pushed himself up into a sitting position. Beside him, Karen slept on, oblivious.

"Hey, sugar," Luke said. It was three a.m. according to the digital clock on his bedside table. Another day, another dollar. "What's the matter?"

"I keep hearing noises," Lydia said through a yawn. She was struggling to keep her eyes open. Luke wondered whether she even knew what she was doing. She had been known to sleepwalk on occasion.

Luke stood, picked up his daughter, and slowly made his way across the room. The floorboards creaked beneath their weight, but Karen didn't wake. Luke was grateful for that; she had a huge day tomorrow, the culmination of a big case that had been going on for the better part of two years, and she had worked tirelessly to make sure everything went accordingly. A rough night's sleep, however, would throw a spanner in the works, or at least take the shine off what would most likely be a successful outcome.

"What kind of noises, sugar?" They were on the landing now, and Luke knew to be careful out here. This was where his daughter liked to play before bedtime, where she set her toys out—like traps—to trip intruders or midnight toilet-visitors. But Luke had a technique. *Skating*. So long as you didn't lift your foot from the carpet, you were okay. Toys were easily brushed aside. Sure, it was noisy, but not nearly as noisy as a pained scream, followed by several curse-words, and the sound of

Barbie's stable hitting the wall.

"I don't know," Lydia said. "Like a tinkling."

Into his daughter's bedroom they went, Lydia wrapped around him like a reverse backpack. "You don't know, huh?" Luke laughed quietly. "Well, if you don't know, how am I supposed to track the noise down?"

He eased her down onto her bed, peeling her arms from his shoulders, and pulled the duvet up to her chest. He sat there next to her. It was light in here; across the room, Lydia's nightlight—perpetually on—pumped out just slightly less light than the moon. One half of his daughter's face was illuminated, while the other half remained in the shadows. It gave her an ominous mien, which was ridiculous as she was the cutest thing he had ever seen in his life.

"Daddy?"

"Yes, sugar?" Running a hand gently across the light side of her face, he realised he was no longer tired. How long would it be—how long would he lie there, staring into the darkness and listening to Karen's nasally snore—before he drifted back off? Part of him knew it was best to go downstairs, put the TV on, and hope for the best. Sleep did not come as easily as it once had, but it was amazing how quickly he sank into the dark depths of unconsciousness if one of those awful late-night gambling shows played in the background.

"Do you hear it?" Her eyes were shut now; Luke was almost positive she was sleepwalking, or sleeptalking, or something...

Tilting his head just a little, he said, "I don't hear anything, sweetie." He was whispering now, hoping there would be no follow-up questions, that his daughter would forget he was even there.

Almost thirty seconds later, when Luke was about to stand and creep toward the door like some Universal monster in an attempt to make it to the landing without waking her, Lydia said something which chilled him to his core.

"Pop goes the weasel."

Luke froze, could only watch his daughter's face as a tiny smile crept onto it.

Just a coincidence, he tried to assure himself. There was no way Lydia could know about that song, about what had happened to Daddy when he was a child. It was just one of those random things that come back to bite you when you least expect them. Like a song playing on the radio reigniting memories, feelings, of an old lover, or something olfactory—a passing perfume-drenched neck or a late-night campfire—returning to haunt you. Those things happened all the time, and—

"He's coming back for you," Lydia said, only now it wasn't Lydia. Where one side of her face had been illuminated just a moment ago, and one dark, there was now only shadow, and from within that shadow, two burning red orbs flickered and smoked like burnt-out bulbs.

Luke tried to blink the vision away, for that's all it was, all it could be. He must have been tired after all. But when he reopened his eyes, he was shocked to find the nightmare visualisation remained.

He tried to call out for Karen—to hell with her sleep! He needed help—but only a weak whimper trickled from his mouth. And on the bed, the thing that once was his daughter began to rise up, dark oily tendrils dancing through the air as she—*it*—shook free of the duvet and continued to rise, up and up, and...

Half a pound of tuppeny rice.
Half a pound of treacle.
That's the way the money goes.
Pop goes the weasel.

Up and up she went, and Luke shrank down, and down, watching as his daughter became something ancient and evil and ethereal. Something he never thought he would see again.

The thing that took Ryan.

* * *

OCTOBER 31ST, 1988, HAVERING, LONDON

Luke sat on the sofa in his dimly lit living-room, unable to make eye contact with either of his parents, whose eyes were boring into him like lasers. But why? He hadn't done anything wrong.

Would they have preferred it if he'd laid down in the road, allowing the wheels of the ice cream truck to go over him? It wasn't his fault there was a maniac on the loose, his weapon a two-tonne van. All he and his friends had done was run from it, and yet his mother and father were looking at him as if he was somehow responsible. *What did you expect, Luke? You go out after dark on Halloween, it's only a matter of time before someone tries to crush you in a Mister Whippy van...*

"I've just got off the phone to Mrs Fielding," Anne Davis said, lighting a cigarette and exhaling a plume of blue-grey smoke into the room. Luke's father, Jack, coughed uncomfortably, the way he always did when his wife lit up a cigarette, or as he liked to call them: cancer sticks. "She says Ryan still hasn't come home. The police are over there right now taking statements, and they're going to want to talk to you again, you *and* your friends."

"That's *fine*," Luke said, but it wasn't fine. Nothing about this was fine. Ryan was gone, had either been squashed by that murderous prick or... or what?

Taken?

The latter didn't bear thinking about. Why would anyone want to kidnap a twelve-year-old boy, other than to fulfil some deviant urge? Twisted images of Ryan Fielding, strapped to a gurney in the back of that ice cream truck, ran through Luke's mind like one of his View-Master reels. Here, Ryan screamed as some faceless sicko joyfully removed his teeth; there, Ryan howled as the sonofabitch drove nine-inch-nails into his kneecaps with a mallet. The bile rose in Luke's throat, and he forced the grotesque thoughts from his mind.

"It's *not* fine, Lucas," said his mother, and Luke knew how angry she was, for she had used the name printed upon his birth certificate, rather than the hypocorism. "That could have been you. It could have been us" —she motioned to herself and then Jack— "sitting here, waiting to hear from the police that you've been found... that it's not good news." She paused there, the soft light of the table-lamp across the room reflecting in her teary eyes. Jack ran a comforting hand the length of her arm, and she composed herself before continuing. "We're just glad you're okay. You're grounded, of course—"

"But we didn't do anything wrong!" Luke said, a little more indignantly than he'd anticipated.

"You almost got yourselves killed," his father said, wafting smoke away from his face with an open hand. Any moment now, Luke thought, his mother would erupt with a 'For Christ's sake, Jack, it's just a cigarette!', but for now she remained stolid.

"We were Trick or Treating, Dad!" Luke said. "It's not like we were looking for trouble."

"No," said his mother. "But trouble always seems to find you, for some reason." She was shaking, such was her anger. Luke had never noticed before, but his mother had several witchy qualities—pinched nose, wrinkles around her mouth, unkempt hair—that belied her real age. She was thirty going on fifty.

Luke had had enough for one night. He could take no more chastisement, especially since he and his friends were innocent. "Can I go to bed now?" It was almost midnight, and Luke was pretty certain his parents would expect him to go to school the following day, despite what had happened tonight. After all, it wasn't him currently lying in the back of an ice cream truck while some lunatic went at him with a chainsaw...

"Go on up," said his father. "And no TV. If I hear that damn Teenage Turtles Mutant whateveryoucallit theme tune, I'm taking the thing from your room, along with your VCR."

Luke didn't warrant the threat with a response. He had no intentions of watching TV tonight. He was too tired, too confused, and all he wanted to do was sleep and hope that things would be better come morning.

They might find Ryan, he thought. They might find him alive and well, and he would be at school tomorrow, just like his friends, and they would all have a jolly good laugh about it.

Somehow, even as the optimistic thought developed, he knew he was wrong. There would be no lunchtime laughter at school the next day, no banter amongst friends, no jokes about how Ryan had run like a sack of potatoes, because Ryan was dead.

Ryan was dead and he knew it, just like he knew the fucker

behind the wheel of that ice cream truck was pure evil, just like he knew that Tom and Marcus knew it, too.

Making a point of not bidding his parents goodnight, Luke made his way upstairs and into his room.

Just a moment ago he had been tired, but not anymore. Perhaps he was just tired of being treated like a little kid, an eight-year-old instead of the almost-teen he now was. He couldn't wait to be sixteen so that he could get the hell out of his parents' house. He would get a job down at the sorting-office, just like his uncle Ted; the pay wasn't great, and it would be even less for him as a school-leaver-cum-apprentice, but Luke didn't care. All he needed was four walls and a place to rest his head at night. There were bedsits out there; he could rent one of those, come and go as he pleased. At least in a bedsit he wouldn't have to listen to the constant bickering between his parents, the unremitting back and forth which sometimes culminated in one of them—usually his father—disappearing for a few days. And then, as if nothing had happened, his father would return and things would go on as normal.

Until the next time.

Luke couldn't understand why his parents stayed together. If they were so unhappy, why persevere? He was pretty sure it wasn't for his benefit; he would have been just as miserable if they divorced. At least if they separated, he would get twice as many birthday presents, twice as many Commodore games at Christmas.

Speaking of which, his father had made it perfectly clear that there was to be no television tonight. Strictly speaking, his Commodore 64 was not TV, and he wasn't quite ready for bed now that the opportunity presented itself.

He seated himself at his desk and powered up the computer. The monitor screen turned green, casting an alien glow into his bedroom. He pushed the *Ghosts and Goblins* floppy disk into the drive and typed LOAD "$" ,8. Then he typed LIST, which loaded the contents of the disk. He located the file he needed, then typed the command to load it.

Computers were amazing to Luke. So sophisticated. He could imagine what the computers of the future would be like, how quickly they would load games, how fantastic the graphics would be. He envisioned a computer that could be controlled by the mind; a cable inserted into a port somewhere at the rear of one's head would make gaming much more fun. There would be no more sore hands from manipulating the stubborn joystick, and if the cable was long enough, it would reach all the way across his room to where he slept. He could play without even getting out of bed.

"Come on," Luke whispered, urging the game to load. It was hit and miss; sometimes the commands would work and the game would be up and running in no time, other times there would be an error and the whole thing would freeze up.

Luke hoped this was not one of those freeze times.

There appeared on the green screen, the word '**ERROR**', and Luke deflated somewhat. Computers of the future wouldn't be this recalcitrant; there would be no errors or malfunctions. Whenever you wanted a computer of the future do something, it would damn well do it, and in super quick time.

Luke was about to remove the floppy disk and try another— *Invaders*, perhaps—when another word appeared on-screen.

WINDOW

"Window?" Luke said, frowning. What the hell did that even mean? Window to what? A window of opportunity? What?

He hit the DEL key, hoping to expunge the word, but it remained. After trying three more times, growing more impatient and confused with each attempt, Luke realised that the only way to fix this obvious error was to reboot, to switch the computer off and start from scratch. He reached for the switch on the side of the keyboard, and that was the moment a second, more ominous message, appeared.

GO NOW

And then:

WINDOW

Realising these weren't standard computer commands, Luke stood, glancing down at the green screen with a strange feeling of dread.

Something weird was happening. His computer, for whatever reason, wanted him to go to his window.

GO NOW

Across the room, his bedroom window waited beyond its curtains. Luke's heart was beating so rapidly he could hear it, or at least the quick *hush-thump* of blood in his ears. Standing there, between computer and window, fear washed over Luke. It was still Halloween, or thereabouts, and his computer was talking to him, not only that but giving him commands the way he had once commanded it.

A shrill beep emanated from the monitor speaker, and then three new words appeared in staccato bursts.

IT'S
ME.
RYAN

Luke's legs turned to jelly, for he must have fallen asleep at his desk. That was the only possible explanation for what was happening. Ryan Fielding was not talking to him through his computer, was not insisting he walk to the window. It was not possible.

But what if it was?

What if Ryan was dead, murdered by that sadistic ice cream truck's driver, and was trying to now communicate from beyond the grave? What if Ryan could help Luke, lead him to the murderer? If Ryan was dead, and that sonofabitch had killed him, then Luke wanted nothing more than to bring the sicko to justice.

He leaned across and tapped out a response on the keyboard. The fear he was experiencing led him to make one or two mistakes, but he doubted it would matter in the grand scheme of things. He was talking to a ghost, after all, and ghosts are omnipresent, or something...

DID HJE KILL YU, RY?

He felt silly for even entertaining the possibility that his friend was now some sort of spirit, utilising a Commodore 64 as a less-rudimentary Ouija board, but that was the only thing that made sense. If he wasn't asleep, dreaming this whole thing—and he no longer believed that to be the case, since everything was so lucid, so real—then he really *was* standing in front of his computer waiting for the ghost of his dead best friend to respond, and when a response did come, Luke took it like a punch to the gut.

YES

Downstairs, Luke's parents were fighting; a full-on slanging match was underway, but Luke pushed it away, turning down the volume inside his own head so that he could concentrate, so that he could accept what his friend had just told him.

Ryan was dead. His friend, gone, run over—or *worse*?—by that lunatic. Things would never be the same again; their group was down a member, and—

LUKE
WINDOW
HELP

No longer scared (it was Ryan, the boy who had been dressed as Pugsley Addams just a few hours ago, his cheeks reddened and shiny with sweat as he forced chocolate and blackjacks into his mouth) Luke made his way toward the window.

The caterwauling of his mother, seemingly angrier than his father, as was often the case, drifted up the stairs. On any other occasion, her plaintive keening would have unnerved Luke, but in that moment he didn't feel anything.

He reached the window.

He separated the curtains slightly where they met.

He peered down into the darkness.

He saw Ryan, still dressed as the tubby young offspring of Morticia and Gomez, staring up to the window, a sorrowful look painted across his face, and Luke whimpered.

For the longest time, Ryan just stood there, and Luke just watched him. His friend—one quarter of their gang—did not look like a ghost. There was no spectral aura surrounding him, no unnatural hovering as the wind buffeted him from the south. Ryan looked as solid as he ever had, and for a moment Luke wondered if his friend was dead at all.

But then Ryan lifted an arm and waved; Luke saw ghostly black tendrils trailing behind the boy's arm, and it was then that he knew he was looking at something from the other side.

Something crashed downstairs; his mother screamed. The front door slammed shut, and a few seconds later, Luke heard the family car reverse speedily out of the drive and roar away into the night.

The computer beeped noisily, urgently, and even from where he stood Luke could make out the large capital letters which had appeared.

**COME
DOWN**

Suddenly, Luke was besieged by fear. It was one thing gazing down at the ghost of his dead friend from his bedroom window; it was quite another going down there.

He turned back to the window. Ryan was now waving him down. *Come on down, mate. Just because I'm a ghost, doesn't mean we can't play...*

Sense urged Luke to go downstairs and tell his mother. She would protect him, for that was her job, wasn't it? To keep him from harm, to shield him from danger, to tell him when he was being silly...

And that was the thing, right there. She wouldn't believe him. She would tell him, in no uncertain terms, that ghosts aren't real, and that he'd better get the fuck to bed before she lost her temper. His father had already stormed off; Luke had no doubt that his mother had already opened a bottle of wine. She would be distraught and unapproachable. Certainly not in the right frame of mind to humour her son and his fantasies about dead best friends.

**I
KNOW
WHO**

KILLED
ME

Luke stared at the computer monitor, watching in awe as the words appeared.

"Oh, Ryan!" he whined.

I
WILL
TELL
YOU

Luke knew, then, that he had no choice. He made his way across the room, eased open his bedroom door, and stepped out onto the landing.

The door leading into the living-room at the bottom of the stairs was shut. Luke could just about make out the music his mother was listening to—Gene Pitney? Roy Orbison?—and it was the same music she always played when his father left.

The front door was unlocked; the keys still swung gently to and fro, as if to demonstrate just how hard his father had slammed the door as he went. Luke slipped out like a burglar, stealthy.

Quiet.

It was still raining, but not as heavily as earlier. Thunder rumbled off in the distance. A storm was on its way or had passed them by. Luke hoped for the latter.

Standing in the same place he had been a moment ago, Ryan brightened as Luke emerged from the house, as if he was seeing Luke for the first time in years, when actually they had been together only a few hours ago.

A lot had changed since then.

Ryan was dead.

Ryan was dead.

Ryan was a ghost.

Who killed you? Who killed you, Ryan?

Nothing would come out, though. Luke couldn't even breathe properly, let alone speak.

As he approached slowly, past the tyre-swing, past the row

of firs which contained their gang's den, Luke felt suddenly exposed. Apart from him and his dead friend, the street was deserted. His brain urged him to turn, to turn and run back to the house, to barricade himself in his bedroom until morning.

"You look frightened," Ryan said when Luke was close enough to hear him. His voice was not much more than a whisper, and yet it echoed around inside Luke's head as if played through a speaker. "Why?"

Why?

Luke had heard some stupid questions in his short life, but that one took the biscuit. *Why are you scared of a ghost? Why have you wet your pants, Luke?*

For he had; a warmth saturated the front of his boxers, quickly turning ice cold.

Seeing the dark patch appearing around Luke's crotch, Ryan erupted with laughter. "Oh! Deary me! You've pissed your panties, Luke!" As if it was the funniest thing he had ever seen.

Luke couldn't move, no matter how hard he tried. He knew he had had an accident, and yet it didn't bother him.

"Poor Pissy-Pants Davis! That's what they're going to call you at school! Pissy-Pants David! Pissy-Pants Davis! Pissy-Pants..."

This isn't my friend!

Luke knew—was he too late to do anything about it?—that this was not Ryan Fielding; this was something wearing his skin, an imposter—

The thing which killed him!

Luke turned and ran; the thing behind him wearing his friend's skin roared gutturally. "I'll come back!" it bellowed. "I will have you!"

Too terrified to turn around to make sure the thing was not chasing after him, Luke flung open the front door to his house, no longer mindful of the noise he made. His mother had turned the music up—"*Something's got a hold of my heart*"—so he doubted she would hear him as he slammed it shut behind him and turned the key. Without pause, he flew up the stairs and into his room. Across to the window, he peered through the crack in the curtains, but there was no *thing* pretending to be Ryan.

There was only the distant tinkling of an ice cream truck—

Pop goes the weasel

—and when Luke turned to his computer, he saw one word, flashing repeatedly and filling up the whole monitor screen.

MINE

* * *

OCTOBER 25TH, 2016
LUTON, BEDFORDSHIRE

"What the fuck are you doing, Luke!?" Karen screeched, and then she was rushing across the room through the semi-darkness, arms outstretched, reaching for their daughter and the hands wrapped tightly around her throat.

When Luke realised what he was doing, he quickly released his daughter and watched as, with eyes and mouth impossibly wide, she sucked in huge lungfuls of air. After a few seconds the colour returned to her cheeks, to her lips, which had turned an awful shade of blue.

Luke stood from the bed and backed into the corner housing Lydia's gigantic doll's house. Karen was still screeching at him as she pulled their daughter up from her bed and, after checking her over and asking if she was okay, hugged her tightly.

Then she turned to Luke—Lydia just hung there in Karen's arms like a ragdoll, or one of those ultra-realistic reborn things barren women put their life savings into—with an expression of fear and confusion etched across her face.

Luke shook his head. He didn't know what to say, couldn't remember how his hands had come to be around their daughter's throat, didn't want to admit that he had almost strangled her to death in her bed, half-covered over with her pink sheets.

"What the... fuck, Luke!?" It was Karen's turn to back away now; she moved toward the door without taking her eyes from him, as if he might suddenly snap and lunge for her. After all, he had just tried to kill their daughter, hadn't he? Who knew what he was capable of?

"I didn't..." Luke trailed off there, for he did, and there was no denying it. But why? Why had he almost throttled the life out of his precious daughter? How long had his hands been crushing her throat? Long enough for his knuckles to turn white and Lydia's lips to turn blue.

"Get the fuck out of here before I call the police!" Karen was hysterical, as was her wont, but this time she had good reason to be.

"The police?" Luke swallowed; it felt as if a handful of razorblades slipped down his throat. "Karen... I would... I would never hurt..."

But Karen was gone, through the bedroom door. Luke listened as she rushed downstairs—thump, thump, thump—and then he knew she wasn't messing around; she was going to call the police, and they would come to arrest him for attempted murder. He would spend the next decade or so staring at four walls and trying not to get raped by some overzealous muscleman from D-Block.

Before he knew it, he was rushing for the door, down the stairs, and into the living-room, where Lydia sat upon the sofa, rubbing a tiny hand over the soreness of her neck while Karen paced back and forth. Her mobile phone was clenched tightly in her right hand.

"Please, Karen!" Luke was about to approach, but when Karen shrank back like an abused housewife, summoning their daughter to her side, he decided to remain where he was. Calmly, he said, "I don't know what just happened. I... I took her back to bed, and then we were listening... listening for something..."

Pop goes the weasel.

We were listening for Pop goes the weasel.

Red-faced with anger, Karen placed herself between Luke and their daughter. "You don't know what *happened*? I'll tell you, shall I? You almost killed our daughter, Luke? If I hadn't heard her choking and come to check everything was okay, you would have succeeded!"

Luke only now realised his wife was naked. "I must have blacked out," he explained. "I would never hurt you, Lydia." He was talking directly to his frightened little girl now, appealing, hoping Lydia would explain that this was all some kind of fucked up misunderstanding. But Lydia was petrified, and seemingly glad that her mother was shielding her from further harm. Luke hated the idea his daughter was scared of him. He had never, in her eight years, laid a finger upon her, would never so much as raise his voice if it wasn't absolutely necessary, and now that was all gone—spoiled—all that trust down the drain, for now he was the man who had tried to murder her in her bed, surrounded by her favourite things.

"I want you out of this house right now!" Karen screamed. She was crying now, perhaps resigned to the fact that their marriage—the majority of which had been filled with happiness and love—was over in the blink of an eye. How could she remain with the man who had almost strangled their daughter? No amount of counselling could ever put that right.

Luke decided to give it one last shot, for there was something there, something which told him his wife knew he would never cause Lydia harm. "Something happened up there, Karen," he said. "I don't know what, but one minute... she wasn't Lydia."

Lydia was crying now, too. Luke felt like an absolute monster, a bastard, the worst father in the world.

"Lydia, do you remember what happened? While we were listening for Pop goes the weasel? Do you remember?"

"Stop it, Luke!" Karen said. "You don't get to talk to her, not after what you just did up there."

"I would never hurt her, Karen," Luke said. "You know that! You know I would never knowingly harm a hair on her head, so why don't you believe me?" He was becoming frantic, the thought of checking into some seedy budget hotel at this time of night—or worse, sleeping in the car—made him feel physically sick.

Karen wiped the tears from her eyes. "Just go," she said, composed now. "I don't... I don't know what's going on, Luke, but it's best if you just leave, until..." She left that hanging, although Luke had a good idea of what it meant.

Luke wanted to argue his case, but he knew it was no good.

Whichever way he looked at it, he had tried to kill his little girl, his princess, and Karen had every right to want him as far away as possible.

"I'm sorry," he said. The only two words he could manage.

He left the house, stopping only to grab the car keys from the hallway table.

It wasn't until he was sitting in a layby three miles away, staring at the rear end of an overnight UPS truck, that he began to cry.

Pop goes the weasel.

NINE

The kitchen was chaos. Jayden and Justice were fighting over which one of them got to eat the last of the Cheerios; Joel and Oscar were wrestling over by the counter. A tiny black-and-white TV played the early morning BBC news, and from what Danielle could gather, there had been yet another atrocity committed in some foreign country. Nothing new there, then.

While the kids wrestled and bickered and punched and tussled, Rebecca toiled away at the cooker. On the counter to her right, a stack of burnt toast looked precarious and not at all appetising. Just looking at it turned Danielle's stomach, so she turned her gaze back to Jayden and Justice sitting across the table from her, tugging a cereal box back and forth as if it contained some valuable Pokémon card, or whatever it was the kids were into these days.

"Knock it off, guys," Danielle said, and even though there was a hint of playfulness in her tone, she meant it. "Why doesn't one of you have chocolate pops? Huh?"

Justice screwed his face up. "Ergh. Because they make the milk all chocolatey, and then it doesn't taste right."

Danielle shrugged. "I thought all kids loved chocolate?" Or was that just another fallacy she had been led to believe. After all, what did she know? It wasn't as if she had any kids of her own. It wasn't as if she was a mother, or knew what kids liked and what they didn't. Thanks to Tom, the selfish bastard, she was childless and growing older by the day. And he was showing no sign of capitulation. In fact, he was stubborner now than when she'd first met him.

"I like chocolate when it tastes like chocolate," Justice

explained. "That stuff they coat the corn in? That ain't chocolate. That's the dust from Satan's nutsack."

Unable to help it, Danielle burst out laughing. "Justice!" she said. "Oh my God!"

From the cooker, and without turning away from the pan of steaming baked beans on the hob, Rebecca said, "Are you being rude again, Justice?"

"Just telling it like it is, Mom," Justice said.

"He was just telling me about Satan's balls," Danielle said.

"Snitch," Justice replied with a tiny smirk.

Rebecca, now buttering the burnt toast, said, "Justice knows all about Satan's balls, don't you, son?"

At this, Jayden punched Justice in the arm, hard enough to make him drop his spoon. "That's because Justice has had Satan's balls on his chin."

"Jayden Lebbon!" Rebecca said, placing the toast and beans on the table. "I will not have that kind of talk at the breakfast table, understood?"

Jayden nodded sheepishly, perhaps embarrassed he had been reproached in front of his Auntie Danielle. A few minutes later, though, they were all eating, all except for Danielle who really couldn't stomach anything.

"You have to eat," Rebecca said, motioning to Danielle's empty plate. "You think Tom's over at your place right now, starving himself to death with worry?"

"That's exactly what he's doing," Danielle said. She knew Tom better than anyone, knew that last night he would have drunk himself into a blind stupor and fallen asleep on the sofa. There would be no breakfast for Tom, not unless it came in a brandy glass.

"Are you and Uncle Tom going to get divorced?" Joel asked before forcing a whole slice of singed bread into his mouth.

"Joel!" Rebecca said. "Grown-ups are talking. And don't chew with your mouth open. It makes you look like a retard."

"It's okay," Danielle told Joel. "No, Uncle Tom and I aren't going to get divorced. We're just having a few problems at the moment, that's all." That's all? As if it were nothing. As if Tom's refusal to impregnate her was nothing; as if Tom's constant nightmares and walking hallucinations were nothing.

"Good," Joel said, mouth finally empty. "I like Uncle Tom. He makes me laugh."

"He makes my blood boil," Rebecca muttered under her breath. Only Danielle was meant to hear that gut-punch.

"Uncle Tom is a very funny man," Danielle said, sipping at her coffee, which was just a few shades above freezing. There had been a time, when she and Tom first got together, that everything that came out of his mouth was either a joke or a terrible pun. He always made her laugh, sometimes trying *too* hard to elicit some form of response from her, and she had loved him for it.

Now, the jokes were few and far between; Tom was either too drunk to bother, or simply didn't care whether his wife found him amusing.

"I think I should call him." Danielle added an extra sugar to her coffee and gave it a stir. If it was cold, it might as well be unhealthily sweet. The sugar, though, probably wouldn't even dissolve. She would spoon it out at the end.

"No," Rebecca said, with some finality. "You do that, he's going to think you've got nothing better to do than worry about his sorry ass."

"I don't have anything better to do than worry about his sorry ass."

"Yes, but *he* doesn't need to know that." Danielle crunched into her toast, sending black crumbs down onto her plate. With a mouth half full, she went on. "He's an adult, sis. I know, it's hard to believe it sometimes, but Tom can look after himself for a few days, or weeks, or however long it takes to get his shit together. If he's drinking as much as you say he is, then it's going to be better if you're not around. I mean, I'm not being funny, or anything, but you know how to push his buttons, and that—"

"Push his buttons?" Danielle didn't know whether that was an insult or not. "What, like I get off on making him angry?"

"I didn't say that," Rebecca said. "I just meant that your relationship is a little intense at times, and if you're around him while he's still got his head buried in the sand, it's just going to make things worse."

Her sister had a point. And if anyone knew about toxic relationships it was Rebecca, whose ex-husband Warren—father to the four boys sitting at the table, and lord knows how many others sitting at countless tables across the country—had beat her seven shades from Sunday the last three years of their marriage. Danielle had never liked that sonofabitch, not since he'd cornered her in the bathroom during a Christmas party six years earlier.

"I'm going to call him," Danielle reiterated. There was no way she could go through the day without picking up the phone to at least make sure Tom hadn't hanged himself from their faux chandelier. It would just be a courtesy call, she told herself. A quick check-in, and then she would forget about him, help Rebecca around the house, maybe go on the school-run with her, anything to keep busy.

"At least wait until we've finished breakfast," Rebecca said. To the boys, she said, "You lot don't want to hear Aunty Danielle being all lovey-dovey with Uncle Tom, do you?"

In unison, the four boys groaned and made disgusted noises. Danielle took that as a no.

"It can wait," Danielle said, her appetite returning slightly. "So, boys. Any of you got girlfriends at the moment?"

"Justice has!" Jayden said suddenly. "I've seen them holding hands."

"No, you haven't," Justice calmly said. "Because I don't have a girlfriend. Mom, tell Jayden to stop telling lies."

Rebecca shrugged and continued to eat toast. "Hey, it's nothing to be ashamed of," she said. "Unless her parents are Tories. Are her parents Tories?"

"Her parents aren't *anything*," Justice said, "because she doesn't exist." He spooned cereal into his mouth and crunched. Danielle guessed it was to drown out the ridicule his older brother was piling upon him.

"What was the name of that young lass you brought here last weekend?" Rebecca asked Jayden. "The one with all that glitter up her face?"

"Glitter?" Danielle said, smirking.

"Oh, you should have seen it, sis!" Rebecca said. "Looked

like she'd fallen into a machine at the Christmas card factory."

Jayden clearly didn't find the conversation amusing, for he sat there, shaking his head and huffing, the way teenage boys are wont to do when things aren't going accordingly. "Her name is Lena," he said, defensively, "and she's just a friend. And anyway, she prefers girls."

Danielle couldn't quite believe she was having this conversation with a boy barely out of nappies. "And how do you know that?"

"She *told* me," Jayden said. "She fancies Katie Guerlain from Science class, but I don't think Katie swings that way."

With a shocked expression, Rebecca said, "Things are changing so fast. I mean, when your Aunty Danielle and me were your age, we were throwing sticks into the canal and making a damn good afternoon of it. Kids these days already know if they're gay or lesbian or bi. If Aunty Danielle had put on a shirt, a tie, and a pair of trousers when we were kids—and I believe she did on several occasions—it was called dress-up. You do that nowadays, you're transitioning." She shook her head and sighed; Danielle couldn't help but laugh.

"I'll be sure to pass that little story on to Lena when I see her in Science this afternoon," Jayden said, rising from the table and transferring his empty bowl to the sink. Justice did the same. Joel and Oscar were manoeuvring matchbox vehicles across the table, oblivious to everything else going on around them.

Just then, someone's phone began to ring, and it was only after several seconds that Danielle realised it was hers. "Shit!" she said, fumbling for the phone in her pocket. What if it was Tom? What if Tom was contemplating doing something silly? What if she missed it, and he went ahead and killed himself? She would never be able to live with that; she was already regretting leaving him in the first place.

"Just let it ring," Rebecca said. "If it's Tom, he'll call back later. Remember, you're trying to play it aloof."

"You're trying to play it aloof," Danielle said, finally wrestling the mobile phone from her pocket. "I'm trying to save my marriage by whatever means necessary." She pushed the button to answer the call. "Hello?"

It was Tom.

It was Tom and he didn't sound as if he had been drinking, but he was good at hiding it, had always been pretty high functioning when it came to alcohol.

It was Tom and he was talking like he was going to do something, telling Danielle that he loved her and that, whatever happened, he wanted her to know that he was sorry. Sorry for everything. Sorry for being so goddamned stubborn. Sorry for drinking. Sorry for not treating her the way he should have.

It was Tom and he was sorry.

And then before Danielle knew it, Tom was gone, and she was listening to the monotone shrill of the dial-tone wondering what the hell had just happened.

"Something's wrong," Danielle said, staring at the phone in her hand as if she had no clue how it got there.

Now even Rebecca looked concerned. "What is it?" she said. "What did he say?"

Danielle shook her head. "I don't know, but he didn't sound right." She placed the phone down on the table. There was no way she could see this through, no way she could leave Tom alone while he was so vulnerable. "After we drop the kids off at school," she said, "can we swing by the house, just to make sure...?"

Make sure Tom wasn't lying in the bathtub, the water pink with his blood, his arms slashed to the wrists, wide open and congealed with blood.

"Sure," Rebecca said. "He's okay, though. You know that. Probably just feeling sorry for himself. It's probably only just sunk in that you're not there, and you're not coming home any time soon."

"Maybe," Danielle said.

But that wasn't it.

She knew Tom; something terrible had happened or was about to.

The next two hours—of Jayden and Justice and Joel and Oscar wrestling as they readied for school, wasting precious time, fighting over nothing in particular—were going to be the longest two hours of Danielle's life.

> *Please be okay, Tom*, she thought.
> *Please be okay.*

TEN

Tom showered and changed, brushed his teeth and applied a healthy dose of anti-perspirant. He felt a little better for doing so, but not much. The pins-behind-the-eyes beginning of a migraine made him want to crawl into bed, to pull the covers up over his eyes and wait for the pain to subside, but he knew he couldn't do that.

He had things to do.

After smoking three cigarettes and finishing a percolator of coffee, he locked up and began the mile-and-a-half walk to Redbridge Central Library.

It was a chilly morning; Tom's breath crystallised in front of his face as he walked. But at least it wasn't raining. The cold he could deal with; soaking wet clothes he could not.

The morning crowd were out in force. Old men made their way to the local corner-shop for their daily fix of tabloid propaganda; health freaks jogged and cycled and walked preternaturally fast through the streets; animal lovers waited patiently as their dogs cocked their legs or stooped to shit, small scented bags in hand ready to pick up after their beloved mutts. Shop shutters were noisily lifted as shopkeepers prepared for another day at the grindstone, while at the corner of Cowley Road, where Valentines Park's gates yawned open like some portal to a magical place, workmen were dropping cones and cordoning off a whole strip of pavement ready to start work, laying new tarmac or whatever pointless job the taxpayer had funded this week.

Cutting through the park, Tom thought back to his conversation with Danielle earlier that morning. Had he sounded desperate? Crazy? Had he come across as distracted?

The last thing he'd wanted to do was worry her—had in fact called her up to reassure her everything was going to be okay—but now that he thought about it, he realised how the call might have sounded from her end.

An elderly couple walking three Yorkshire terriers bade him good morning, and Tom countered with a smile and a grunt.

Would the library even be open this early? He hadn't really thought this through. The council were making cutbacks, getting rid of valuable resources in order to have enough cash in the kitty to make sure the MP's and MEP's got their annual rise come April. And the library was the first to suffer the council's wrath. At first there had been only minor changes—not opening until ten on Fridays and Saturdays, closing at noon on Sundays, the closure of the DVD documentary section—but within six months the alterations had become wholesale. Staff were made redundant, positions were filled by volunteers (old ladies with nothing but spare time and whinging husbands at home) and there were a whole lot less literary events and a whole lot more sugarcraft classes.

What if things had changed even further since Tom's last visit? Maybe they opened at seven p.m. now on Thursdays, for half-an-hour, and only then the Gardening and Cooking sections? As Tom had washed and dressed that morning, it hadn't occurred to him that the computer café would be off-limits for whatever reason, that he would be unable to do what he needed to.

Screw Danielle for taking the car, he thought. On foot, Tom was extremely limited as to where he could go and the things he could do, but he was determined to make a start.

He had to.

Tom arrived at the library and was pleasantly surprised to find the lights on. He could just make out, through the library's front window, some old biddy slipping books into spaces on half-empty shelves, smiling as she worked.

Of course she was smiling. Poor Arthur back at home wouldn't be smiling this morning, though, while his wife of fifty years put the free hours in just to get a moment's peace.

Inside, the library wasn't much warmer than outside. A

small convector heater, clearly too tiny to heat such a large environment, hummed away in the corner. From the counter where he stood, Tom could see that the desktop computers in the adjacent room had yet to be switched on.

The woman, who appeared to be working alone this morning, saw Tom standing there and, after emptying her arms of books via their corresponding shelves, made her way toward him.

"Good morning," she said, far too cheerfully for Tom's liking. Why were old people always so happy? Was it because they knew they didn't have long left, that death was just around the corner, and so there would be just a little more pain, a soupcon of misery to go, and then boom! Into the ground we go, not a problem or a care in the world?

"Morning," Tom said, noncommittally.

"Is it still raining out there?" she said, motioning to the door.

Tom didn't think it had rained all morning, but he must have been wrong, otherwise the woman wouldn't have been asking. "Not at the moment," he said.

The woman clucked her tongue; Tom didn't think it would be the last time she did it today. "It's that time of year again," she said. "You don't think you need an umbrella, but you do." She smiled, her too-white dentures reminded Tom of the scene from The Snowman, when the titular character tries in Jamie's father's falsies. "So, what can I do for you, or are you just here to browse?"

"Actually," Tom said, gesturing toward the room with the black-screened computers, "I was hoping to use one of the library computers for a few hours. I've got some stuff I need to look up."

The woman's artificial grin disappeared. "Oh, deary me," she said. "The computers are down at the moment. We've got one of them technician fellas coming in this afternoon to get us back up and running."

Shit! Tom had worked himself up, and was ready to go at it, and now this. "That's a shame," he said, unable to keep the disappointment from his voice.

"The microfiche reader's still working, if that's any good to you."

"The what?"

"It's the newspaper archive machine," the old woman said. "I'll bet you've never used one before, have you?"

Used one? Tom thought. *I didn't think they still made them.* However, a newspaper archive machine was perfect; better, even, than the computer, which would try to distract him at any given opportunity, leading him away from the job at hand with its promises of money-saving advice and one-pound auction sites. "I've never used one, but if you've got a few minutes to spare, I wouldn't mind a quick lesson?"

The woman, it turned out, had all the time in the world, and was only happy to assist. It must have felt extremely stranger for her, giving someone younger than her a guided tour of a piece of technology. Most old people Tom knew were frightened of microwaves; you so much as mention a Blu-Ray player, it's likely to result in a life-changing stroke.

But this woman, whose name—when she finally introduced herself to Tom when he was seated in front of the microfiche reader—was Margaret Banks, knew her way around this particular piece of machinery. Tom, not for the first time in his life, felt useless.

But Margaret explained how everything worked, how to load the film-rolls, how to navigate the pages, and how to rotate the image on the screen (but that, she said, shouldn't be necessary).

"This thing is amazing!" Tom said, and it was. Who would have thought, with the advancements in technology—and the readily available plethora of information provided by the World Wide Web—that an archaic machine reading microfilm would get him all excited?

"The library wants to get rid of it," said Margaret, disappointedly, "but not on my watch."

"You stand your ground, Margaret," Tom said, instantly realising how ridiculous he sounded. Margaret didn't seem to notice, for she brightened, as if he had given her crusade to retain the microfiche reader more purpose. "Well," Tom said after a few seconds of silence. "I think I'll be able to manage now."

"In that case," Margaret said, "I'll get back to my alphabetising and leave you to get on with it. If you do need any help, just give me a shout. I'm thinking the weather's going to make my day a relatively simple one."

Tom smiled, wished her well with her alphabetising, and watched as she waddled away, seemingly pleased she had been of service to at least one of a younger generation.

Right.

Down to business.

Tom cracked his knuckles—it sounded unnaturally loud in the otherwise silent library—and began scanning.

The Romford Recorder was first up, and it didn't take Tom long to locate the front page from November 1st, 1988. There, at the foot of the article, was a photograph of Ryan Fielding, looking happier than Tom ever remembered him being. The headline read: HAVERING BOY MISSING. The subtitle read: LOCAL BOY, 12, FEARED DEAD.

It hit Tom hard in the gut. He remembered reading that front page all those years ago, remembered how his mother had snatched the newspaper out of his hand and ordered him to his bedroom, recalled—with perfect clarity—how she had come up not long after and held him while he'd cried.

His entire childhood was made up of bad memories but sitting there on his bed while his mother rocked him gently back and forth... that was one of the only times he had ever truly felt safe.

As he began to read the article, mumbling out loud at first and then reverting to reading it in his head, Tom felt everything come flooding back. The pain, the uncertainty, the feeling of loss amongst the community. He remembered how, just a few days later, there had been a special assembly at school. Hundreds of kids, his age and older, gathered in the main hall for prayers. Mrs Coulter, the Head, had stood at the front of the assembly and sobbed as she read messages of hope, messages of sadness, of denial. Tom had had no idea just how popular Ryan Fielding was until that day; it seemed every kid in school had something to say about the boy whose final action was running away from a phantom ice cream truck dressed as Pugsley Addams. Marcus and Luke had sat beside Tom, shaking their heads, still unable to comprehend what had happened to their friend, listening to sad story after sad story and—if they were anything like Tom— wondering just who the fuck the madman behind the wheel of that chiming death-trap was and why he had done what he had done.

Madman?

That was not right.

The thing behind the wheel of that ice cream truck was no man. Tom knew that now. As a twelve-year-old boy, he had doubted what he saw—what he *thought* he saw. His imagination as a child had always been wild. But what he'd seen in Kurian's office yesterday, what he felt when he heard that familiar Nursery Rhyme coming from the doctor's mobile phone, that was real.

It had taken almost thirty years, but now Tom knew he wasn't going mad. What he and his friends had witnessed as kids was no product of an overactive imagination.

The Ice Cream Man was real.

I'm coming back...

He read and reread the article from November 1st and, once he knew he could glean no new information from it, moved on. There was no mention of Ryan Fielding in the November 2nd edition, or even the 3rd. But there, on the front page of The Romford Recorder November 4th edition, next to an article about fireworks safety, was a new photograph of Ryan beside a headline reading: HAVERING BOY, 12, STILL MISSING.

He would be missing for a lot longer, Tom thought.

Ryan Fielding, the local boy who went missing on Halloween, is still missing. His parents are appealing for any information which might lead to the boy being found. While the disappearance is being treated as a missing person, Sergeant Wood of Romford Police Station has not ruled out abduction.

"We are working closely with the Metropolitan Police, as well as Essex Police, in order to locate Ryan Fielding quickly and safely, however we would also like to talk to the owner of an ice cream truck, seen in the area at the time of Ryan's disappearance," Wood said in a statement released yesterday.

It was an appeal. Sergeant Wood had nothing at all, not a morsel of information, and was relying heavily on the input of local people for something—*anything*—to point him in the right direction.

It had been another waste of time. Tom thought back to those weeks following Ryan's disappearance, remembered how the police scoured the area over and over before moving on to the next. There had been a Panda parked outside the Fielding house for weeks, or so it seemed back then, and the local constabulary were even questioning students in the nurse's office at school.

Sergeant Wood had returned to question Tom on no less than three occasions, once when his mother was there. That was the time Tom remembered the most, because his mother had threatened to sue Wood for harassment, even though he was just doing his job. And besides, Tom had been there at the time of Ryan's disappearance. It made sense that Wood kept plumbing him for information, pestering him with the same tedious questions: *what was the ice cream truck's number plate*? It didn't have one. *What did the driver look like?* A shadow. *Anything suspicious about the truck?* Yeah, it was going about a hundred-miles-per-hour in a thirty zone. It was all so damn repetitive, and yet all so damn necessary.

Tom sighed. The number at the bottom of the article was several digits too short to actually work now, but he wished he could ring it. He wished he could ring it and Sergeant Wood circa 1988 would answer in that belligerent fashion Tom had grown used to back then. He would tell Wood he might as well stop looking for Ryan, for the boy was long gone, had been kidnapped by the Devil.

Or something just as evil and ethereal.

He would tell the Sergeant that search parties would prove fruitless, and that the money collected by the local churches (donations amounting nothing, in the grand scheme of things) would be better spent on a paranormal investigator, or a fucking exorcist.

Tom angrily navigated to the next page, and the one after that, and one more. There were no more articles about Ryan Fielding. Not even updates. The boy was gone, let's just all try to forget about him, yeah? Here's a nice heart-warming story about a prostitute beaten to death with a shoe. No? How about this one, December 16th, about an old lady found half-eaten by her own cats? Three months they reckon she'd been there. How's that story grab you?

Tom changed the microfiche and began looking through the Havering Post. This one featured even less on Ryan's abduction than The Romford Recorder. There wasn't even an accompanying photograph of the boy, just one of Sergeant Wood looking like he hadn't slept in months and serious as hell.

How was anyone supposed to find the boy if they didn't even know what he fucking looked like? What good would it do to let the concerned public know what the inept copper in charge of the investigation looked like? No one was looking for him. He could easily have been found in any number of pubs after finishing his shift. It was no wonder Ryan had not been found.

Again, there was a statement from Sergeant Wood, seemingly just as artificially optimistic in this one. It was his job to remain positive in the face of adversity; it was everyone else's job to call bullshit.

"Once again we are asking people for any information leading to the whereabouts of Ryan Fielding. Ryan was last seen Trick or Treating on Halloween with his friends. He was dressed in costume, that of the Addams Family's Pugsley."

There followed a whole list of Ryan's traits: height, weight, eye- and hair-colour, as if that would help. By this point, Tom knew that even Sergeant Wood had given up hope of finding Ryan alive.

'In one piece' would have been the best they could hope for, and twelve-year-old Tom thought that, though it was a macabre submission, even *that* would have been a miracle. An open casket would have been small consolation.

The Havering Post had no more news in the weeks following Ryan's disappearance, and Tom was running out of ideas. The microfiche reader was good for its time, but if you were unsure of exact dates or it didn't have what you were specifically looking for, you were screwed. At least with the World Wide Web you could sometimes fluke it. He returned to the front page with the last article on Ryan, hoping to find something he might have missed.

"Everything going okay?"

Tom almost leapt out of his skin, which seemed to amuse Margaret no end. She stood beside him, a cup of something steaming in one hand.

"Thought you might like a nice cup of tea," she said, presenting him with the cup. Tom took it and was grateful for it. "Find what you were looking for?"

Tom sipped at the tea, burning his tongue in the process and trying not to cringe at the complete absence of sugar. He hadn't always taken his tea sweet, but by god once you got used to it, it was hard to take it any other way.

"Some," Tom lied. For some reason, he didn't want to tell the old librarian the microfiche reader had turned up nothing new, that he could have gleaned more information from an outdated copy of Fortean Times. He figured it would upset her somewhat, though perhaps he was underestimating the mettle of Margaret Banks.

"Glad to hear it," she said, stooping to see what he was looking at. Part of him was embarrassed, as if the librarian had caught him with a screen full of porn. "Hey, that's Trevor!" she said, excitedly and pointing at the black-and-white photograph on the screen.

"Excuse me?" Tom frowned and leaned in to see what Margaret's liveried finger jabbed at. "You know Sergeant Wood?" It had never occurred to him that Sergeant Wood would still be around after... after what happened. As far as Tom knew, the poor bastard had retired the year after Ryan Fielding went missing; it must have been one of his last cases, and perhaps the straw that broke the camel's back.

"Know him?" Margaret snorted. "He's our number one borrower. Oh, yeah, Trevor comes in all the time, takes out a lot of stuff on..." She let the sentence trail off, as if she had already said too much. "Well, let's just say I don't approve of his choice of reading."

Tom felt as if he might be getting somewhere; where that was, he didn't know. "Don't tell me. *Harry Potter and the Half Blood Prince?*"

Margaret shook her head. "I wish." She reached for the tiny cross hanging around her neck. Tom was only now seeing it for the first time. She fairly grasped it until her bony knuckles whitened. "He takes out books on..." Another pause as she considered the confidentiality of her number one borrower. "He takes out stuff on the occult, witchcraft, supernatural stuff, a load of old hogwash, if you ask me."

How bizarre, Tom thought. Sergeant Wood had never shown any interest in that stuff when he was on the force. But every man needs a hobby when retirement comes a-calling, and surely it was more interesting than flying model aircraft on an empty field in the middle of fucking autumn.

It occurred to Tom, just then, that Margaret Banks—she of the unsweetened tea and propensity to jump out on you when you least expected it—might be able to help him.

It was worth a shot.

"Margaret, I'm going to be honest with you," Tom said. "I'm really struggling to find out what I need to know with this machine—"

"But you said—"

"But if I knew where to find Sergeant Wood—I mean, Trevor—then I really think I'd be able to get to the bottom of my little problem."

Margaret released the cross and regarded Tom with no small amount of suspicion. "I really don't think I can help you," she said. "I'm not supposed to give out lender's details, and—"

"You'd be doing me a huge favour," Tom said. "You see, Sergeant Wood and I go way back. A friend of mine went missing when I was just a kid, and Wood was the fella in charge. I just need to ask him a few questions."

"I really can't give out that kind of information," Margaret said, "but if you want, Trevor comes in most Wednesdays. Wednesdays and Saturdays are his days, and he always takes out the maximum number of books allowed. I honestly don't see how he has the time to read all of them. Unless he doesn't sleep at all, I'd say it was impossible."

Tom thought about pushing for Trevor Wood's address, but he didn't want to infuriate the librarian, who had been nothing but wonderful to him from the moment he set foot in the place. "Do you know what time he usually comes in on a Wednesday?"

Margaret nodded. "Around noon," she said. "He likes to spend the afternoon in the pub, poring over his new borrows. You'd do better to catch him there, to be honest. If he doesn't come in today, chances are he'll be there, working his way through whatever blasphemous tome he's got to hand. The Walnut Tree, it is. You know it?"

Oh, Tom knew it alright. Cheap beer, one of those smoky huts out back covered over by a three-metre parasol. It was a proper geezer's boozer, the kind of place you could catch a good fight—or be in one—if the mood struck you.

So, if Wood turned up at the library on schedule before making his way to The Walnut Tree, it would be around one by the time he arrived.

Three hours from now, Tom thought, checking his watch.

"Margaret," Tom said, pushing himself up from the chair. For a moment he forgot he was holding a cup of molten lava disguised as Breakfast Tea; over the rim it went, dripped down his knuckles. He hissed and was about to curse when he caught sight of the cross around Margaret's neck and quickly edited himself. "Ah, shiiiiii...silly me."

"Oh, dear!" Margaret said, taking the cup from him and placing it down on the desk next to the microfiche reader. "Did you burn yourself?"

"I'm okay," Tom said, wiping his hand on the seat of his jeans. "What I was going to say" —before I almost melted my fucking knuckles, he thought but didn't say— "is that you're a lifesaver. Thank you for the information, and for teaching me how to use this thing." He motioned to the antiquated machine in front of them. "And would you do me a big favour?"

"If I can."

"If Sergeant Wood—Trevor—does pay you a visit today, I'd really appreciate if you didn't mention me. I want to surprise him, if I can."

"My lips are sealed." And Tom knew they would be; Margaret was a woman of God, it seemed, true to her word as well as her religion.

"Thank you."

Three minutes later, Tom was heading for The Walnut Tree. It was early—far too early for alcohol, not that he felt like it anyway—but The Walnut Tree, like most places these days, opened early for breakfast.

Tom was desperate for a coffee.

One with sugar.

It was going to be a long day.

ELEVEN

OCTOBER 25TH, 2016
REDBRIDGE, LONDON

By the time Rebecca pulled up next to the kerb, Danielle was nervous as hell, for she had no idea what she was walking in on, what state Tom might be in. He'd sounded sober enough on the phone earlier, but that didn't mean he would be now. A couple of hours had passed since their conversation—if you could call it that—and Danielle knew Tom had access to a surfeit of spirits.

As she and Rebecca made their way through the gate and up the short path toward the house, Danielle prayed, not for the first time that morning, that Tom hadn't done anything stupid, that he was simply feeling remorseful and it had drove him to call her so early on a Wednesday morning.

"Won't he be at work?" Rebecca said just before they arrived at the front door.

"I don't think so," replied Danielle. "Tom never needs an excuse for time off. If he went to see the psychiatrist yesterday, like he said he did, then I should imagine he's taken the rest of the week as holiday, just to recover."

Rebecca sighed. "How the other half live," she said, sardonically.

Danielle thought about knocking, but then realised this was still her house, too. All her stuff was in there, including her mixed-up husband; there was no way she was going to knock on her own front door.

Still, as she pushed the key into the lock, turned it and eased the door open, she felt like a trespasser.

"Do you want me to go first?"

It was a strange thing for Rebecca to say, but Danielle knew immediately why she had said it. Do you want me to go first just in case? In case Tom's lying in a pool of his own blood? "Don't be silly," Danielle said as she ushered her sister inside and closed the door behind them. Then she began to call out. "Tom? Tom? It's just me. Is everything okay?"

No answer.

Danielle's heart began to race.

Rebecca, seemingly bored by the whole thing, paced quickly down the hall and into the living-room. "Tom?" she said. "It's Rebecca, your favourite sister-in-law." She was, in fact, his only sister-in-law, and by far his least favourite.

Danielle caught up to Rebecca and they stood there in the living-room, staring around at the furniture as if trying to figure out if any of it was missing.

After a few seconds—seconds which seemed to go on forever, Danielle thought—Rebecca said, "He's not here, but it smells like he was not too long ago."

There was a stale smoke smell lingering in the air, and the ashtray on the coffee table was filled to overflowing. Danielle grimaced at the sight of it, for Tom knew how much she loathed him smoking in the house. He would never even consider it if she was there.

But you're not, Danielle reminded herself. Tom had every right to smoke in his own house when she was staying with her sister for an unstipulated amount of time. So long as the mustiness was gone by the time she returned.

Danielle quickly realised that Tom was not home; not downstairs or up. She should have realised it the moment her key slipped effortlessly into the keyhole. If Tom *was* home, his own key would have been in the door, and her key would have met resistance.

"Where could he have gone to?" No longer concerned with the possibility that Tom was swinging from the rafters in their marital home, Danielle was now worried that he was sitting on the edge of a bridge somewhere, a few inches from the edge while he contemplated doing it.

"Could be anywhere," Rebecca said. "Should we call his work? He might have gone in, sis..."

Danielle considered Rebecca's words. "He might," she

ceded, reaching for her phone. "I just didn't think he'd be up to it, after..." She trailed off as the call went through; waiting for a reply, she didn't know what she would do if he wasn't there.

"Michael & Michael," a voice Danielle recognised as belonging to Bob Wilcott cheerfully announced. Bob was Tom's boss; typical Estate Agent manager, all confidence and bluster. Danielle had met him once or twice on Tom's work's annual Christmas dinner, and to say she didn't like him very much was an understatement.

"Hey, Bob! It's Danielle. Tom's wife—"

"Don't tell me," Bob interrupted. "Tom had a little too much to drink last night and he's not going to be in today. He's late as it is, and he knows we've got two viewings of the McKenzie place this afternoon."

Danielle closed her eyes. Tom hadn't turned up for work.

And he wasn't at home.

Then where the hell *was* he?

"Actually," Danielle said, "I was ringing to let you know that Tom's not well. He's not well at all today. He was up all night being sick. It might just be a twenty-four-hour thing, but he wanted me to tell you he's sorry about not being able to make the McKenzie viewings."

"Too sick to call and explain himself, is he?" Bob said. "I'll have to cancel those two viewings now. Did he think about that? Did he think about the commission he was about to lose on that place? I'll bet he did. Now I'm going to have to give it to someone else, and do me a favour, Danielle, since you're his messenger."

She was growing angrier by the second. How dare this prick talk to her like something he just trod in; how dare he put Tom down when Tom was having a hard time of everything at the moment. How fucking dare he!

"Tell him if he doesn't turn up for work tomorrow, he can consider himself fired, okay?"

Danielle was about to argue Tom's case when there was a click, followed by the monotonous drone of the dial-tone.

The sonofabitch had hung up on her.

"Sounds like a real nice guy," Rebecca said. She must have heard the whole thing, which didn't surprise Danielle as Bob

Wilcott only had two volume settings: loud and louder.

"He didn't show for work," Danielle told her sister, though her sister already knew that, of course. "Where the fuck is he, Bec?"

"I think we need to calm down a minute here, okay?" Rebecca said. "Despite being a selfish asshole most of the time, Tom's a sensible man. Maybe he decided to go see that head doctor of yours, what's his name?"

"Kurian."

"Yeah. If Tom's feeling like shit at the moment, wouldn't it make sense that he booked himself another session with Kurian Freud?" She smiled, seemingly pleased with herself for that one.

Danielle slowly nodded. Maybe Rebecca was right. Perhaps Tom had woken feeling a little crazy, or what if he'd had another one of those nightmares? If Tom had spent the entirety of last night being chased by imaginary ice cream trucks, wasn't there a chance he'd decided to take the bull by the horns and called up Kurian to make an urgent appointment?

Swiping the screen of the phone in her hand, Danielle navigated to Tom's profile and hit CALL. It rang, and rang, and eventually the answer machine kicked in: "Hey, this is Tom Craven. Leave a message, or don't, and I'll get back to you, or won't." It was a recording Tom had made years ago, when he'd been happy, when they had been happy. His voice had changed in the meantime; now it was tinged with melancholy and despair and, more often than not, a little fear.

Danielle waited for the beep before speaking. "Hey, Tom. Please call me as soon as you get this message, okay? Don't do anything stupid. I love you." She hung up.

"Heart-warming," Rebecca said, sarcastically.

"Come on," Danielle said, moving toward the hallway.

They left the house, and as Rebecca drove away, Danielle couldn't help looking back, just in case Tom was watching from one of the upstairs windows, waiting for them to leave before getting on to the good cutting.

TWELVE

OCTOBER 25TH, 2016
REDBRIDGE, LONDON

Tom couldn't help himself. He made it to three coffees before deciding he needed something a little stronger. After ordering a single malt from the bar, he wandered across to an empty table and sat down.

The Walnut Tree was teeming with old folk and the unemployed. It wasn't so much as a 'happy hour' more of a 'resigned despondency hour'. The atmosphere was steeped with misery as old men worked their way silently through the Times crossword, as much younger men wearing tracksuits and trainers plumbed what little money they had into one-armed-bandits. Occasionally the jackpot would drop, but instead of walking away, satisfied they had beaten the machine, in it would go again, until nothing remained. Tom had never understood the fascination with those damned machines. The games were often tedious—line up three fucking lemons, line up three 7's, three cherries gets you your money back—and the chances of winning were slim. Even slimmer if you didn't know what you were doing. As someone who fell into that category, Tom steered well clear.

Now the quiz machines he could really get behind. Those general knowledge trivia machines had become ubiquitous over the past few years, and Tom had been known to dabble when the mood struck him and he was feeling particularly clever. At least there was an element of skill involved with those games. Pop Trivia, TV & Film, History, all things Tom knew a little bit of something about. He seldom walked away without at least breaking even; many times he had even made it all the way to the jackpot questions, such was his general knowledge prowess.

The Walnut Tree didn't have one of those machines, for that would mean getting rid of one of the money-stealers, the one-armed-bandits which stripped already destitute folk of what little they had left and sent them home to their wives or girlfriends without so much as a note explaining why the kids didn't have any school dinner money next week.

Tom finished his drink and, leaving his jacket on his chair so that he kept the table, went to the bar to order another.

Upon returning, he set his drink down at the table and made his way outside, to where the filthy, the rotten, the cancer-ridden—or so the government would have you believe—crowded around a single ashtray underneath what looked like an old bus shelter. Mutterings of 'Alright, mate?' and 'Shit weather, innit?' were exchanged, and then Tom was smoking along with the rest of them, feeding his disgusting habit and trying not to make eye-contact with anyone in case it incited an unwanted conversation.

Some of the men were happy for such interaction. Tom listened as the smokers discussed the state of the country, how the Tories were only out to help the rich and to hell with the rest of the populace, how sexy Holly Willoughby was (especially on that programme with that unfunny northern muppet), and how, no matter which way you looked at it, the Russians were a terrible race of people. It was standard pub banter, not to be taken seriously. Even the vitriolic slights against the Russians were accompanied by jokes about vodka and President Putin.

Finishing his cigarette and managing to get through the whole thing without becoming party to the misogynistic and xenophobic dialogue, Tom went back inside to where his whiskey sat waiting.

Just then, as he settled back into the cushioned seat at his table, his phone began to ring. It was Danielle.

Part of him wanted to answer it, to tell her he was okay, just had a few things to take care of, but he knew she wouldn't understand. He let it ring out, and a second later the phone beeped to announce a new voicemail message in his inbox.

He listened to it, sighed, and cancelled the call.

So, she was worried about him, after all. And here he was thinking he was all on his own, that his wife had left him for good and was probably already on the lookout for a decent replacement, one who would happily give her the child she so desperately desired.

Even though the message was short, Tom felt better for having received it.

He would call her later tonight, let her know everything was okay and that he was sorry he missed her call. His phone was dead, or something like that.

The fruit-machine to Tom's right started beeping and spitting coins into the bucket. The player—a middle-aged man with a ridiculous comb-over and too-short trousers—punched the air with joy. Had he just been given the funds to pay this week's rent? Had the machine fortuitously just prevented him from getting evicted?

Obviously not, for the man began feeding the coins back in, as Tom knew he would.

Checking his watch, Tom turned his attention to the double-doors across the pub, beyond which more smokers gathered to shoot the shit and put down whichever race or religion was today's flavour of the month.

If Margaret the librarian was right, Trevor Wood's arrival at The Walnut Tree was imminent. Tom began to wonder if he would even recognise the man who had once sat in front of him at Marcus Berry's house with a look of bemusement etched across his face. Wood would be pushing seventy now, for it had been almost twenty-eight years to the day that Ryan Fielding disappeared, since the Ice Cream Man—

took him

—tried to run them all down as they knocked doors for sweeties. Things about the man would be different, not least the fact he was no longer a policeman. Thirty years could change a man. Wood's hair would be silver by now, if indeed he had any left, and the man would undoubtedly be shorter. It was a common fact that most men lose an inch by the time they reach their seventies. Then, of course, there is the height lost through stooping over, through the myriad afflictions more commonly known as 'bad back syndrome' that people of a certain age are stricken with.

Shit, he might be five-foot-nothing by now, Tom thought. Coupled with the grey or no hair, the thinning lips and inevitable jowls, and Tom began to consider his chances of recognising the ex-copper as less than good.

His glass empty, Tom quickly fetched a drink from the bar, and it was as he returned to his table that the double-doors swung open and...

It was him. It was Trevor Wood—formerly Sergeant Wood— but he was shorter even than Tom had anticipated, for he was seated upon a mobility scooter. At the front was a white basket, and within the basket were a stack of books. Wood had been to the library, just like Margaret said he would, and now he was here at The Walnut Tree looking not much different than he had back in '88. If he had walked in, instead of steering that electric contraption clumsily through the doors, Tom would have guessed the man had figured out the secrets of immortality or had a map leading all the way to the Fountain of Youth.

Shielding his face from Wood, Tom watched as the former copper traversed the tables and chairs peppered around the pub floor, apologising every now and then to those seated.

Nothing had prepared Tom for this. Why hadn't Margaret warned him? Why hadn't she told him what to expect?

Why the fuck was Trevor Wood riding around on a Geri-Jeep?

At the bar—when he finally made it—Wood didn't even have to order. A drink just suddenly materialised in front of him, as if by magic. Tom watched as Wood fished around in his jacket pocket before replacing the full pint-glass with a stack of coins.

The table across from Tom had recently been vacated, though the staff of The Walnut Tree were apparently in no rush to clear away the empty glasses, the peanut packets, the free newspaper open to its Sudoku page. Still, it was the only free table, and Tom watched as Wood pointed his scooter in its general direction, not stopping even as people said hello as he drove past the tables they were seated at. It seemed, to Tom, that Wood knew almost everyone in the pub. Didn't necessarily like any of them, judging by his indifferent countenance and the fact he blatantly ignored most of them, but knew them all the same.

By the time Wood arrived at the vacant table, much of his ale's froth was in his lap, and he cursed as he wiped it away. Tom felt bad for the guy; something terrible had happened to him in the years since that fateful Halloween night in '88, something which had resulted in his cruel disability, and it wasn't just age.

Or it might be, Tom thought, watching Wood surreptitiously and sipping at his drink. That Wood didn't look a day over fifty-five made it improbable—though not impossible—that Wood had simply succumbed to senescence more tragically than most.

Wood glanced his way, but there was nothing in it; no shred of recognition, no hint that the man sitting at the table across from him was anything but a stranger; just another jobless bum passing the time of day with cheap alcohol and scarcely edible food.

Tom was tempted to get up and leave, just put the whole thing down as a bad idea and go on with his life, but most importantly let Trevor Wood get on with his. Lord knows he looked like he needed a blast from the past like he needed a bout of septicaemia.

But Tom hadn't spent the better part of the morning waiting for Wood to show only to get up and leave.

This was important.

I'm coming back...

This was inevitable.

Pop goes the weasel.

Tom slowly stood, picked up his jacket and drink, and walked toward Wood's table, upon which the old man was now rearranging beermats as if it was the most important task of his day. It might very well have been. It might be the only important thing he does today, Tom thought.

In the next second, Wood had placed his drink down on one of the perfectly placed beermats and was about to start reading from one of his library books.

Keep walking, the voice in Tom's head said, though it was not his own voice but one he recognised. One which caused every hair on his body to stand on end, one which turned the saliva in his mouth to dust. *Don't stop, Tom Craven. He hasn't seen you yet. Out the door and up the street, back to your empty house. Wait for me there. I'm coming back...*

The voice of the Ice Cream Man.

It wasn't real, of course; at least, Tom didn't think it was. Truthfully, he was uncertain what was real and what was not anymore.

What was definitely real was the chair in front of him—one of four, since Wood remained seated upon his scooter—and the man sitting, reading the back cover of some nonfiction book and licking beer froth from his upper-lip stubble.

What was definitely real was the feeling Tom had in the pit of his stomach, almost as if he knew this had to be done. Wood had something for him, something which would help, and now was the time to found out what it was.

Tom reached Wood's table, and Wood looked up at him. "Sorry," he said. "Someone's sitting there." He motioned to the empty chair whose back Tom had placed a hand upon.

Tom smiled, hoping Wood recognised him. He didn't. "Trevor Wood?" he said. For some reason it came out as a question, even though he knew for a fact who the man was.

Wood frowned. "Do I know you?"

"You probably don't recognise me," Tom said. "I was just a boy when we last saw one another. Tom Craven?" He held out his hand, expecting Wood to shake it, if only out of courtesy. He did no such thing; instead he just stared at Tom's face, his bottom lip quivering slightly, his frown a seemingly permanent thing now.

"Tom Craven?" Wood said. "Name rings a bell, but I..." He trailed off there, and then he snapped his fingers and said, "Hell! Not Tom Craven from Havering? It *is* you, isn't it? Shit, you got old!"

Not as old as you, Tom thought but didn't say. He had always been taught to respect his elders, and no matter what, Trevor Wood would forever be an elder to him. "You haven't changed a bit," Tom said, which was a lot kinder than the alternative. "I was... erm, I was just sitting over there, wondering where I knew you from, and then it just clicked."

"I saw you when I came in," Wood said. "You were watching me, weren't you?" Tom didn't answer. "Yeah, I thought so. In fact, I knew you were. You see, Margaret Banks from the library told me I might bump into you here today. 'Lovely chap called Tom Craven, or something,' she said when I went in there to pick up some new reading material, 'came in this morning, played with the microfiche, told me he knew you'."

Tom felt incredibly uncomfortable all of a sudden, but then he realised that, despite the old crow at the library snitching on him—when he expressly told her not to—Wood had still turned up. That meant one of two things.

Either Wood was here to kick his ass, or he was here to listen to what Tom had to say.

"Look," Tom said, "I didn't know you were living in Redbridge. I was using the microfiche when the librarian looked over my shoulder and saw a picture of you on the screen. She told me she knew you, and that I—"

"I don't give two shits about any of that, Tom," Wood said, the frown lines in his forehead disappearing momentarily. "It's actually not terrible to see you after all these years. After what happened to your friend, I thought you kids might go off the rails.

So, he remembered what happened to Ryan Fielding. He had come here to see Tom, and was not, it seemed, as angry as he'd initially appeared to be. "Do you mind if I sit down?" Tom said. "I want to ask you a few questions, you know? About some of the stuff that happened back then? If that's okay with you."

Wood shook his head. "I didn't come here to talk about that stuff." He picked up his beer and swallowed half of it down in three gulps before placing the glass down on the table. "I came to see if you were okay, that's all. And you look alright, so my work here is done."

Tom took a seat anyway, placed his jacket and glass down on the table and leaned in so that only Wood heard what came next. "I'm not okay," he said. "I don't know... I don't know what's going on, but I've got a really bad feeling that whatever happened to us when we were kids is going to happen again—"

"Trust me," Wood said impatiently. "You don't want to drag all that shit up again. I mean, what happened to your friend was terrible, and all, but it was a long time ago, Tom. We didn't figure it out then, we didn't figure it out the second time, and I wasn't even there for the third or fourth. So let's just talk about sport, or—"

"What do you mean the second time?" Tom was confused. Were they even talking about the same thing? "I'm talking about Ryan Fielding. I'm talking about when Ryan went missing."

Now Wood seemed apprehensive, as if he had put his foot in something dirty and he was looking for somewhere to wipe it off. "Look, forget I said anyth—"

"Are you telling me Ryan wasn't the only kid to go missing?" Tom's heart was racing as if he'd just necked several energy drinks in quick succession. Wood couldn't even make eye-contact with him.

"I'm saying drop it," Wood said. "You were a good kid, Tom Craven. A good kid in a shitty situation, but it's best to let sleeping dogs lie, okay?"

"Trevor, I need to know," Tom said. "I saw the sonofabitch. I saw him when I visited my doctor."

"That explains a lot," Wood said.

"You know as well as I do that whatever happened to Ryan, it wasn't just a kidnapping, or a murder. He just straight up disappeared, and the thing that took him was no man." He looked into Wood's eyes, and yes! He knew it, too. Had he always known it? Had he always realised the Ice Cream Man was something else entirely? "You know something," Tom said. "You know something and you're scared to bring it up in case..."

In case he comes for you, too.

Wood sighed, turned his beer-glass around and around on its mat, anything to distract himself from the conversation. Eventually, he said, "You know I left the police force in 1989?"

Tom nodded. "Yeah, but none of us knew why. Marcus reckoned you'd lost your marbles, and Luke said he'd heard you'd run away to join the clergy, or something like that."

This elicited a tiny smirk from Wood. "The clergy, huh? I wonder where he got that from."

"Kids can be cruel," Tom said. "You drop off the map, you'd better have a decent backstory."

"Well, I'd like to say I ran away and joined the clergy," Wood said, "but it was nothing like that." He picked up his half-full glass and proceeded to wipe the condensation from its side as he spoke. "After your friend went missing, things went downhill for me fast. I don't know how much of the truth you heard—if any— but that was the worst time of my life, right there. I was married, both to my wife and to my job, but there was apparently only room for one. Pity I didn't realise that until it was too late. After Emily left me, I put all my efforts into finding Ryan, but there was no evidence, no nothing, to suggest he'd been hit by your phantom ice cream truck. We went over that street with a fine-tooth comb, more times than you could ever imagine. Some days I had three constables out there, searching for trucks like the one you described to me during that first interview. Do you have any idea how many white-and-yellow ice cream trucks there are out there? I'll give you a clue; it's a lot. We questioned so many ice cream men they all forged into one, and the only way we could be sure it was none of them was by having them play us their truck chimes. We were trying to catch them off-guard; you see. Figured we'd nail the sonofabitch by turning up unannounced and marching him out to his truck, forcing him to run the music through the speaker. Pop Goes the Weasel and we would have him, or at least enough to arrest him for questioning. But that song never came, Tom. We had 'Do Your Ears Hang Low?', 'The Entertainer', 'Turkey in the Straw'. We had 'Greensleeves' and 'It's Now or Never' and 'You Are My Sunshine'. But it was never 'Pop Goes the Weasel'. Did you know, Tom, that ice cream trucks can only play their chimes for four seconds at a time? That's all. Any longer than that and they're breaking the law. I don't think it's a law that's enforceable, but it's a real thing. Anyway, I started to lose my mind. I was letting the whole thing consume me. Mrs Fielding killed herself in '89, did you hear about that?"

Tom nodded. He knew that Ryan's mother had climbed into her car while it was still locked up in the garage, and he knew she had started the engine, slowly poisoning herself in the process. Losing Ryan had done that to her. Less than a year later and she was dead—just like her son, Tom had thought at the time.

"I don't know what happened, but I knew that the only way to get away from it all was to quit. When Cassie Fielding took her own life, it was as if I had been handed a 'Get Out of Jail Free' card. I could stop looking for Ryan now, because his mother was dead. I was angry at myself for being such a selfish prick, but I just wanted to make a clean break of it, and since I had nothing to prove to anyone now that Cassie was gone, I worked my three months' notice and retired with a half-decent pension and fifty percent of the equity from the house Emily and I used to live in together."

Tom finished the whiskey in his glass, savoured the burn as it reached his stomach. How could he be angry at Wood for abandoning the search for Ryan, for taking the easy way out? "So, that's why you left? Because Cassie Fielding killed herself?"

"I knew I'd never be able to give her the news that Ryan had been found, alive safe and well, or that some jogger had found his body, half-covered over with foliage in the middle of the woods." He seemed to grimace at the thought. "Either way, the only person who wanted to know what had happened to Ryan was gone—"

"Not the *only* person," Tom said, reminding Wood that Ryan had friends, too, people who cared deeply about him.

"You know what I mean," Wood said, defensively. "Family."

Tom nodded.

"So I quit, became a little bit reclusive, I suppose you could say. There were days when I didn't leave my flat, days when I would lie on my bed and just stare at the cracks in the ceiling. I knew it couldn't last. Eventually I would have to get up and go out. My pension was paying the bills, but I was going crazy in there. I had to make myself busy. I felt like I had to work again, and it didn't matter what I did so long as it helped me block out the guilt."

"A busy mind is a happy mind," Tom said. He'd heard that somewhere, and it made perfect sense. But did it also mean that you couldn't be happy just existing? That you had to occupy your brain just to attain some sort of contentment was disconcerting.

"I worked six years as a school caretaker," Wood said. "Nice school, smart kids, parents with more money than sense. I was part-time, which meant less than four hours a day, fixing lights, painting walls, chasing stray dogs from the playground before the kids got too excited." He took a huge gulp of his beer and set it back down. "I wasn't happy, but I was getting there, you know? No more drug busts, no more murders, no more rapes; the dirtiest job I had back then was unblocking the boys' toilets.

"Just when I thought everything was going to be okay, well…"

* * *

OCTOBER 31ST, 1995
BROADFIELD PRIMARY SCHOOL, LONDON

"Goddammit!" Wood cursed as his wrench slipped off the radiator valve and he skinned his knuckles on the wall. Whoever thought stippled paint was a good idea for a school classroom was an idiot; not a day went by when Wood didn't leave a slice of flesh or a piece of skin hanging there next to the colourful paperchains and class photographs.

"Having problems?"

Wood started. He turned to find Henry Baker—Mr Baker to the kids, or Big-Beak-Baker to the naughtier lads on account of his massive nose—standing there with his arms crossed. "Oh, I didn't hear you come in," Wood said. Motioning to the radiator, he said, "This whole thing's rounded off. I don't think I'm going to be able to fix it with the tools I have."

"I wouldn't worry too much about it," Baker said, scratching that huge hooter of his, which looked to Wood like something athletes skied down at the Winter Olympics. "It's rare I turn it on. This room's stuffy at the best of times, and the kids are warm enough, what with their shirts, jumpers, and blazers on."

Wood nodded and climbed to his feet, dusting his knees off in the process. "I'll be able to mend it by Friday, but it's going to need a whole new valve. In the meantime, I'd keep the windows shut. Don't want the kids coming down with colds."

"Cheers, Trevor," Baker said. Wood assumed he was thanking him for not quite fixing the radiator, which was strange. "You were in the police force, weren't you?" Baker said. "Before you came here?"

The question caught Wood off guard. It was a well-known fact that Wood had made it all the way to Sergeant before throwing in the towel; he would love to be a fly on the wall in that staffroom to hear what everyone thought about him, to hear their postulations as to why he was now a caretaker at a primary school. "Eighteen years, give or take," he said.

Baker brightened. "I *thought* so," he said. "Look, I was wondering if you could do me a favour? You see, I'm writing this book—a novel, actually—and there are some things I need to fact-check with regards to police-work. Nothing major, but I want it to be as accurate as possible."

Wood shrugged. "What do you need to know?" It wasn't as if he had anything better to do in that moment; the boys' toilet was blocked again, but that could wait half-an-hour or so.

"I have a list back in the staffroom," Baker said. "Give me a minute and I'll be right back, that okay?"

Wood nodded. A list, huh? A whole list of things he needed Wood to verify? This wasn't a spur of the moment thing; Baker had sought him out. For some odd reason, Wood felt nervous.

What if I can't answer the questions?

What if Big-Beak-Baker wants to know something I'm not allowed to tell him?

What if I just run away right now? Just run and hide before Baker gets back with his list?

Placing his tools back in their box, Wood thought about what Baker was going to ask him? How many days does it take for a body to rot completely? What's the maximum amount of weed you can get away with before it becomes an imprisonable offence? How many constables can you fit into a Mini?

It was while he was working out just what kind of novel Baker was writing anyway, that he heard it.

Distant at first, the chiming of an ice cream truck.

An ice cream truck in October?

On Halloween?

Pop goes the weasel.

And Wood's heart skipped a beat. More than one, in fact, as the distorted melody drew closer and closer, louder and louder, a nightmarish cacophony, a symphony composed by demons, and before Wood knew it, he was running from the classroom, barrelling along the deserted corridor toward the school's main entrance.

It was him!

It *had* to be. The fucker who kidnapped the Fielding kid seven years ago, back for more, still plying his trade on the same streets he liked to snatch helpless fat kids from.

Out through the front entrance and down the three steps to the playground, Wood didn't even think about what he was doing. He was no longer a police office, had quit years ago, and yet all he wanted to do was catch a glimpse of the fucker in the yellow-and-white ice cream truck. If he just saw... something— anything—he could take the description to the lads at the station. Brownlee was in charge there now, and Wood was certain he would appreciate some new information.

Out through the school gates and halfway along the street when the yellow-and-white ice cream truck, spotted with rust and without a number-plate, appeared at the junction just ahead.

The chimes were deafening now. Those kids had been right all along. It was a noise that would haunt him for the rest of his life.

Still running toward towards the truck even though it was coming toward him. They would meet somewhere in the middle.

I could pretend I just want an ice cream, Wood thought. *Just a Whippy with a flake, and no syrup, please, thankee very much.*

Would he stop for a grown-up?

Wood didn't think so. This prick was only interested in children. Defenceless kids that he could man-handle into the side of his truck.

Close enough now to see the driver, and yet Wood didn't see a damn thing. Where there should have been a man there was just a... shape. A blackness, as if someone had cut around a man with scissors in the fabric of time and space and thought 'fuck it, that'll do'.

It didn't make sense; Wood's brain couldn't figure out just what he was supposed to be looking at. There are a few things in this world we are not able to comprehend; the Universe, quantum particles, feeling blue for absolutely no reason.

And this thing driving along Lawnwood Street in a beat-up old ice cream truck.

Wood stopped running as the truck approached, squinted through the drizzle, his brain still playing catch-up.

What was it those kids had said on the night the Fielding kid went missing? They were sitting there, all three, in the black boy's living-room—

just a shadow

—and Wood had questioned them about the driver.

Just a shadow.

And they were absolutely right, for that was what peered out at him through the truck's windscreen as it drove slowly past. A shadow with trailing tendrils which looked and moved like smoke.

From somewhere—the rear of the ice cream truck, where there were no ice creams or lollies, Wood thought, just a rack of surgical implements, meat-hooks hanging from the ceiling, body-parts strewn across the floor—there came a scream.

A girl.

The bastard had another kid in there, and she was screaming for help.

"Stop!" Wood cried, and he threw out a hand, hitting the side of the truck with his open palm. But then it was past, and quickly moving away from him. The words **MIND THE CHILDREN** seemed out of place on the back of this particular ice cream truck. It should have read **KILL THE CHILDREN**.

Those words got too small to read in less than ten seconds, by which time Wood had fallen to his knees in the rain and was hammering at the wet tarmac with his fists.

Just a shadow.

Just a shadow.

Just a shadow.

* * *

OCTOBER 25TH, 2016
REDBRIDGE, LONDON

Tom listened to Wood's story without interrupting once. This was exactly what he needed right now; an ally, someone who believed what he had to say, who had seen the evil sonofabitch with his own eyes. "So you saw it?" Tom finally said, wishing his empty glass was full to the brim, and hold the ice. God, he needed a cigarette after that.

"I saw it," Wood said. His own glass now stood empty, yet he still cradled it as if it contained a miracle elixir. "I didn't know what the hell it was, and I still don't. But you were right about all that stuff when we interviewed you back in '88. It took seven years for me to realise you and your friends had been telling the truth all along."

Tom didn't know whether that was an apology, of sorts. *Sorry I didn't believe your crazy story about the shadow who likes to drive around in an ice cream truck. It's perfectly plausible...* "You said you heard a girl screaming from the back of the truck as it drove by?" Tom said. "Were there any missing girls at the time?"

"Cheryl Mitchell," Wood nodded. "It was all over the papers the next day. Eight-year-old girl snatched from the corner of her street in broad daylight. She was on her way to a friend's Halloween party. Dressed as a cat, according to her parents. A black glittery cat." He paused, shook his head with disgust. "And that thing just took her. Drove around the streets with her in the back of its truck with the music on full blast."

"Looking for more," Tom said.

"I think so," Wood replied. "But there were no more missing kids reported that year. I guess it got one: Cheryl Mitchell. Still not been found, as far as I'm aware. I made a statement, told Brownlee and the boys what I had seen, and they said they would look into it, but I think they were just humouring me."

Tom thought he saw a glimpse of something in Wood's face; was he contrite? Now that he knew how Tom and his friends had felt in '88 when Wood had all but laughed at their tall tale, exactly the way he had been treated by Sergeant Brownlee seven years later, was he regretful?

"I'm going to get a drink," Tom said. He asked if Wood wanted another ale, and Wood told him yes, yes, he would very much like that. When Tom returned a few minutes later, Wood picked right back up from where he left off.

"I've never been able to put that fucking trucker and its driver out of my mind, Tom. I dream about it, a hear that creepy-ass music in elevators and when someone puts me on hold. It's like it imprinted something on me.

Tom knew exactly what that felt like; he'd wakened almost ritualistically three times a night for the past twenty-eight years with that sicko's discordant theme tune running through his head.

"Then it all happened again," Wood said. "Twice more, in fact. In 2002 a young boy named Harvey Poulson was snatched from outside a shopping centre while his mother was inside trying to get hold of some last-minute pumpkins to carve. There were no witnesses, despite it being the store's busiest time of the evening, but several of the people questioned remembered seeing a white-and-yellow ice cream truck moving slowly around the carpark. When asked whether any of them had seen the driver, it was a resounding no. But they heard that fucking tune. Pop Goes the Weasel." He picked up his glass and clinked it against Tom's. "I read about that one in the newspaper. The last I heard, Brownlee moved up north with his wife and kids, so there was no one at the station I could talk to, not without them taking the piss. When Rochelle Chambers was taken from her bedroom in 2009, I didn't even need to read the rest of the article. I just knew it was that thing, and I was right. Down there at the bottom of the page, the reporter mentioned the ice cream truck, which had been seen parked outside the Chambers house just a few hours before she was taken. Her parents had even heard the chimes but thought nothing of it." He smiled sardonically. "I think it's one of those sounds, you know? Your brain tunes it out. You hear it so many times in the summer, in the spring, that when it happens in the autumn you don't think anything of it, not unless you stop and really think about it."

"Four kids," Tom said. "Over the course of twenty-one years? Spaced out like that, as if it was content with what it had and didn't feel the need to overdo it."

"Every seven years," Wood said. "Did you realise that? This thing, it comes back every seven years and takes a kid. That last one, the Chambers girl, she wasn't even in London. They lived in Glasgow. Harvey Poulson and his family lived in Brighton."

Tom was still running through the dates in his head. 1988, 1995, 2002, 2009; every seven years, just like Wood said.

And this year was 2016.

Seven more years.

"When Margaret told me she'd met you at the library just this morning, I knew I had to come and see you," Wood said. "I think... I think that sonofabitch, whatever the hell it is, is coming back, Tom." Tom was already nodding. Had Wood experienced a Kurian moment of his own? "It's been seven years since Rochelle Chambers vanished into thin air while she combed the hair of her favourite doll, and unless this is just some sort of coincidence, and the dates are not correlated at all, then we're running out of time."

Tom knew the dates weren't coincidental; every seven years, and this year was one of his. That was why he had watched Kurian transform into the Ice Cream Man (such a silly name!), why the nightmares had become more frequent, inasmuch as he'd been having them at work during the day.

Work?

Shit! Bob's going to fucking crucify me! Or fire me. Either would be bad. The latter would be more likely.

"Like I said earlier," Tom said, "I saw him—it—come through my doctor, and I knew it was real. More than just another nightmare. It's as if the bastard's gearing up for what's to come, drawing power from us, testing us." The thought sent a chill the course of his spine, and he shuddered, the same way one might when sitting alone in a room late at night and, suddenly, there are eyes on you. Whose?

"I never thought I'd say this," Wood said, "but I really wish I was thirty years younger. I don't know how much use I can be confined to this stupid scooter, or my ridiculously expensive wheelchair."

Tom thought about asking how Wood had ended up the way he had, but it wasn't the done thing, especially with someone you hadn't seen for the better part of thirty years. Wood, however, must have seen the question lingering upon Tom's lips, because he smiled slightly, and said:

"Car accident. Back in '14. Even crueller is that there's nothing actually wrong with my fucking legs? There were no breaks, no sprains, nothing like that. Head went through the windshield first, hit the pavement before the rest of me. Traumatic Brain Injury fucked up my coordination and voluntary movements." He patted his useless legs. "They're not paralysed, but they're about as useful as tits on a fish. Been having physio three times a week for the last two years."

Tom felt for him. He'd been through so much, what with his wife leaving him, early retirement from the force, major car accident, and now this: the return of the Ice Cream Man. Truthfully, Tom was just glad he didn't have to fight this thing alone.

They spent the rest of the afternoon talking about more pleasant things; about how they had both watched Marcus Berry's rise and rise, from his Olympic bronze to Heavyweight champion of the Midlands, and how Wood always knew that kid had it in him. Tom told a few of his anecdotal stories about the weirdest things that happen when you're an estate agent; he told the one about how he'd arrived to a country-house viewing once, only to discover a trio of squatters had taken over the upper floors. They had even brought gas bottles and camping stoves, because although you don't own the house, a nice fried breakfast first thing in the morning goes a long way to helping forget the fact. He told the one about how he'd been showing a nice young Christian couple around a three-bed semi when they'd stumbled upon what could only be described as a sex dungeon. The previous owners, it seemed, had had a thing for wall-chains and ball-gags. And he told the one about the couple who he watched implode right in front of him at one particular viewing. Everything had been going swimmingly, right up until it was time to make a decision. The girl loved it; the guy hated it. The girl slapped the guy. The guy called the girl some of the worst things Tom had ever heard fall out of a human's face. He told all those stories to keep from thinking about the alternative, and they both knew it.

When the time came for Wood to leave, Tom didn't want to let him go.

THIRTEEN

OCTOBER 25TH, 2016, BROMLEY, LONDON

The children were being good for a change. Danielle and Rebecca helped them dress for bed, and there were no tantrums, no fights or arguments with one another. Just four boys doing what they were told with a minimum of fuss. Danielle was grateful for their cooperation; she couldn't get Tom out of her mind, had tried to call him seven times throughout the day, and each time it went through to that stupid answer machine message of his.

She'd tried to convince herself that it was a good idea to drive over there to see if he'd made it home, but Rebecca had talked her out of it. *You've just got to let him get on with it for a while,* she'd said. *If he loves you, he'll do the right thing.*

If he loves you?

Danielle didn't doubt Tom's love for her. That wasn't even an issue. The issue was whether she had done the right thing, leaving him along like this. Was he in the right frame of mind to get the help he needed? Was he prepared to do whatever it took to save their marriage?

If he loves you...

With the kids in bed—Jayden and Justice in one room, Joel and Oscar in another—Danielle and Rebecca went downstairs and Rebecca opened a bottle of red wine, which Danielle wasn't really in the mood for, but she accepted a small glass, nonetheless.

"Do you think he's okay?" Danielle asked, concernedly.

Rebecca sighed and rolled her eyes. "Sis! What have I told you? You've got to put it out of your mind. He's an adult, for fuck's sake. I'm pretty sure he can cope on his own for a few weeks."

"Not if he gets himself fired," Danielle said. The smell of the wine was nauseating, and she placed her glass down on the glass coffee table. "If he doesn't show for work tomorrow, Bob's going to get rid of him. And then what?" Tom didn't love the job, not really, but Danielle knew he needed it. He needed something to keep him focussed. They needed the money to pay the mortgage—Tom's one major bill—and Tom needed the money to fund his smoking habit. It was bad enough him trying to tone down his drinking without him having to face an involuntary battle against nicotine.

"Tom's a smart guy," Rebecca said. "If that prick fires him, then I shouldn't imagine it would take long for him to find something else. I mean, who knows, it might be just the kick up the arse he needs."

Danielle nodded. Why did her sister have to be the sensible one? It was because she wasn't invested like Danielle was; she was a spectator watching two grown adults throw their toys out of the pram and then figure out how they were going to pick them back up again.

Just then, Rebecca's phone started to ring, and she frowned as she looked down at the screen. "It's Tom," she said. "Why's he ringing me?"

Danielle's heart began to race. Thank God he was okay. He was okay, and he was—she checked her own phone and saw that it was dead—trying to call Rebecca because, apparently, it was the only way to get in touch with his wife.

Rebecca answered with a curt "Hello, Tom?" She sounded, Danielle thought, like that evil computer from the Kubrick film. *Hello Dave. You're looking well today...* "Yeah, she's right here having the time of her life. You want me to put her on?"

Danielle cursed at her sister—the time of her life? —and leaned in to take the phone.

"Ignore her," Danielle said when she had the phone to her ear. "Where have you been all day? I've been trying to get in touch since nine o'clock this morning. And why didn't you go to work? Bob's going to fire you if you don't show up tomorrow." She knew she had made a mistake; she should have kept it to herself that she'd known about his nonattendance at work, to see if he lied. *I was at work, babe. Had a couple of important viewings, but you already knew that...*

"Shit!" Tom said. "Did he sound angry?"

"He sounded like he'd already made up his mind," Danielle said. "So, where were you?"

"I was at the library," Tom said, which was not what Danielle had expected to hear. She wasn't even sure Tom had a library card.

"The library?"

"Yeah. I had to look some stuff up."

"For ten hours?" Danielle said.

"Well, it didn't take that long, but I went for a walk afterwards. I haven't been drinking, I swear. I'm getting my shit together, Dani. Just like we talked about."

Danielle sighed. She didn't know what to believe anymore. "So, what was more important at the library than work?" It was a damn good question, and one she couldn't wait to hear the answer to. But when it came, she wished she hadn't bothered.

"Ryan Fielding wasn't the only kid abducted by that lunatic," Tom said.

"Oh, for crying out loud, Tom, how is that helping things between us, huh?"

"This isn't about you and me," Tom argued. "This is about the fact that Ryan wasn't the only kid to go missing—"

"Hundreds of kids go missing every week, Tom," Danielle said, though she didn't know whether that was true. It seemed about right, though, if you considered fourteen or so a day.

"It was the same yellow-and-white ice cream truck, Danielle. Snatched kids from Glasgow, from Brighton, from—"

Danielle couldn't help herself. She fairly screeched down the phone, and across from her Rebecca almost spilt red wine down her favourite green dress. "Stop! Just stop with all this Ice Cream Man bullshit, Tom! It's taken over every facet of your life. Is that why you don't want kids? Because you're afraid that someday, someone's going to pull up to the kerb and take them away?"

Silence.

"I don't believe it," Danielle said, and she didn't. All this time, all these years she'd pleaded with him to give her a child, to make them both parents, and the reason why he wouldn't was because of something which had happened when he was a kid. Almost thirty years ago.

"It's not like that, Dani," Tom said. "This... thing is real, okay? I spoke to someone today, someone from back then, an ex-policeman, and he—"

"I don't *believe* you!" Danielle said. "Tom, I told you what to do, I told you what you *needed* to do for me to come home, and you've been out there pulling some sort of... some sort of Poirot shit on the locals and raiding the library for information on things which happened before you had hair on your body!" She was losing it, and Rebecca was finding it amusing, for some reason. "Did you even go to see Kurian?" she said, for now she was beginning to doubt everything he'd told her.

"I did," Tom said. "I went to see him, and do you know what happened, Dani? That fucker stood up and transformed into a demon right in front of my eyes." It was apparently Tom's turn to rant now; they had done this so much over the past years, it seemed to be the only way they could communicate. "You know what, Dani? I went to see your precious Doctor Kurian because you made me believe that I was deluded, that the things I was dreaming about were just remnants of a past I needed to forget, to block out, to come to terms with, whatever the hell you want to call it. But today I found out that it's all real, just like I knew it was. The ex-policeman from way back when, he knows it's true, too. This thing is coming back, Dani, and it's going to take another kid—fuck knows who—and then it's going to vanish again for seven ore years—"

"Have you even *heard* yourself, Tom?" Calm again now. There was no point, Danielle thought, trying to outdo one another. They were both raving lunatics to the outside world, and to Rebecca, who was at least seeing the funny side of things, even if Danielle wasn't. "Seven years? What does that even, I, Tom, this is ridic—"

"I don't expect you to believe me," Tom said. "You never have, not about what happened to Ryan, not about the shadow behind the wheel, none of it. But it doesn't matter, Dani, because

I'm going to make things right. We're going to stop that sonofabitch this time around. We're going to put an end to it."

"Who's we, Tom?" Danielle half-expected him to say, *We! Me and the voices in my head. We're going to stop it, and then we're going to have a nice game of chess, because Tom 2 is good at chess, aren't you, Tom 2?*

There was a pause, and then Tom said, "Trevor Wood and I," as if he didn't quite believe either of them, was only just realising for the first time that neither of them, were up to the task.

"Sergeant Wood?" Danielle said, if only to prove that she had been listening all these years, all those times Tom recounted the story. She had been listening, and it was his turn to listen now. Listen to her. Get some help. Stop being a fucking cuckoo!

"Wood knows about the thing," Tom said. "He was there when the second girl went missing, and he's been doing research into it ever since. He believes me, Dani. Why can't you?"

"Because ghosts aren't real, Tom," Danielle said, and for the first time she had the urge to cancel the call. It would have been the easy thing to do. But it wouldn't make a difference. Tom's problems would persist; their problems would persist. "Don't you see how crazy you sound?"

"I don't expect you to believe me," Tom said. "It's not as if you ever have, not about what we went through."

That cut to the bone. How *could* she believe him? He was talking about something beyond the realms of science, a metaphysical being—a fucking monster! She wasn't wrong for finding it a little difficult to swallow.

"I only called to make sure you were okay, Tom," Danielle said, trying to compose herself. "Clearly you're not, but at least you're not dead. Do me a favour, will you?"

A grunt.

"If I call you, please answer the phone, okay? We're still married, you're still my husband, and I care about you." *More than you'll ever know.*

"I'll answer," Tom said. Two words which, quite frankly, Danielle didn't think sounded sincere.

When the call ended a minute later, Rebecca was right

there, shaking her head in disbelief. How much had she heard? You didn't have to be a genius to fill in the gaps. "Is he—"

"Losing his mind? Going bat-shit crazy?" Danielle felt bad for talking about Tom like that to her sister, but what did he expect?

Rebecca filled both their glasses, even though Danielle hadn't touched her drink. "On the bright side," she said, "we get to take the kids to the Sealife Centre this weekend."

Danielle smiled.

On the bright side...

FOURTEEN

OCTOBER 27TH, 2016
HAVERING, LONDON

Luke pulled the car over to the kerb and sat, for a moment, looking at the house he used to live in. It was so different to how he remembered it. There were no net-curtains, for starters, and the windows had been leaded; a criss-cross lattice which made the house look far more extravagant than it actually was.

The small front garden was meticulous. Even though an early morning frost covered the grass, it was clear that the present owners took great care of it. The row of firs which Luke, Tom, Marcus and Ryan had once constructed a den in were now gone, replaced by a pair of fruit trees Luke thought were apple. Where there had once been a tyre-swing, there was now a wooden trellis with some unknown—to Luke, at least—species of flower snaking up it.

It was only right that Luke should visit the house first. It had been such a huge part of his life, even after that thing took Ryan. Though Luke could not remember much happiness taking place there after '88, or even before. His parents' constant arguments, his father's propensity to leave for days on end, his mother's loud music as she sobbed into her cheap wine, it was no wonder the house caused him to shudder at the mere sight of it.

And yet he was home.

He had returned and, sitting there in the car while the engine idled and staring at the house of bad memories, he felt *right*, and it was as if nothing had changed.

Nothing and everything.

He turned off the engine and stepped out of the car. Just a few feet away was the space upon which that thing had stood pretending to be Ryan. Pissy-Pants Davis! Pissy-Pants Davis! Luke remembered it as if it were just yesterday.

The messages appearing on the computer screen— WINDOW, MINE, HELP—and the bickering between his mother and father as he'd stared down from his bedroom window at the thing wearing the skin of his friend.

The thing that wasn't Ryan.

Luke walked slowly over to the spot, unsure why, or what he was expecting to achieve from it. Was it merely a macho thing? A gesture to prove he wasn't chicken, to prove he wasn't Pissy-Pants Davis?

He stared up at the bedroom window, the one through which he'd looked as a child from the other side. A dog-walker on the other side of the road watched him suspiciously as she went by, and Luke waited until she was out of earshot before muttering a few choice words about 'nosey old cunts'.

Now what? Luke thought.

He had come all this way, had spent last night in one of the most squalid hotels he had ever had the displeasure of staying in on the outskirts of the city, and now he was here he was at a loss.

It was as if he'd been pulled toward Havering by an unseen force. He had felt it last night at the hotel, growing stronger with each passing hour, a tugging at his stomach he had mistakenly assumed to be a case of too much vending-machine food. Driving into Havering had been a strange moment, for the sensation— the pull—had grown even stronger.

I'm fucking here! Luke thought. *Now what?*

As much as he wanted to, it was far too early to knock the door, to speak to the new owners of the house he used to live in, to ask them if it was okay for him to take a little look around the place, you know? For old time's sake? Was there ever a good time to do that, though? When was that *ever* acceptable? Not since the turn of the century, Luke imagined. People didn't like letting strangers into their house nowadays, especially if they were going to get all teary-eyed. There was, of course, always the possibility that he wasn't telling the truth, that he had never lived there and was only casing the place for some future burglary.

The new owners would probably call the police, just on

general principle, and things were bad enough without getting arrested on account that he wanted to take a little looksee at his old bedroom.

So, what then? Luke thought. Why had he come all this way? Apart from the strange pull in his stomach? That irrepressible feeling that he had unfinished business in Havering. But what was it? He was one man, and he was clueless.

There was no way he could walk up to the house and knock the door. Not a chance in Hell; he felt like some sort of voyeur just by looking at the place.

He had one more stop to make, though even that now seemed like a bad idea.

He walked back to the car, terrified to look back at the house over his shoulder in case someone was peering through the curtain, phone in hand, waiting for the police to arrive.

The drive to his parents' house, just a few short miles from where he was now parked, would hopefully help him clear his head.

But then he started thinking about how they were with one another, how much water had passed under the metaphorical bridge that was their marriage, how they had almost disowned him in the weeks and months following Ryan's disappearance, and by the time he arrived twelve minutes later, he was even more wound up.

His parents' house was a large white affair in a much better neighbourhood than the one he had been brought up in. All of the houses here, including his parents', were detached, and with more than enough land surrounding them to make neighbourly disputes a thing of the past.

Luke pulled into the driveway, crunching gravel under his wheels, and stopped just short of the red TR7 in front of the house.

"Fucking hell, Dad," Luke said, shaking his head as he tried to figure out what had possessed his father to buy such a ridiculously impractical car, but then it all made sense. The car was just about big enough for his father, therefore he wouldn't have to take his mother out in it, because there was not a cat in Hell's chance she would stuff herself into such a tight space, not unless it was worth her while.

Luke climbed out of his own car and eased the door shut. He didn't slam it, and the only reason he could think why was that it was still not too late to change his mind. His parents probably hadn't heard him pull up—it wasn't as if he was driving a clapped-out TR7, after all—and he was well within his right to turn around and head back to Luton without popping in to say, 'Hey, folks! I'm all grown up and mentally unstable. Thanks for that."

By the time he reached the front door—they even had one of those tawdry bells hanging there as if to prove their gaudiness—Luke was ready for it, surprisingly. He had no idea how they would react when they saw him, for it had been a long time since his last visit.

Lydia's first birthday, in fact, over seven years ago. It was during that visit that things got a little testy—his father had instigated an argument with his mother, Lydia had become upset, his father had shouted at Lydia for crying "like a fucking baby", Karen had dropped one of his mother's favourite crystal glasses—and Luke had parted on bad terms. Luke remembered the drive home on that eventful afternoon; Karen was livid and swore never to let them see Lydia again.

And that was that.

Now here he was, the prodigal son returning, his own family in disarray while he was on the verge of madness.

He rang the bell and waited.

An aeroplane thundered across the sky overhead; a cat appeared through the hedgerow to Luke's left, mewled once or twice, then buggered off again; it started to rain yet again, which Luke only noticed because of the noise it made as it rattled a million skeletal fingers on the aluminium bins sitting outside his parents' garage. All these things seemed to happen at once, and then...

The door opened a crack, just as far as the chain on the inside would allow it, and there, filling the tiny opening, was the face of a man.

A man who wasn't his father.

"Not interested, mate," said the man, whose reddened

cheeks suggested he'd recently been exerting himself.

On your mom, Luke thought as the rage inside him grew.

"Who the fuck are you?" Luke said, unable to control himself. The man was lucky he hadn't already had a hammer-fist to the temple.

The man's eyebrows knitted together, forming an angry V. It would have been comical under different circumstances. "Hang on a minute, you cheeky prick," he said. "You knocked my door. Who the fuck are you?" He didn't wait for a response; instead the door shut, and then there came the sound of the chain being slid across, before the door flew wide open and the bullish gimp stepped forward. Even though he was twenty years older than Luke, he was stockier, and had huge hands, Luke noticed, which were peppered with blue and green tattoos.

Prison tats, Luke thought.

Despite the man's size, Luke wasn't in the mood for this. He had been expecting to see his father, his mother, but for some reason this fool had answered the door. "Anne Davis," he said, holding the big guy back with one hand. But the big guy, whoever he fucking was, had obviously been looking after himself, and he twisted Luke's arm as if it were made of spaghetti.

Luke dropped to his knees—he'd had no choice; the sonofabitch was one step away from breaking his wrist—as the man called back into the house, "Anne? Anne? Someone here to see you, love."

"Let go of my fucking arm!" Luke said. His knees were now soaked through with rain, and it was all he could do not to scream out in agony.

Just then a woman's voice came from back in the house. "Who is it, Dave?" it said. And then there she was. His mother, looking as if she'd been made up by some French whore teaching her the ropes. Her skin was old and leathery, and golden. Far too golden for a human. She looked like a gangster's moll, or whatever the 21st century equivalent was. When she saw Luke, down on his knees, his right hand reaching for a terracotta plant-pot he planned to use as a weapon against the brute, she gasped. "Luke! What are you doing here?"

The big man—Dave, apparently—eased up on Luke's arm.

"You know this prick?"

"Let him up, Dave," Luke's mother said. "That's my son."

Dave's frown said it all; this was the first he was hearing about a son. Luke didn't know what was worse, the fact that his mother was clearly boffing this thug, or that she was so embarrassed by Luke that she had decided not to mention she had a son.

When Luke was back on his feet, breathless and angry as all hell, he turned to his mother and threw her a fake smile. "This might be a stupid question," he said, "but is Dad in?"

* * *

His parents had been separated for almost three years, and neither of them had thought to let him know. His father now lived with some floozy by the Thames—*a whore,* his mother said, but Luke didn't believe that was accurate—while his mother and Dave were planning on marrying once the divorce was finalised.

Dave owned a rock-themed pub in Camden; Luke had probably walked past it many times, not once thinking to stick his head in just in case his mother was planning on marrying the proprietor. Funny, that.

"Sorry about what happened outside," Dave said. They were now sitting opposite one another in a living-room whose primary décor was porcelain dolls. So many goddamn porcelain dolls.

"S'alright," Luke said, rubbing his reddened wrist.

"I thought you were being a smart-mouthed fucker," said Dave, folding his huge arms across his chest. Printed upon his tee-shirt was a British Bulldog, everyone's favourite patriotic/xenophobic mascot.

"I thought you'd killed my parents and buried them underneath the patio," Luke said, being a smart-mouthed fucker. "So pleased you're just shagging my mom."

Dave took that as a compliment, somehow. "She never told me she had a son," he said. "It's come as a bit of a shock, if I'm being completely honest."

"That's funny," Luke said, "because she never told me I had a future stepfather. Do you think we should call her on it when she's done butchering the tea?" Luke was not in the mood for this. He had always wondered what life would be like if his parents split, and ostensibly this was it. Dave and his mother. Big Dave, as they no doubt called him down at his Camden boozer. His mother looking like a tangerine, with huge hoop earrings clattering noisily against the side of her face. Luke was hardly in a position to criticise anyone's relationship—it was only a couple of days ago Karen had ejected him from the marital home for trying to strangle their daughter in her sleep—but this was a farce.

An unexpected travesty.

"He wasn't nice to her, you know," Dave said, and for a few seconds Luke wasn't sure who he meant. But then it hit him. His father. His father wasn't nice to his mother. "He was knocking her about—"

"You don't know anything about my father," Luke said. He was unsure why he was leaping to his old man's defence— perhaps because he wasn't here, in the home he had bought with his wife, to defend himself—but it seemed the right thing to do. "You only know what she's told you. They're as bad as each other, and I'd be more likely to believe that Mom was the one knocking Dad about."

Dave lit a cigarette, and the room quickly filled with a grey fug. Luke remembered back to the night—Halloween '88—Ryan went messing. His father had lit a cigarette and his mother had, as she always did, reproached him for it. Did Dave get the same treatment or was that simply something she had reserved for his father; it wasn't the smoking that bothered her, it was the smoker.

"Hate to say it, son," Dave said, putting far too much emphasis on the last word for Luke's liking, "but your father's a prick what likes to knock defenceless women around."

Luke shook his head; he wasn't rising to the bait. It was already clear that he and Dave were never going to get along. There would be no father-son camping trips with this one; no fishing or golf expeditions, which suited Luke just fine as he'd only met the man ten minutes ago and already hated being in the same room as him.

Just then, his mother walked in carrying a tray laden with

china. Cups and saucers rattled as she traversed the furniture, trying desperately not to spill a drop, and she finally set the tray down on the coffee table between Luke and Dave. Luke noticed his mother's garish nails as she poured out three cups of tea. They were nails which didn't belong on a human, not unless said human hid in treetops and hunted voles at night. It was a wonder she could even pick up the teapot.

A deathly silence had descended upon the living-room, and Luke turned his attention to the carriage clock on the mantelpiece, either side of which sat two more ugly fucking porcelain dolls. It was almost eleven, not that Luke had anywhere else to be.

"So..." his mother said as she settled herself down onto the sofa next to Dave. He placed a huge hand on her thigh and gave it a squeeze. Luke couldn't have been less bothered by the action. These assholes, he thought, are perfect for one another.

But then, he'd thought that of his parents for so long, too.

Eventually, his mother went on. "How's Lydia?"

Lydia? His beautiful daughter who he was missing something rotten? The best thing in his life who he had tried to murder because she had turned into something pure evil? Just hearing her name out loud caused his heart to skip a beat, and it was all he could do not to break down in tears right there in front of his mother and big Dave, the arsehole.

"She's doing well," Luke said, for she was, as far as Luke was aware. "She's good at school, and she's just joined the Brownies. Absolutely loves it." *I tried to fucking kill her, Mom! I tried to kill Lydia because the Ice Cream Man—you remember him, don't you?—possessed her and made her levitate off the bed.*

He almost said it, too, managing to pull himself back at the last moment.

"You could have brought her to see us," his mother said, slurping noisily at her watered-down tea.

"Oh, that would have been a lovely surprise for her!" Luke said with mock enthusiasm. "You can never have enough grandfathers, as far as she's concerned. I know she would have just *loved* big Dave—"

"There's no need to be like that," said his mother, placing

teacup into saucer and wiping her lips with the back of her hand. "Is it wrong that I want to see my granddaughter once in a while? What happened all those years ago, it was silly, Luke." She waved a hand dismissively through the air. "I never wanted any of this. I didn't want to fall out with anyone."

Always the victim, Luke thought. "Pity you hate Karen then, isn't it," he said.

"Pity she hates *me!*"

"Who's Karen?" Dave asked.

"Don't worry yourself about it," Luke told him. "One new name today is enough for you. Don't want to go overdoing it."

Dave snorted. "I'll knock that smug look off your fucking face, you little—"

"Dave!" gasped his mother. "Just leave him alone, okay? It must have been incredibly hard for him to come here at all today."

"I was just passing through," Luke said, just in case his mother made the mistake of assuming he had come all the way to Havering just to see her. "Thought I'd stop by, make sure my parents hadn't killed each other. Turns out they haven't, because they're getting divorced. Oh, Happy Days!" He almost sang the last part.

There was another brief silence, far more uncomfortable than the last, and Luke wondered what the consequences of him standing up, crashing his cup-and-saucer down on Dave's melon head, and leaving with his pride intact might be. What was the worst that could happen? Another seven years of not seeing his mother. Bring it on. She might not even make it that long, for she was already looking impossibly tan, and there was only so much sun-damage the body could take before deciding to start punishing.

"Passing through?" His mother reached forwards and poured herself a second cup.

"Huh?" Luke had been too busy picturing Dave pulling shards of china from his bald head to hear properly.

"You said you were just passing through," said his mother. "From Luton? Without Karen or Lydia? Passing through to where?"

Luke shrugged. He didn't know what to say, what he could tell her and what he should keep to himself. She hadn't believed him the night Ryan Fielding had been plucked from the street, never to be seen or heard from again. What could he tell her now, all these years later? That he had a strange feeling in the pit of his stomach. A burning, almost, and it was tugging him inexorably toward Havering. That he believed—no, that he was certain, albeit without proof—that the Ice Cream Man was not a man at all, but a demon, a thing from another realm, and that it was coming back. That he had wrapped his hands around his daughter's throat and had attempted to choke the life out of her because he was having some sort of breakdown. That Karen had asked him to leave, and he had done so because she was right, goddammit! She was right to want him out of the house because he had tried to kill Lydia and needed to be punished. That he feared the police were already after him, pursuing him from cheap hotel to cheap hotel, and that he was terrified to stop moving in case they caught up and threw him in jail for what he had done.

That he was terrified.

That he was cold and hot all at the same time.

That he wanted to die.

That he feared he might.

His mother waited patiently as he tried to figure out the words, and in the end, he simply repeated himself. "Just passing through."

Dave sighed deeply and dipped a biscuit in his tea before forcing the whole soggy thing into his disgusting mouth. *I hope you choke in it,* Luke thought.

"I hope you choke on it, huh?" said Dave, but then it wasn't Dave at all. Sitting there, next to Luke's mother, was the Ice Cream Man. Black tendrils licked at the sofa, teased his mother's hair from behind. She didn't seem to notice; she simply smiled wistfully at the shadow-person, as if her beloved Dave was still sitting there and not some malevolent kidnapper in his place.

This isn't real! This can't be real!

"Oh, it's real, all right," said the Ice Cream Man. "I'm being big Dave. I don't know which of us you hate more."

"I hate you!" Luke said.

"Luke!" his mother said, shocked. That was when he knew he was the only one that could see the foul creature, that big Dave was still there, underneath, and that his mother thought Luke had just voiced his animosity toward her future husband, and not the thing only he could see.

The black shape's red eyes darted around the room, and it hissed. *"Sssssuch a ssstrange fassscination with dollsssss. Creepy, don't you think?"*

Luke knew he was wasting his time talking to the thing; not only that, but his mother was looking at him as if he had lost his mind. He didn't want to give her the satisfaction of believing he had.

Slowly he stood, placed his lukewarm tea down on the coffee table, and thanked his mother for the hospitality.

"Going already?" she said, sounding genuinely upset.

"Yeah, you're not going already, are you?" said the creature sitting beside her. *"Ssssoooo much to dissscusss... ssoooo much to reminissssce about."*

Luke ignored it, instead aiming his response at his mother. "Yeah, Lydia's got Brownies tonight, and if I'm not back to take her, there'll be hell to pay."

"Issss that the name of the girl you almossst killed?" The Ice Cream Man said, the oily tendrils of its torso dancing languidly in time with its voice. It was enjoying this. It seemed to be getting pleasure from watching Luke squirm.

Once again Luke ignored it. "I'll see you again soon," he told his mother, knowing it was a lie. He didn't know when he would see her again—didn't know *if* he would ever see her again—but if he did, it would most probably not be 'soon'. And the look on his mother's face suggested she knew it too. "Nice meeting you, Dave," Luke said to the man behind the demon. He didn't think Dave would hear him, part of the reason why he kept it civil. "I'd shake your hand, but..." *But there's a fucking monster sitting on your lap and you probably don't even know it.*

"I'll show you to the door," said his mother. She started to stand.

"It's okay," Luke said, holding out a hand: don't get up. "I know where it is, but Mom?"

"Hm?"

"Look after yourself, yeah? And if you see Dad, tell him the same."

"I won't see that sonofabitch as long as I live," his mother said, her face contorted into something like pure anger. She was about to continue her tirade when Luke cut her off.

"Next time I come," he said. "I'll bring Lydia." Just another lie. And why not? He was on a roll.

His mother smiled. "That would be lovely."

And all the time the creature sitting beside her listened, sneered, licked its thin black lips with an even blacker tongue.

Luke left the living-room and, once he was out of sight, he ran to his car. The thing wasn't in the passenger seat as he pulled off the driveway; it was waving from the living-room window, net curtains flapping around it like a superhero's cape.

"Fuck you!" Luke yelled as loud as he could, hoping the Ice Cream Man could hear him over the roar of the engine, the crunching of gravel, the screeching of tyres as he sped away from the house.

Luke was driving so fast, so wildly, that he forgot to brake when he came to the junction at the end of the street. Although it was too late, he pulled the wheel hard to the left, hoping he'd done enough to prevent crossing over into oncoming traffic.

He hadn't.

He saw the BMW for a split second, and then there was an almighty crunch, by which time Luke had closed his eyes and braced himself for impact. The car seemed to travel for an age, hitting things that hadn't been there a moment ago, and then it was flipping, turning over and over. Luke didn't know what was the sound of twisted metal and what was the sound of his own screams as pain wracked through his entire body and the seatbelt cut into his shoulder and chest.

I'm dead, he thought, and it was the last thing that occurred to him before the darkness came.

FIFTEEN

The library was a little busier than the last time he'd been here, which, Tom guessed, might have had something to do with the working computers and the fact it was Saturday. This was where jobseekers came to look for work, where adulterous husbands and wives came to contact their chat-room lovers, where the older generations came to learn how to fill in spreadsheets, save word documents, print manuscripts and type with both hands at the same time, where immigrants new to the country sought to learn a new language so that the next time they were in Starbucks they could order precisely what they wanted without looking like a complete dick and pissing off the irate queue building up behind them. The library was a commune, a kibbutz of wannabe-betters, a gathering of the general populace, from Ahmet the Barber to Sir Steven the cheating Lord.

This was where it all happened.

The library.

"Did you find him?"

Tom turned from the shelf he had been staring blankly at for the past two minutes to find Margaret, the librarian who couldn't even hold her own water even if the CIA told her it was classified, standing there, smiling thinly. "Oh, Sergeant Wood?" he said. "Yes, I caught up with him in the pub, just like you said I would."

Margaret slipped a thick hardback book on UFO's into an empty space on the shelf in front of her. "Hope you didn't mind me telling him you were looking for him," she said. "Trevor's a good man, and I'd only just met you. For all I knew you were going to give him a good hiding."

Tom laughed at that. "Wouldn't that have been something," he said. "And you would have pointed me straight at him."

It was Margaret's turn to laugh. "It was only fair I should warn him, just in case," she said. "Don't think I would have been able to live with myself if he'd turned up here the next day with a black eye and teeth missing."

"I'm sure Wood can look after himself," Tom said, and he meant it. Even though Trevor Wood was now confined to a wheelchair or a mobility scooter, he still had about him a formidability which Tom found quite overpowering. You could take the man out of the police force, it seemed, but you couldn't take the police force out of the man.

"He's certainly a tough cookie, that one," Margaret said, and for the first time Tom wondered if she harboured something for the old copper, a secret love, perhaps, or something more than just friendship. "I see he's got you into his way of thinking," she said, motioning to the books sitting on the shelf in front of Tom and frowning. "Is he starting some sort of supernatural club? Somewhere you lads can go to talk about ghosties and flying saucers and things that go bump in the night?"

Clearly, Wood hadn't shared with Margaret the way she ostensibly did with him. This woman had no idea what Wood had been through, what had happened to them all those years ago—what was *still* happening. If Margaret saw an ice cream truck, she wouldn't run away from it, afraid that the bogeyman was behind the wheel; she would, like most people, pucker up for a creamy treat.

And that was just the thing: Tom and Wood were so alone in this that it was almost impossible to find anything out.

"Don't you believe in ghosts, Margaret?" Tom asked, trying to keep the tone light. His question was accompanied by a smile which said, *Didn't you watch Casper?*

"I believe in... *something*," she said, "but not that we die and become poltergeists and headless horsemen."

Tom wanted to tell her that you would have had to have been a horseman, killed by decapitation, for that to happen, but decided against it. "But you believe in God?" Tom said, motioning to the necklace she wore.

"Very much so," she said, "but does that mean I'm going to start hanging around supposedly haunted hotel rooms, like they do on those asinine TV programmes, waiting for something to blow into my ear just so I can say I had an encounter?"

"I guess not," Tom said. "But there are people out there who have already seen things that can't be explained, and Trevor Wood is one of those people."

"Ah, I *like* the man," Margaret said, "but that doesn't mean I believe a word he says. He once told me that he got run over by a petrol tanker. That's how he ended up in his chair. It wasn't until almost a year later that he told me the truth, that he'd fallen down a well trying to rescue a little girl. Since then, I've taken everything that man says with a pinch of salt."

Fallen down a well?

Tom almost shit himself laughing.

"So, what's he got you looking into?" Margaret said, perusing the spines of the titles on the shelf. "Cryptozoology, whatever that is? Haunted Ireland? The Bermuda Triangle?"

"Something a little closer to home," Tom said. On your own doorstep, in fact. He didn't want to terrify the woman, so he kept that part to himself. "I may have to use one of your computers, if that's okay?"

"You should really be a member if you want to make use of the facilities," Margaret said. "Do you even have a card?"

Tom told her that he didn't, that he would like very much to be a member, that he had time to fill out the forms and that, no, unfortunately, he didn't have photo identification on him, but could he bring it next time?

Ten minutes later he was sat at one of the whirring machines in the computer room. To his left and right, people checked their social media, something that Tom had never had an urge to become embroiled in. He didn't have any friends in real life, and he had even fewer willing to speak to him digitally.

He had acquaintances, people at work he liked to bullshit with at the water-cooler or while waiting for specs to print, but could he call them friends? Not really. His last real friends had all grown up and moved on with their lives—apart from the one who never made it. Marcus was a renowned boxer, had fought some of the best. Tom had even saved all the newspaper clippings, kept them in a folder with the name MARCUS BERRY scribbled across its front. Marcus had made something of his life, had moved to the Midlands and become a superstar of sorts. Then there was Luke, who Tom had not seen since school. Tom often wondered what Luke was up to, whether he would even remember Tom if they were to meet in the street. Perhaps not. So much had changed, lives had chuntered inexorably onward, and memories had faded like a photograph left out in the sun for too long. Even Tom now struggled to picture what they had once looked like, all four of them, riding their BMX's or hammering together pieces of wood and calling it a den.

They had looked happy, that much he was certain of. Happier than they ever had been in their lives? At least that was true for Tom. Sure, he had Danielle—or not, as the case might be—but he had never felt so damaged, so unsure of himself, feelings that had never been present as an eleven- and twelve-year-old boy.

As he sat there, Tom began to wonder what his friends were up to right now. Marcus would probably be training; Tom had read in an article recently that he was thinking of coming out of retirement. According to Marcus, he had at least three more fights in him, and by God he would have them.

But what of Luke? Was he married? Did he have children? Did he ever make it as an Aerospace engineer? Tom wished there was a way he could get in touch, let them know what was happening in Havering once again. That the Ice Cream Man was coming back—every seven years, it seemed—for more children. And how, Tom thought, might that conversation go? *Hey guys. Guess what? The ghost that took Ryan when we were twelve is still active, still driving around in that beat-up yellow-and-white ice cream truck, and I'm pretty certain he's going to return this year. So, how are things with you? Kids? Wives? Do you like Game of Thrones?* They would tell him not to contact them ever again; at best they would shrug him off as mentally disturbed, tell him to get some sort of help.

Tom sighed and clicked the browser icon, waited for the screen to load.

The girl to his right answered her phone with what Tom liked to refer to as 'wilful ignorance'. As she began to regale the caller—a girlfriend by the name of Rochelle, apparently—with a story about the immense size of her current squeeze's genitals ("Seriously, girl, I couldn't walk right for three days after!"), Tom navigated to a search engine and sat, fingers hovering over the keyboard, trying to decide what to do first.

The world at his fingertips, and he was at a loss. Once again, he realised just how old he was getting. Kids all around him were typing at the speed of light, their fingers a blur as they worked the keys. Tom wasn't the slowest typist in the world, but these fuckers made him look like Stephen Hawking. As the cursor blinked in its little box, Tom typed three words he hoped would bring up some results.

Ice cream murders.

Two million and something results, most of which were about some turf war in the East End of Glasgow during the eighties which came to be known as the Glasgow Ice Cream Wars. Tom had never heard of it, but he was curious, nonetheless, and read through the Wikipedia article. Turns out a bunch of criminals were using ice cream vans to sell drugs and stolen goods, using the sale of regular ice creams as a front. It was, as far as Tom could tell from the article, all very farcical, the behaviour of the belligerent gangs akin to something one might see on a BBC sketch show—something by Hale and Pace, perhaps, or Little Britain.

Tom clicked the arrow at the top left of the screen, which took him back to the search results. The girl to his left was now telling Rochelle what she was wearing for tonight's party. A slutty black dress, apparently. No doubt to impress her big-dicked suitor, Tom thought miserably.

The next article Tom found himself reading—for no other reason than he had three hours to kill before meeting Wood at The Walnut Tree to discuss their respective findings—was about a woman called Goidsargi Estibaliz Carranza, or 'Esti', an ice cream parlour proprietor who had done things to two men—her ex-husband and her lover—that would have made The Krays reach for their nut-sacks in sympathy. She had shot the men in the backs of their heads at close range, cut up their bodies with a chainsaw, stuffed them in a deep freeze, and then later interred them in concrete under the cellar of her store. In other words, she was a bit of a maniac. The pictures accompanying the article, however, revealed her to be somewhat photogenic, a regular thirty-four-year-old woman who just so happened to need psychiatric help. By the time he reached the end of the article, Tom felt sorry for Esti.

The girl to his left laughed boisterously at something she had seen on her monitor. Tom had a surreptitious look, saw a plump-looking girl on screen—a picture taken during a holiday, it seemed—and shook his head with disgust as phone girl began to ridicule and fat-shame the poor girl while Rochelle seemingly did the same from her end.

Tom could feel the anger rising within him, but he swallowed it back down and went about his business, hoping Margaret, who was lurking somewhere between the stacks like that thing from the opening minutes of *Ghostbusters*, would pluck up the courage to ask phone girl to leave, and take her uncouth attitude with her.

On and on the results went: there was an article about a 1919 murder in Monmouth, one from a clickbait page which had somehow concluded that there are more murders when sales of ice creams go up. Tom didn't quite understand the correlation between the two—something to do with heat driving people crazy, perhaps—and he didn't really care. There was an article about an episode of *Murder, She Wrote* entitled 'Frozen Stiff', plenty of stuff about Richard 'The Iceman' Kuklinski, a mafia hitman who liked to freeze his hits to obscure their time of death; there was an article about a pair of ice cream vendors who had been hacked to death in Iloilo; an article about Constable John Larmour, shot dead by the IRA as he helped out at his brother's ice cream parlour. There were lots of articles, but none of them were relevant.

Tom worked his way back to the search engine and typed in: ice cream kidnapping.

The girl to Tom's left must have seen what he had typed; she was whispering into the phone now, telling Rochelle about the man sitting at the computer next to her looking at weird shit. It was an opportunity, Tom thought, not to be missed.

He turned to the girl.

He smiled.

"Do you like ice cream?" he asked, sounding a little like Hannibal Lecter, a little like Donald Pleasance.

The girl looked terrified, and for the first time in fifteen minutes she was speechless. When Tom flashed her another, even more maniacal, grin, she got up, slung a bag across her shoulder, and headed for the exit as quickly as she could, daring to look back over her shoulder only once as she went.

Childish? Tom thought. Yes, indeed. Worth it? You betcha!

He turned his attention back to the screen in front of him, began to scroll down the page, looking for something—*anything*—to jump out at him. A YouTube video was the number one result. Someone had put together a rather elaborate social experiment to prove just how easy it would be for an Ice Cream Man to kidnap your kid. Tom didn't need to watch the video to know that was true.

He'd lived it.

There was a Snopes article about a Mr Softee driving around, chloroforming the living shit out of young girls, but Snopes called bullshit, so that was the end of that one.

There was an article whose title was simply: Does Ice Cream Man = Pervert? Tom didn't need to read that one, for it was like saying, Does Window Cleaner = Voyeur? Or, Does Grass Mower = Frog Murderer?

Tom clicked to the next page, and that was when he saw it. The very first article at the top of the second page—**ICE CREAM VAN POLICE CHASE ENDS IN TRAGEDY**—was accompanied by an image: an ice cream truck being pulled from the Thames, yellow-and-white with more than a little rust. The article was dated October 31st, 1987, a year—to the day—before Ryan's disappearance.

Although he couldn't be certain, Tom thought his heart had stopped beating. Everything around him was now deathly silent. Even the click-clacking of the manic typists, their fingers all a blur, faded into the distance as Tom clicked the link which pulled up the article.

He began to read.

> Tragedy unfolded yesterday when an ice cream van, which had been pursued by the police for more than thirty minutes through heavy traffic, plunged into the River Thames. Its driver, Frederick White, 46, and Isobel White, 7, were pulled from the vehicle but were pronounced dead at the scene, despite the best efforts of paramedics.
>
> Police had earlier been called to a domestic dispute after White's wife, Laura, barricaded herself in an upstairs bathroom of their South London home, allegedly fearing for her life. By the time police arrived, Frederick White—a local ice cream seller—had fled with their seven-year-old daughter.
>
> It is not yet known whether Frederick White intentionally drove into the river, or if he lost control of the vehicle during the pursuit. Local councillor, Ann Markham, called the events "truly harrowing" earlier today, and has called for an inquest into the tragic loss of life.

When Tom finished reading the article, he read it again, and then a third time. Frederick White? Was that the real name of the Ice Cream Man, the thing which had returned to claim children's souls? Tom looked closely at the picture; it was definitely the same truck, right down to the **MIND THE CHILDREN!** vinyl decal on the back. Tom could almost hear the atonal chimes now.

Pop goes the weasel.

This was *something*. After all these years, Tom had made progress, but was it a case of too little, too late? If this sonofabitch was coming back on Halloween, where would he be?

Who would he go after? The possibilities were limitless. The fucker had millions of children to choose from, in hundreds of cities and towns across the country.

And yet Tom knew he was coming back to Havering. The recent torment, the nightmares which left Tom in a pool of his own sweat most mornings, the terrifying incident with Kurian, it all pointed to the return of the Ice Cream Man.

The thing was mocking him, plaguing him day and night, haunting his dreams and toying with him while he was awake.

I'm coming back...

The creature had even said so itself. If not Havering, then one of the surrounding boroughs, but where, and how would Tom and Wood know when the truck appeared? Would they hear the discordant chimes from the pub?

So many likelihoods, all disparate, and Tom could feel himself growing increasingly frustrated as he stared at the screen, his heart now thumping hard in his chest, and tried to work out his next move.

Laura White.

Frederick's widow.

That's it, Tom thought. The woman shouldn't be too difficult to track down, not with all this modern technology at his fingertips. He would find the address of Laura White, maybe he and Wood could pay her a visit, find out as much as they possibly could about the man behind the demon. Tom didn't see the flaw in his design, however, at least not until her really thought about it. Laura White might be reluctant to discuss the man who had, ultimately, either intentionally or accidentally, killed their daughter. It was one of those sore points, Tom thought, which people didn't like dragged back up, especially twenty-nine years after the fact.

Tom took out his phone, pointed it at the screen, and took a picture. The words were just about legible, enough for him to read out to Wood later on.

How had Wood not heard about this incident? Surely, he had. London's big, Tom thought, but it's not so big if you're a copper. This kind of thing would have been the talk of all the stations around London; at least, that's what Tom would have thought. Maybe Wood was off the week it happened. Maybe it was just another death in London, throw it on the pile, let's never speak of it again, let's go get some of those salt-and-pepper crab claws you like so much, Brownlee...

"You do know we have a printer for that kind of thing?"

Tom turned to find Margaret standing just behind him, smiling in that motherly, and yet condescending way she was really good at. She was looking at Tom, and not the screen behind him, which Tom was grateful for. The last thing he needed right now was more questions. "Excuse me?"

"The printer," Margaret explained. "It's hooked up to all the computers. All you have to do is right-click on the page you want printing, and it'll come out over there." She motioned to an antique-looking crème box across the room. "I wouldn't leave anything important lying around on there for too long, though," she said. "Identity thieves... they're everywhere."

"Thanks for the advice, Margaret," Tom said, and then she went about her business. Tom turned back to the computer and followed her instructions. It was relatively simple, and a minute later he held in his hand a crisp, warm printout of the article.

Next, he found a site which promised to locate any person living in the UK with just a name and a street, town, or postcode. He typed Laura White's name into the first box, and then Havering into the second. A list appeared on screen, and Tom cursed. There were eight Laura Whites living in Havering or the surrounding areas. But then Tom noticed a new column containing the names of the other occupants of those Laura White's respective residences, and Tom brightened once again.

There, in the 'other occupants' box of the third result down, was the name Frederick White. Thanks to the electoral register, Tom had figured it out. He felt, in that moment, like a superspy, an agent of CSI, Sherlock Holmes on his very best day, and yet the information he had gleaned was readily available. He had done nothing, really.

7 Burke Street was the last known address of Laura and Frederick White, the house from which Frederick had fled the police with their daughter. There was a good chance Laura White had moved on, was actually one of the *other* Laura Whites from

the results, now living at a different address—one without so many awful memories—but Tom didn't really have anything else to go on. He would speak with Wood, and together they would decide whether it was a good idea to pay White a visit. If Tom knew Wood as well as he thought he did, they would be on Burke Street by that very afternoon.

Satisfied, Tom logged off the browser and the computer returned to its homepage, which featured the library's insignia and details on how to get started.

And he was about to leave when he noticed the computer to his left—the one Little Miss Chatterbox had been sitting at—was still logged in to some social media site.

"Okay," Tom said quietly to himself, checking around to make sure no one noticed what he was about to do. If Margaret was watching, she was doing it from between the stacks, a library ninja.

Tom shifted seats, clicked on the search box at the top of the social media page, and entered a name.

Luke Davis.

He hit enter and was immediately bombarded with a thousand Luke Davises. "Shit." Of course, there would be lots of them, far too many to work through. The tiny thumbnail profile pictures next to the names didn't give much away, either. Tom quickly realised he was wasting his time.

He typed Marcus Berry into the search box, and there, in the very first two results, was his old friend. The first result was for a fan page—the little blue tick, Tom thought, made it a verified account—but the second was his personal profile. The profile thumbnail showed Marcus, arm around his old man, standing in front of some run-down gymnasium. Marcus looked happy, while his father fairly scowled at the camera. It was just the way he was, Tom thought, remembering back to how Clive Berry had been when they were just kids: a cantankerous bully with a heart of gold, a pushy sonofabitch who could break your skull one minute and then drive you to the hospital the next. Deep down he was a good man, but Tom was surprised to see him looking so old and frail. The years had not been terribly kind to Clive Berry, unlike his son, who showed none of the usual signs of middle age. There was no unfortunate spreading of the midriff to see here, no drooping of the man-tits, and no slowly shrinking into dotage, like some withering plant. Marcus and Tom were the same age, give or take a couple of weeks, and yet Marcus looked better now than Tom had twenty years ago.

Sonofabitch.

Although Tom didn't know what he was doing with regards to this stupid site, he clicked on the personal profile of Marcus and hoped for the best.

What he got was Marcus's most recent public posts. Photographs taken at the gym, posters promoting his forthcoming fight with Samuels Jr. (which was no longer forthcoming, Tom noticed; had already happened, in fact, and according to the stream of condolences on the post, it hadn't gone in Marcus's favour), a couple of comments about films he'd watched recently and would recommend.

To the left of the feed there was a sidebar, and Tom found a link which would lead to a list of Marcus's current friends.

He clicked it.

Wow, there were so many of them! Not real friends, of course, but people who wanted to be able to say they were acquainted with 'The Banger'. The sycophancy was strong with these ones.

Fortunately for Tom, the list was in alphabetical order, and he scrolled down to the L's. There were several Lukes, but only one Luke Davis. Tom saw, even from the tiny picture, it was the right Luke. He hadn't changed that much, really. Got a bit older, wore a bit more stubble around his chin and jaw, but it was Luke, all right.

Tom clicked the link and was immediately, by the magic of the internet, taken to Luke's profile.

This profile is set to private, the text below Luke's face said. *The user must add you as a friend to see his/her profile.*

"Same old Luke," Tom said, smiling. He wasn't even disappointed, for he knew his friend was okay. A helluva lot older, but still kicking. *Maybe,* Tom thought, *when this is all over, I'll sign up to this stupid site and add the fucker as a friend.*

When all this is over...

Tom logged Little Miss Chatterbox out of the site and closed the browser. On his way out, he thanked Margaret for the help and told her he would probably see her in a couple of days, all being well. The library had become his home from home, now, a place to escape to when he was bored with the emptiness of the house, tired of the inane chatter of the senile clientele at The Walnut Tree, and fed up with not hearing a peep from Danielle, who was probably already expunging the last few years from her memory with the help of her meddling sister.

"Will you be seeing Trevor at any point today?" Margaret asked, hopeful. Tom felt for her, for he didn't think the feelings were mutual; Wood was a good man, a strong man, but a ladies' man? Maybe once, but not anymore.

Tom nodded. "You know, when I was a kid, if you'd told me I'd grow up and spend hour after hour with Sergeant Wood, I'd have told you to get lost and stop winding me up."

"Well," Margaret said, "when you see him, tell him the book he ordered has come in. Tell him I don't approve of its content" —she made the sign of the cross over her chest— "but who am I to judge?"

"You want me to take it to him?" Tom said. "I'm meeting him in a few; save him coming in here to bother you for it." But she liked that. She liked it when Wood came in to bother her, wished he would do it more often. Tom half-expected Margaret to vehemently decline his offer.

"That would be most kind of you," she said. She bent down behind the counter and came back up with a large tome, brand new, ordered in especially for Wood, Tom thought. Of course! Margaret would order the man *The Satanic Bible* if she thought it would get her into his Y-fronts. She handed the book to Tom. "I've already stamped it," she said.

"Thanks," Tom said, tucking the book underneath his arm. He wished her a pleasant afternoon and left the library with Wood's book and his article printout. Not a bad haul, considering.

Tom sheltered from the rain—which was coming down in sheets—for a few minutes, lit a cigarette—on the fourth attempt—and decided to take a look at what was next on Wood's reading list.

The book was heavy, but its cover gave no clue as to what it contained. A single line of text, with awful kerning, was its only feature. There wasn't even an author's byline.

GHUUL: THE CHILDREN-EATER

"Holy shit!" Tom said. Was this fiction? It certainly didn't look like it. Where the hell did Margaret even find this book? It was like something someone had self-published, only to decide they didn't want their name on it after all.

After examining the book more closely while the rain hammered the pavement six feet in front of him, Tom realised this was a relatively serious investigation into some Babylonian deity. The writing was scientific; to Tom, it was like reading the instruction manual for the Large Hadron Collider, but he had no doubt Wood knew what he was looking for.

The Children-Eater?

Did Wood think this had something to do with the Ice Cream Man? That wasn't possible. Frederick White was no Babylonian deity; he was just a spurned husband making a run for it.

Maybe Wood knew something Tom didn't. He'd been researching for so long, perhaps the old guy had turned up something useful, something which Tom would never have considered possible in a million years.

Maybe, Tom thought for the very first time, *I need Wood more than he needs me.*

SIXTEEN

OCTOBER 28TH, 2016
ST. GEORGE'S HOSPITAL
TOOTING, LONDON

Screaming. Women screaming. Men moaning. Agony? Pleasure? It was hard to tell the difference. Beeping. Machines whirring and screeching. The sound of a squeaky trolley-wheel zipping by somewhere to his right.

Open your eyes, Luke...

But he couldn't. Not just yet. It was far too bright, and his eyes felt brand new. Fluorescent lights hovered above where he lay; he could hear them buzzing, could see their glow through his eyelids.

Pain in his left arm. An IV, perhaps? What was happening to him? How had he come to be here, in this room with its incessantly beeping appliances and, just beyond, a whole army of lamenting souls?

He had been in an accident. That much he knew. But what? What accident? It was just out of reach, the explanation he desperately sought. He could almost taste the words on his lips—car crash—but not quite, not just then. It would be several more hours before the doctor arrived to tell him what had happened, that he was very lucky to be alive, and that the man in the other vehicle was doing well. *Uninjured*, would be the word the doctor used, uninjured and doing just fine, "But we're keeping him in for observations," and Luke would nod and thank the heavens he hadn't killed someone.

But for now, he needed sleep. He needed to go back under, let the doctors and nurses do their thing all around him while he fell deeper into the darkness and his pain washed slowly away.

He slept.

* * *

Ghuul.

"What?" *Luke was in a tiny room, surrounded on four sides by brick walls. He was seated at a table, upon which sat a fruit-bowl, its contents seemingly ripe and fresh for the taking. There was a strange scent in the air—vanilla?—and Luke knew straight away that this was a dream. It was far too surreal to be anything but.* "What does that mean? Ghuul?" *Now that he had established this was fantasy, what the Scottish might call a Dwam, he relaxed a little, for nothing could hurt him here, could it? Nothing could hurt you in a dream? Luke had read, once, that if you fell from a great height in your dream and didn't awaken before you hit the ground, then you died in reality. However, he knew that to be complete bullshit; he had hit the ground on many occasions. He had fallen from skyscrapers in the wake of 9/11—too much TV footage, he ascribed that to—and had woken to feel pretty damn bad about himself the next morning. He had survived flayings and beheadings, gunshots and war.*

You simply could not die as a result of a dream.

Ghuul.

"I heard you the first time," *Luke said, standing from the table.* "But what does it mean, and who are you?"

One question at a time, Luke thought, otherwise this could all get a little confusing.

When no answer came, Luke explored the four walls, dragged his hands across the coarse brickwork, feeling for... what? A secret passageway? A loose brick that would send one of the walls sliding aside to reveal a hidden room? This wasn't Indiana Jones, and Luke certainly wasn't Harrison Ford, even in his dreams. There would be no ancient artefact discovery here today. Just confusion and nonsensical mindfuckery, what the old folk liked to call 'Bamboozlement'.

The fruit—apples, pears, bananas, peaches, grapes, all perfectly formed and reflecting a light-source which didn't exist anywhere else in the room—was wholly appealing, even though it wasn't real, and Luke knew it wasn't real.

This is a dream, he kept reminding himself.

And yet, just because it was a dream, did that mean he had to starve? Did that mean he should ignore the fruit his mind had put out for him?

The mind works in mysterious ways. What if that fruit bowl was his only chance of recovery, and the eating thereof would see him rise from the ashes like a Phoenix, ready to soar again over the houses and treetops of London?

What if the fruit was poisoned, and the eating of just one piece sent his recuperating body into a coma? Would Karen visit with their daughter? Would she change his soiled nappies, massage his seized-up limbs, read to him his favourite poets? Would Lydia grow into a woman while he lay there, cabbaged, unable to comprehend the world still moving all around him?

Luke decided not to eat the fruit.

"Ghuul."

Luke turned around, but it was like moving through water and took wholly longer than it should have. There, sitting upon a wooden bench which hadn't been there a moment ago, was his daughter. She looked so happy, so innocent, and in her hand, she held her favourite dolly, Katie.

"Lydia," Luke said, moving across the room towards her. "What are you doing here? You shouldn't be here. Where's your mother?"

Lydia giggled. Even though her voice was tiny, it seemed to echo around the brick chamber. For a moment, Luke was angry. There was nothing funny about what he had said, nothing remotely giggle-worthy about leaving an eight-year-old girl to go off a-wandering. But then Luke remembered that this was just a dream, that Lydia was probably at home, in her own bed, sleeping well and entirely unaware of what had happened to him.

"Does your mother know about the accident?" *Might as well play along, Luke thought.*

Lydia nodded. "She said you were probably speeding; probably drunk, too. Were you, Daddy? Were you drink-driving?" She looked solemn, disappointed in him.

"No, sweetie!" Luke said, dropping to one knee so that he

was level with her. He took her by the hand—it was like ice—
and said, "Daddy doesn't do things like that, despite what your
mother tells you."

"She's on her way to the hospital right now," said Lydia.
"To see you. She's very upset, Daddy. She dropped me off at
Inderjeet's house, which sucks because I really wanted to see
you."

"You're seeing me right now," Luke reminded her, but she
wasn't, really. The dream was so vivid, Luke had to keep
reminding himself it wasn't real. Lydia wasn't here right now
talking to him; Karen wasn't rushing to the hospital to be at his
bedside. They were both at home, oblivious. Karen was still
angry with him for what he had tried to do.

If anything, Luke thought, it was the police who would be
on their way, if they were not already waiting outside his room
for him to waken so they could slap the cuffs on him and drag
him off to wherever it was you went for attempted murder.

Prison.

"Ghuul," Lydia said, her lips curling into a tiny smile.

"You keep saying that," Luke said, "but what does it
mean?"

Lydia laughed, and there was nothing cute about it. In
fact, Luke shuddered. "He's coming back, Daddy," she said.
"He's coming back and he's going to make you pay."

"Who?" Luke said. "Who's coming back, sweetie?" But he
already knew the answer. This was quickly turning into a
nightmare; his subconscious was toying with him. The Ice
Cream Man's sudden reappearance was sending him crazy.

"You know who, Daddy," Lydia said, the smile growing
wider.

Luke nodded. Of course he knew. He was lying in a
hospital bed, having this bad dream right now, because of the
Ice Cream Man. He wouldn't be here if it weren't for that
monster.

"He's angry, Daddy," Lydia said. "He's angry with you for
escaping him, you and your friends." She began to comb the
long blonde hair sprouting from Katie's plastic head. "He is
Ghuul, Daddy, and you're going to wish you'd never crossed

him."

There came a strange hissing noise from behind, and when Luke turned, he saw the fruit on the table beginning to rot like so many deflating balloons. Flies punched out through the putrid fruit flesh, took to the air in swarms.

Lydia was laughing now, as if this were a show put on merely to entertain her.

The flies still came, a thick dark fog in the air above the decaying fruit bowl, the incessant droning enough to drive even the sanest man to the brink of madness.

"He's waking up..."

Luke began to swat at the flies, trying to keep them away from his daughter, who was once again nonchalantly brushing her dolly's hair as if nothing untoward was happening. The brick walls on all four sides began to break apart; cement crumbled down like water from a burst pipe. The whole thing was going to come crashing down.

And still the flies buzzed.

"Luke? Luke? Hold him down..."

The fruit was now nothing more than blackened pulp; the glass bowl in which it sat exploded, showering shards of crystal down upon Luke and his daughter. Flies were attacking now, and Luke could not keep them off. There were simply too many.

Ghuul.

"Luke, wake up..."

Who is that? Luke thought, of the voice that he kept hearing. It sounded familiar. A man's voice he had heard many times before.

"Don't fight it, Daddy," Lydia said. "And when he comes for you, let him have his way or this will never end."

"NO!" Luke cried, his mouth now full of buzzing flies.

"Should we call a nurse?"

Luke spat out the flies, but there were more, and they began to fill him up, crawling and flying and creeping into every crack of his body. He could feel them within him, and he howled out in agony as more and more sought entry to his temple.

"I'm coming for you, Daddy," said Lydia, only now it

wasn't Lydia at all. The Ice Cream Man looked incongruous and never more evil sitting in her place, combing the hair of his daughter's favourite doll.

"NOOOOOO!"

"He's awake! Luke! Calm down! Luke, you were just having a bad dream! Luke!"

* * *

Luke bolted upright and immediately regretted it. His ribs were so sore, and his left leg throbbed as if someone had placed it in a vice and turned the handle until it would go no further.

Hands.

Hands were holding him in place, easing him back down, and it took a long time for him to realise who the hands belonged to.

"It's okay, Luke," Karen said. "Everything is going to be okay. Please, just lie down. The nurse is on her way."

"Ka... Karen?" Lydia in the dream had been right; his wife had come to visit him at the hospital. Just another subconscious/unconscious trick, he thought. He must have heard Karen's voice; must have known she would be here when he opened his eyes. That's what it was.

"You're going to be okay," Karen told him, leaning in and kissing him lightly on the forehead. "Just try to relax, yeah?"

"Should I go?" It was the voice Luke thought he recognised, the one he had heard in the dream, and when Karen moved back, Luke saw the man standing there between the bed and the door.

"Marcus?" It was! It was Marcus, his old friend come to visit him. Shit, how bad was this?

"Long time, mate," Marcus said, forcing a smile. He hissed a little, as if even that small gesture pained him.

"What... what are you doing here?"

Marcus stepped closer to the bed, seemed to ask Karen for permission to speak—she nodded, *Go right ahead*—and said, "Who'd have thought it would take a car crash to get the old team back together, huh?"

Confused, and still seeing things through blurred vision, Luke said, "You were there?"

"There?" Marcus laughed. "I was just minding my own business when you came bolting out of that street. You think your car's a write-off? Mine's still sticking out of some poor old couple's living-room. Had that BMW less than a month, so you owe me forty-two grand, unless you're not as dumb as I think you are, and you were insured up to the hilt."

"He's just joking, Luke," Karen said, her smile warming his rapidly beating heart. "He said he was going to say that to you when you came around. Said you'd appreciate the joke."

"He was damn right," Luke said.

Was this really happening? Could this be just another bad dream? The last one had started off just as pleasantly, before turning into something *Lynch*ian. Had he really crashed into Marcus, the friend he hadn't seen in almost thirty years? What were the odds? And if so, what was Marcus doing back in Havering?

The same as you, Luke thought.

He knows what's coming.

"Get some rest, buddy," Marcus said, placing a huge hand on top of Luke's. No wonder he was so good at boxing, Luke thought. His hands were like shovels, could knock out a gorilla, if they connected just right. "I'm going back to my bed. Those nurses are giving me shit about keep wandering off the ward. I think they just know how famous and important I am, and they don't want to have to explain to the press how it is a champ can simply disappear from St. George's." He was joking, of course. Luke had seen hundreds of interviews on the TV over the years; Marcus channelled Ali as best he could, right down to the ego. You had to take everything Marcus said with a pinch of salt, otherwise you'd think he was a complete dick.

"Talk later, mate," Luke said. And just before Marcus reached the door, he said, "Sorry about your Beemer. I'll buy you a new one when I get out of here. You take cheques?"

"Don't worry about it," Marcus said, pushing the door open and stepping through it. Without even breaking his stride, he said, "I've got three more of them." And then he was gone, and the door was whispering slowly shut behind him.

I'll be damned, Luke thought. *Marcus Berry*. And it was

real, too. He knew that now. This wasn't a dream; this was fate.

Bringing them together.

Bringing Karen here to see him today so that they could work through their problems. They had so much to figure out; Luke didn't know where to begin.

"Karen, about what happened—"

"Don't," Karen said, pulling a chair up to the bed and sitting down. "Just rest, okay? That's all that matters right now."

Luke nodded. Karen was right; this was no place to talk about what had happened, what he had almost done to their daughter. That conversation would come in time, but not now.

The machines continued to beep and whir, the nurses and doctors came and went, and Luke slept fitfully as Karen sat watching.

SEVENTEEN

OCTOBER 28TH, 2016, REDBRIDGE, LONDON

Wood read the article one more time before handing the printout back to Tom, a grave expression worrying his countenance. "Why didn't I know about this?" he said, more to himself than to Tom. "I've been looking into this damn case since you were twelve-years-old. You show up and, an hour at the library later, you're all caught up."

Tom shrugged. "I had help from Margaret Banks," he said. "You know, she's surprisingly good with technology."

"That Frederick White stuff, it all happened the year before your friend went missing." Wood swallowed half his pint down in one thirsty gulp before setting the glass down on the table and continuing. "One year exactly, according to the article. If this is the guy we're looking for—"

"If?" Tom said. "You think there's any chance it's *not* White?" He placed the printout down on the table, spun it so it was the right way up for Wood, and pointed at the vehicle being pulled from the Thames. "See? Same yellow-and-white ice cream truck. Unless there's another vengeful ghost out there, driving around in an identical truck, I don't think we even have to consider the possibility that Frederick White is *not* our guy."

Even though he had examined the picture closely several times already, Wood leaned in and took another look. "It is, isn't it," he said. "This is the truck I saw outside the school that night. The night Cheryl Mitchell went missing."

"Only when you saw it," Tom said, "it wasn't real." This was all getting a little confusing; Wood's frown prompted Tom to explain what he meant. "This truck, the one in the photograph, was probably crushed years ago, even before Ryan was taken. I'm guessing, as evidence, it wasn't much use, so wouldn't they just scrap the thing, rather than keep it impounded indefinitely?"

"They would have squashed it," Wood said. "They must have. There's no way that thing would have been kept in an impoundment for thirty years. No way."

"So, the van doesn't even exist, not really, just like Frederick White doesn't exist, at least not as anything we can possibly understand." Tom took out a cigarette and was about to light it right there in the pub before realising, at the last second, the law had changed years ago. That's how much this was all getting to him; he'd forgotten simple things, like the fact you could no longer smoke indoors in public spaces. He took it from his mouth and tucked it behind his ear.

"So, you're saying the truck is a ghost, too?" Wood said.

"I think it's an extension of White," Tom said. "He died in that vehicle, his daughter screaming beside him as it filled up with water and sank to the bottom of the river."

"And now he's taking a new child every seven years, for what?" Wood said. "Nobody killed his daughter. He was responsible for what happened to her, not the Fieldings, or the Mitchells or the Poulsons... it was *his* fault—"

"He was chased into the river by your boys," Tom said. "All blues and sirens, going after him hard, and for what? Because he'd had an argument with his missus and had decided to leave with his daughter?"

"That counts as kidnap, whether you're the kid's parent or not," Wood said.

"Point being, he shouldn't have died there that day. His daughter—Isobel—shouldn't have died there that day, and now he's back, and he's just going to keep on coming until..." He trailed off there, because he didn't know how they were going to stop this sonofabitch. The Ice Cream Man, Frederick White, Ghuul? "So, what's with the book?" Tom said, of the hefty tome sitting in the front basket of Wood's mobility scooter. "Think it has something do with White?"

Wood shrugged. He took the book out of the basket and began to flick through it. "I've been looking into this stuff for so long now, I'm starting to feel like I should have my own show.

You know? Just me, wheeling myself around apparently haunted buildings, screaming every time I run into a cobweb or the wind picks up outside."

"You're no Yvette Fielding," Tom said.

The reference seemed to be lost on Wood, who, Tom thought, probably didn't even own a TV set, just sat there in his one-bed flat staring at the pictures Sellotaped to his walls, trying to figure shit out. "This is the closest thing I could find on our ghost, or demon, or whatever the fuck it is." He searched for a specific page in the book and, when he located it, handed it over to Tom.

There, on the page, was a crude sketch of what appeared to be Ghuul, Eater of Children. All abs and fangs, axe clutched in one hand and the decapitated head of some unfortunate soul in the other. Tom wasn't sure how serious Wood was being with this. "Doesn't look like the thing I saw," he said. *Or the thing that keeps showing up when I least expect it.*

"Ghuul takes whatever form it needs to," Wood said. "All it needs is a tragedy and a willing receptacle."

"And the tragedy in this case," Tom said, "would be Frederick White steering him and his daughter into the Thames."

Wood nodded. "Just a theory," he said, "but if what we're dealing with here *is* Ghuul, then we're fucked. And I don't just mean 'up Shit Creek without a paddle' fucked. I mean 'might as well roll over and die right now' fucked."

Tom sighed. "The Children-Eater?" he said. "Is that what this thing does?"

Wood took the book back and began to flick through it, although what he was looking for, Tom didn't know. "Not in a literal sense," he said. "It's more of a figurative thing. From the small amount of research I've been able to do on this thing—you have no idea how difficult it is to find stuff on this bastard—the Ghuul needs somewhere to take the children, a netherworld, a realm beyond our own, and it's there that he keeps them, devouring their souls over many years." The way he spoke, so matter-of-factly, was almost as frightening to Tom as the concept of the Ghuul itself.

"What are we talking about here?" Tom said. "Torture? Abuse? Cannibalism?"

"From what I understand, none of the above," Wood said, which came as a relief to Tom. That his friend had suffered so inordinately at the hands of this creature was too much to contemplate. "This world, an infinitesimal distance from our own—a gnat's bollock away, to be more precise—drains the children, leaves them paralysed, fighting to survive, and it's a fight they are destined to lose. Just being there is all it takes; it's a world created for one thing, and one thing only. The consumption of souls. It literally sucks the life out of a person, only over an extended amount of time. Years, decades, centuries..." He trailed off there, and Tom was grateful for it. This was all too much to absorb in one sitting, and Tom couldn't help feeling as though he hadn't yet taken enough alcohol on board to even consider the possibility that Ryan Fielding was still being tapped of his essence right now, even after all these years.

"Can I read that when you're done with it?" It wasn't Tom's usual subgenre—child-devouring Babylonian gods didn't appeal to him the same way Terry Pratchett novels did—but if Wood was right, and this was the creature they were going up against, then it made sense to learn as much as they could about it, find out its weaknesses, if indeed it has any, and figure out a way to ultimately stop it from transporting more minors to its soul-sapping world, wherever that might be.

Wood reversed his scooter from the table and made his way toward the bar, stopping only for a second to answer. "You can read it first, if you think it'll help," he said. "Same again?"

"Cheers."

When Wood returned from the bar a little over ten minutes later—The Walnut Tree was severely understaffed—he said, "So, what's our next move?"

Tom took a sip of whiskey before speaking. "We'll need a little bit of luck," he said, removing a scrap of paper from his pocket, "but this is the last known address of Laura White. It's the house she used to live in with Frederick and their daughter."

"Where did you get that?" Wood looked almost impressed. Almost, but not quite. Tom felt as if he already knew Trevor

Wood well, well enough to know it would take more than an address scribbled on a piece of paper to excite him.

"There's this thing," Tom said, "called the World Wide Web. You might have heard of it—"

"Okay, smart-aleck," Wood said. "So you got the Whites' old address from the internet. And what? You think she's still living there?"

Tom shrugged. "We're due a bit of luck," he said. Did he really think it was a good idea turning up on Burke Street with the intention of dragging Laura White once again through the darkest days of her entire life? Of course not. Did they have a choice? Not really.

"And what, pray tell, do you think the wife's going to be able to tell us?" Wood asked. "That her husband was unhinged? That she hates him with every ounce of her being, and that she'll never be able to forgive him for what he did to their daughter?"

"I don't know," Tom said, drawing a finger through the condensation left upon the table by his glass. "She might be able to tell us *something*. Something to better understand how this happened, how Frederick was a father one minute, and an eater of children's souls the next. I don't know about you, but I think that's a helluva leap to make. I mean, could that happen to anyone? To any one of us when we die? Instead of moving on to Heaven or Hell or wherever the fuck it is we're meant to go, we're suddenly employed as demons, told to prowl the streets at night looking for innocent souls to add to the tally? Because that's fucked up!"

"I don't think it happens to just *anyone*," Wood said. "Like you, I think there is more to this than meets the eye. Fine, you want to go pay the widow White a visit? I'm with you. All I'm saying is that, if she is still living there, don't expect her to be forthcoming."

"I expect her to slam the door in our faces almost immediately," Tom said, for he did.

"In that case, you have no reason to fear disappointment," Wood said. "Would you do me a huge favour? Put that book away somewhere nice and safe. People are starting to notice it, and I don't want them to think we're starting some sort of gay cult."

Laughing, Tom secreted the book beneath his jacket, which sat on the chair beside him. They finished their drinks in silence. Tom had no idea what Wood was thinking—the old man's face seldom changed expression—but all Tom could think about was how things had changed so irrevocably in the past few days, how easily his life had descended into chaos, and how much he missed Danielle and wanted her back right there and then, to hold, to kiss, to tell her he loved her.

He would call her tonight to let her know he was still alive, that there was nothing to worry about. He would even throw in a lie or two about seeing Kurian again late next week, just to placate her.

"Ready?" Tom had finished his drink. His glass now sat empty on the table.

Wood put his own glass down—half a pint remaining—and said, "Let's get this over with."

* * *

OCTOBER 28TH, 2016
HAVERING, LONDON

The house was nothing special; just a semi-detached in Havering, like hundreds of others. The only difference being its apparent deterioration, as if its owner cared little for outward appearance. The windowsills were rotten; paint flaked from the building as if it were trying, so so hard, to shed its skin. The front garden—if it could be called such—was overgrown with grass and weeds and unkempt hedges. Buried there, at the centre of the mess, was a child's perambulator, the kind which a daughter would push proudly around while her dolly's eyes flickered open and shut, open and shut. Had that tiny pink pushchair once belonged to Isobel White? Was that thirty years' worth of rust eating away at its paintwork, at the aluminium frame?

"Hate to say it, kid," Wood said, glancing up at the house from the pavement just outside its eroded gate, "but if Laura White still lives here, in *this*, I'm not sure we should be knocking on her door." He sounded reluctant, sure, but also a little afraid.

Tom felt it, too. "She'll be an old woman by now," he said.

"She'd be the same age as me," Wood said. "And if I wasn't in this fucking chair, I'd teach you some manners." He was joking, of course, but Tom made a mental note to choose his words more carefully from here on.

After the pub, Tom and Wood had gone back to the former copper's ground-floor flat to, as Wood called it, 'part-ex vehicles'. In other words, he wanted his wheelchair, which was easier to manoeuvre and made him look less like a lazy fucker and more like a man who could not walk.

Wood's flat-cum-bedsit had been just as Tom pictured it. No soft furnishings, a complete lack of colour, and files and folders scattered everywhere. Wood might have left the police force a long time ago, but old habits die hard. He was still investigating. Still looking into things which shouldn't concern him, and not just the missing children cases. All around Wood's room there were notes and pictures, newspaper cut-outs and scribbled theories. This was the room of a man very much still working—albeit without pay, and with no real jurisdiction.

"We can stand her all afternoon," Tom said, "but I'm pretty sure it's going to start raining in a minute, and we didn't come all this way to look at someone's overgrown garden." For Tom, it wasn't a case of whether they were going to knock the door of 7, Burke Street. It was a case of whether he was going to be doing it alone, while Wood sat out here, waiting, probably getting wet.

"Go on, then," Wood said, motioning to the rust-worn gate. "What? You want me to open the damn thing?"

There was nothing, not even a suggestion, of a pathway leading up to the house, and in places the grass was up to Tom's chest—and the top of Wood's head. Though Wood was adamant he didn't need any help getting through the forest of regular and timothy-grass, Tom latched on to the handles of the wheelchair and pushed through it toward the house.

By the time they arrived at the front door, both Tom and Wood were covered with sticky buds and greenfly, and there was a strong smell of meadow clinging to them, such an incongruity out here in East London. Tom was breathless, for the wheelchair and its contents were heavy, especially over such uneven terrain.

The porch was lined with old, dirty shoes. Here was a pair of filthy stilettos, there a pair of steel-toe-capped work-boots, but it was the tiny pink wellies which caused Tom's heart to falter. Printed upon their side, and just about visible, were a pair of glittery butterflies cavorting around one another.

"Look," Wood said, pointing up at a sign stuck to the front door.

> **NO SOLICITING OF ANY KIND. NO RELIGION. WE WON'T BUY FROM YOU. WE DON'T NEED ANY ADVICE. NO EXCEPTIONS.**

"Looks like someone's had enough of the Jehovah's Witnesses."

"I've got to get me one of those signs," Tom said, and he meant it. He was just about sick of cold callers. The owner of this house—Laura White or not—had the right idea. "But we're not here to sell anything, are we?"

"After a sign like that," Wood said, "you really think she's going to come to the door?"

"Only one way to find out." Tom reached in through the open porch and knocked lightly three times on the front door. There was, he noticed, no bell, no knocker; was that to prevent people from taking liberties? So that those who missed the sign, that great big yellow-and-black thing in the middle of the porch door, realised they weren't welcome to knock at this house. Move along, nothing to see here.

Some time passed, and Tom listened for movement from within. The opening of a door, the insuppressible cough or sneeze of a hiding woman, the oblivious clatters of a lady hard of hearing—for there was always that possibility—working away in the kitchen at the rear of the house and unable to hear the knocking at the door.

"Knock again," Wood said. "Harder." But he didn't wait for Tom to do so. The ex-copper reached down, picked up one of the tiny pink wellington boots, and flung it hard at the door. There was an almighty thump as the boot hit and then bounced off.

"What the—"

"Just wait," Wood said, seemingly unaware of the curious way he was acting. Tom ascribed it to fear. Fear and uncertainty. Neither of them knew how this was going to pan out, whether they had made, what would turn out to be, a wasted journey. Whether Laura White even lived here any longer. This—their being here—was one of their only leads; if it came to nothing, they were back to square one, with nothing but a library book and a newspaper clipping.

Just then, and not a second too soon as far as Tom was concerned, there was movement beyond the door. Tom glanced down at Wood, who arched his eyebrows and smiled.

"Sometimes you've just got to throw a boot at the door," he said.

A voice from the other side of the door—female, cracked, and not at all welcoming—said, "Go away."

Go away.

"Mrs White?" Tom said. Was that even right? Would it still be Mrs White, or would it be Ms White? Tom hadn't a clue, and it was too late now to change it. *Should have just gone with Laura*, he thought.

"Read the sign," said the voice. "I don't buy or bullshit with cold-callers—"

It was Wood's turn to speak. "Mrs White, we're here to talk to you about your husband, a mister Frederick White."

A beat.

Tom and Wood exchanged a glance, one which said, She's not going to open up for us, and if she does it will be a miracle.

"Frederick died," came the voice after the longest time.

"We know that, Mrs White," Wood went on. "That's what we're here to discuss. You see, there have been a couple of new developments, and we really need to speak with you to—"

The sound of a key turning; a chain sliding across, and then the door swung inward to reveal Laura White, standing there with a cigarette in one hand while the other hand teased nervously at her unkempt silver hair.

She looked, Tom thought, like a woman of eighty, and not sixty-three. Her thin lips overlapped one another—Laura White obviously wore dentures, though not today—and dark bags sat beneath her eyes like shadows. The long white dressing gown she wore gave her a somewhat ghostly appearance, as did the gnarled and veiny arms protruding from its sleeves. Her skin seemed to stretch taut over her skeleton and looked as brittle as centuries-old parchment. She was a woman who had lived a hard life, a woman who had not forgiven herself for what had happened to her daughter—her *husband*—and a woman to whom death could not come a moment too soon.

She looked at Tom long and hard, then turned her attention to Wood, who squirmed a little in his chair as she appraised him. Tom could tell the ex-copper was uncomfortable with this whole thing; gone was his usual severity, replaced by insecurity and hesitation. All those years on the police force, questioning people, taking statements and generally making a menace of himself, all now lost. Was he doubting himself? Doubting what they were trying to do here? Tom didn't know, but he knew someone was going to have to say something soon or he was certain Laura White would shut the door in their faces.

"You policemen?" Laura said, taking a long drag on her cigarette before exhaling a plume of blue fog back into the hallway.

"I was," Wood said. "A long time ago."

Tom didn't know what to say. Did he lie, tell the old lady he was a copper, or did he tell her the truth—that he was here as a concerned citizen, concerned that her husband was about to return from beyond the grave once again to wreak havoc and transport children to his netherworld, where he would feast upon their souls for all eternity, or until they were wholly devoured, whichever came first?

Thankfully he didn't have to do either.

Laura White stepped aside and motioned them to enter.

If the exterior of the house was like something from one of the myriad daytime home makeover programmes (the BEFORE stage, not the AFTER) then the inside was just as bad, if not worse. Newspapers were stacked throughout the ground floor;

they lined the hallway, the tiny kitchenette in which no cooking had apparently been attempted for quite some time, and the living-room, which was the worst of the lot. No sooner had Tom followed Laura White into the living-room than he smelt it. An assault on his nose—shit, piss, rotten food, Lord knows what else—made him gag, but he swallowed it back down, for it wouldn't be polite to walk into someone's house and immediately throw up in their most cherished of rooms.

How Wood managed to traverse the decades' worth of junk and tat which filled up the house was a mystery to Tom, but there they were in the living-room, and Wood was the lucky one! He was already sitting down; Tom couldn't see a seat anywhere and resigned himself to standing until one was pointed out to him.

"I'd offer you a drink," said Laura, "but I have no idea where the kettle is."

"Don't worry about it," Tom said. The last thing he wanted here was a drink. Several flies danced around the light fixture at the centre of the room, their buzzing a distraction, their infuriating circling and plunging a good advertisement for flyswatters. "We really appreciate this, Mrs White. There really is no easy way to go about it, so we're going to be as brief as possible."

"You talk funny," Laura said, lighting a new cigarette from the butt of the one she had just smoked. Her grin made her look almost crazy, as if life had managed to get the better of her.

Wood took a deep intake of breath before speaking. "Mrs White... well, there's no really easy way to put this, but..." So hard were the words to find, that Wood seemingly gave up mid-sentence.

"We believe," Tom said, taking over, "that the death of your husband is related to several disappearances in the area, dating back to 1988."

Laura White almost choked on a mouthful of smoke. "What?" she said. "Frederick died in '87. How the hell could he have anything to do with something which happened afterwards?"

Tom and Wood exchanged a glance; they were, Tom realised, doing that a lot lately. "I don't quite know how to explain it," Tom said, "but we're sure your husband's death, and the death of your daughter, are directly related to the missing children."

"Bullshit!" Laura White couldn't have placed any more venom behind the word if she tried; perhaps it was the mention of her daughter. "That day, the day that bastard killed my little girl, was the end of Frederick White. And good riddance! As far as I'm concerned, he can rot, if he hasn't already."

So there was no love lost between husband and wife. Laura White despised the man, had never forgiven him for what he'd done, and wouldn't piss on him if he were on fire right now and standing in that cluttered living-room, screaming for mercy.

One thing was bothering Tom. He had never found out why Frederick White had run from the police on that day, had put it down to a domestic disturbance and nothing more. It was a good idea to clarify that point right now. "Mrs White—"

"Knock it off what that Mrs White horseshit," she said. "Nobody, at least nobody from around here, has called me that in years. It's Laura. Laura Dixon. Has been ever since the coroner signed the papers."

Tom nodded his thanks, for he was finding it increasingly difficult to keep up the formalities. "The last thing I want to do is drag up events from three decades ago, but what happened? On the day Frederick ran from the police?"

Reluctant at first—as if she was considering covering for her ex-husband momentarily—Laura sighed deeply and said, "Frederick was not a nice man." As easy as that. "Oh, everyone who knew him thought he was this great guy, this gentleman, just an Ice Cream Man, hard-working, good with kids, but... there was more to Frederick than that. He had what some doctors would call, I suppose, mental issues." She paused, lit yet another cigarette and extinguished the second in an over-spilling ashtray before continuing. "He kept that part of him hidden from the rest of the world, let everyone think he was perfect when, in fact, he was sick. Of course, I didn't know that when I married him, otherwise I'd have told him to get up off his knee and jump in the fucking river.

"It was less than a month after our wedding that I realised

I'd made a big mistake. He put me in hospital with three broken ribs, a fractured cheekbone, and two black eyes. I covered for him. Of course I covered for him. I told the police I'd tumbled down the stairs, and they believed me. Frederick was even there at the hospital, putting on this great façade, bringing me flowers and grapes, the way any good husband would. The nurses would come into my room after he'd gone and tell me how lucky I was, how much they liked Frederick. 'Such a good husband,' they would say, and I would fight back the urge to leap off the bed, grab them by the throat, and shake some sense into them.

"No one could see it, you see. How this man could be anything but good. He even had me fooled. I left the hospital—I remember it well because we had a really bad storm that day, thunder, lightning, rain, the whole shebang—with the promise it would never happen again. And it didn't, not for a couple of years, but I never truly trusted him after that. I kept a wide berth, you know what I mean? I made sure his dinner was on the table when he got back from selling lollies and twisters to the kids in the neighbourhood. I made sure his apron was clean, ready for the next day, when he'd go out again, putting on smiles and telling the kids all these great stories as he served them. I ran his baths for him and made sure he had the TV remote control on the arm of his chair, just how he liked it, because I was terrified of him. I'm not going to lie to you, I feared for my life, even back then, before Isobel came."

"Is this her?" Wood bent down, picked up something next to the left wheel of his chair, and stared intently down at it.

"Yeah, that was Isobel." The use of past tense was not lost upon Tom. "She never got any older than in that photograph."

Tom could see the face of the little girl behind the glass in Wood's hand. It was a school photograph—the kind every child has to sit for on a yearly basis—only there was no smile here, no real expression in the eyes. Isobel White had been left hollow by the actions of her father, the same way Laura White had. This girl was not happy; she merely existed.

But not anymore.

"I kept the pregnancy to myself for as long as I could. Frederick was out most of the day in the summer months, and luckily Isobel wasn't due until Christmas, so it was easy. When the bump became too difficult to hide, I made sure my mother was with me when I broke the news to Frederick, that we were going to have a baby, that he was going to be a father. I was frightened, you see, that he'd be angry. I had visions of him just punching me, as hard as he could, in the stomach. To get rid of it.

"My mother never suspected anything, other than I wanted her there when I surprised Frederick with what should have been good news. And Frederick took it well. I could see in his eyes that he was genuinely happy. We'd never talked about having a child, and we didn't have intercourse—sex is such a disgusting word—that often, because Frederick often fell asleep in front of the TV, watching snooker. But, like I say, he took it well, and I was so relieved."

Tom and Wood listened carefully. Already Tom didn't like where this was going.

"When Isobel was born, I thought everything would be okay. Frederick had calmed down, somewhat, although I knew not to become complacent. He was always just one step away from a full-blown outburst, and now I didn't just have to protect myself. We had a child, a daughter, and there was no way I would ever let him hurt her the way he hurt me.

"I wasn't ready for what happened next. Isobel's second birthday should have been a happy occasion, but Frederick had had some kids run off with ice creams without paying, and so by the time he came home, he was already cranky. He tore down the banners I'd made, popped all the balloons, and threw all the food I'd prepared in the bin. I think that was the moment I knew he no longer liked children. He suffered them, at least that was how he now saw it, but he hated having to deal with them all day long. I guess it's like any job, really. You spend all day delivering mail, you're going to quickly despise being chased by angry dogs, or getting your fingers trapped in letterboxes.

"Frederick now hated children, and we had one of our own. I never saw him do anything to Isobel—you have to understand that if I had, I would have been out there like a shot—but she was always crying, more often when Frederick was around, and I've never known a baby vomit so much. I'm not just talking about a bit of sick-up; she would really go for it. And diarrhoea, too. 'She's just doing baby stuff,' was what Frederick said when I confronted him about it, but I wasn't convinced and took Isobel to see a doctor.

"Salmonellosis, they said. They asked me if Isobel had eaten any chicken in the last few days, chicken which might have been undercooked. I told them no, of course not, why would we be feeding our two-year-old baby undercooked chicken, but at the back of my mind, all I could picture was the bowl of legs and wings sitting in the freezer, covered over with clingfilm. Frederick had recently made friends with a local butcher, and so the fridge was always stocked to bursting with meat. I had to get rid of all my vegetables, just to make room, because every time he came home from work, he had another bag of stinking chicken or minced lamb."

"He was poisoning her?" Wood said then. "He was feeding Isobel raw chicken?"

Laura nodded. Her lips were drawn tight; the circles surrounding her eyes seemed to have darkened in the short time they had been talking. "I didn't have any proof, but from that moment on I didn't let Isobel out of my sight. I took care of all the feeds, all the baths, everything, because I didn't trust him with her. What kind of sick bastard tries to make his own child ill?"

It happens more than you'd think, Tom thought but didn't say. He had read about it somewhere—a magazine, perhaps, or newspaper article—and they even had a name for it. Munchausen Syndrome by Proxy. Making a child ill to elicit sympathy or for financial gain.

But that's not what Frederick White had been trying to do.

He was trying to kill her.

His own daughter.

Tom was sure of it.

"When I asked Frederick not to bring any more meat home—we'd had to buy a chest freezer for the garage, just so none of it spoiled—he told me to mind my own damn business. 'Don't tell me what the fuck to do, you old witch,' were his exact words. I could see he was on the brink once again, but you know what? It was in his eyes. He was looking for an excuse to kill me, even then. To kill us both. I've never seen such evil in a person before, and it terrified me."

"Why didn't you get out of there?" Wood asked, adjusting his position. *He* was uncomfortable, and yet I was the one still standing, shifting from one foot to the other.

"It wouldn't have made a difference," Laura said, her pained grin revealing two rows of shiny pink gums. "I thought about it. A lot. Just grabbing Isobel in the middle of the night and driving to my mother's house—or just driving anywhere; that was better than spending another day in fear, not knowing whether Frederick was going to blow a fuse and put me in hospital again, or worse. Hurt her. Hurt Isobel.

"Running wasn't the answer. All I could do was safeguard, make sure Isobel didn't get sick again, placate Frederick as best I could. That went on for five more years." She shook her head, as if even she couldn't quite believe she had survived that long, suffered for that long. "He had his moments. Bad days. Days the children called him names or swore at him. He tolerated it with them, but then came home to us, and it was us who suffered for those children, those kids that called him 'creepy' and 'pervert', just because of what he did for a living.

"One thing I know is that Frederick White was not a pervert. He hated kids too much to want to do... that... to them, but I was still wary of him being alone with Isobel, not least because she was growing up to be a fine young girl." She paused here, swallowed hard. Tom could see she was fighting back tears, and for the first time he felt as if they were intruders here, that they had no right to be asking her these things, asking her to recall old and terrible memories.

"That day, the day it happened, I had been to my mother's house with Isobel to discuss a trip Isobel was supposed to be going on with the school. Mom was strange, inasmuch as she didn't understand how anyone could let their seven-year-old go off with a bunch of strangers—teachers and teaching assistants— for a weekend to some remote part of the country, and she'd always said that, when the time came, she would feel a lot better if she went along, too. I'd cleared it with the staff at Isobel's school, who said they'd really appreciate the extra help, although my mother would have to take care of a small group of children, and not just Isobel. Mom said that was fine, so long as she was there, and to be honest I was glad she'd offered to go. I was working part-time at a bakery in town by that point, and there was no way they would let me take a Saturday off.

"So, anyway, when we got back from my mother's—Isobel and I—we started to pack. We even had a little checklist, and every time I read something out from the list, Isobel screamed 'Check!'. It was... it was..." Once again, the sorrow and the anguish threatened to overpower her, and she broke the sentence off there before moving on to the next part.

"When Frederick came home, I knew he'd had a bad day. I asked him whether the children had been giving him a tough time, and he said he wished he could kill them all. Every. Last. One of them. Then he saw Isobel packing her case, and I knew we were in trouble. I hadn't told Frederick about the trip. I'd told my mother, but not Frederick. Lo and behold, he didn't want Isobel to go, to be 'surrounded by a bunch of paedophiles who were, apparently, taking our daughter out to the Forest of Dean for no other reason than to abuse her—and all the *other* children—and hope they got away with it.

"Isobel was gutted, for she was really looking forward to the trip, especially now that grandma was going along, too. But Frederick had made up his mind, and that was that. She couldn't go."

"But she went anyway," Tom said. He knew how this ended, and he was starting to get a good idea of how they arrived there.

"Frederick was at work," Laura said. "There was no way I would let Isobel miss that trip. Her friends were all going, and she was so sad she couldn't because 'Daddy says so'. I had to drive fast, but we made the coach just before it left. Isobel was so happy that day. We both felt as if we had stood up to Frederick— my husband, her father—and that things would be different from now on.

"The more things change, the more they stay the same. I took a beating that night. Boy, did I take a beating. Knocked out most of my teeth, see?" She smiled, but of course Tom and Wood had already seen her glistening gums. Tom had assumed they were missing through lack of proper dental hygiene, that Laura White had allowed her appearance to go the same way as the front garden. "The ones which weren't knocked out that night fell out a couple of weeks later. Luckily, I couldn't see how disgusting my mouth looked in the mirror; my eyes were all swollen up, and I couldn't open them.

"I took a beating that night, and most of the next day, right the way up until Isobel came through the door. Frederick made me sit there on a chair for three hours, just in front of the door so that I was the first thing Isobel saw when she came through it. The fact that my mother would be with her made no difference. Up to that point, my mom still believed the sun shone out of Frederick White's arse, but after this, I knew things would never be the same again. That once my mother knew what he was truly like, once she saw what he had done to me, I would be able to leave him, to put an end to all this. Take Isobel to my mother's, where we would live together while Frederick White went to prison for what he'd done to us."

Tom could feel the beginnings of a migraine, just beneath his right eye. It was a pain he had grown accustomed to over the years, but not one he ever anticipated. They just crept up on him, like middle-age.

"As soon as Mom and Isobel came through the front door, Frederick was on them. He dragged Mom upstairs and left her lying unconscious in the bathroom. I was fighting back by that point, trying to get him to let go of Isobel, who was screaming and crying and not knowing what the hell was going on. She was still wearing her school bookbag. Frederick punched me to get me off his back, and I was out for a few minutes. When I came to, I could hear that truck of his revving up in the garage. He'd even put the chimes on, and they were so damn loud, I thought I was going to go crazy.

"I telephoned for the police before running out the front door to try to stop him from taking her, but... well, I think we all know how it ended." She was crying now; salty tears rolled down her face, changing direction whenever they came across a new wrinkle. Her whole body seemed too tremble. Tom felt guilty, once again, for making her relive the nightmare of her daughter's abduction and subsequent death.

"We're so sorry, Laura," Tom said. Wood remained silent. Tom realised the old man was also teary-eyed. They glistened like polished orbuculum. Was Wood moved by the story, by Isobel's sad demise and Laura's terrible loss? Or was he thinking of other things? The other children (Ryan, and Cheryl, and Harvey, and Rochelle)?

"Why now?" Laura shook her head. "Why, after all these years?"

Tom knew what she meant; *why, after all these years, have you two appeared from nowhere, interested in how my bastard husband kidnapped and subsequently murdered our daughter?*

"You said Frederick is somehow connected to a bunch of missing kids, even though he's been dead for three decades?"

Wood leaned forward in his chair, sighing deeply. "Not just connected, Laura. Directly responsible for."

Tom jumped in and jumped in fast. "Laura, did your husband—"

"Ex-husband."

"—ex-husband... did he ever get into anything strange just before he died?"

Frowning, Laura said, "Like what? Frederick was always strange, always doing things I didn't understand, or didn't *want* to understand."

"Supernatural stuff?" Wood said, and then quickly shook his head, for that wasn't quite the right word. "Occult stuff."

Without hesitation, Laura nodded frantically, grinning that spit-glistening pink gum smile which reminded Tom of the hag-villainess from Snow White and the Seven Dwarves. "Oh, he was always into that stuff." She waved a hand dismissively through the air, parting the smoke from her cigarette like a geriatric Moses. "Used to bang on about it all the time, regardless of whether Isobel was in the room or not."

Tom glanced at Wood, and Wood glanced back. Wood had been right; this was some sort of occult invocation gone awry. "Laura?" Tom said, turning his attention back to the frail woman, old before her years, sitting opposite. "Did he ever mention the word Ghuul?"

Laura shrugged. "I mean, he might have, I don't rightly know. He was always babbling on about demons and death. I should have known when that shit started to pack up and leave. No one wants to be married to someone who thinks they're some kind of... Anton Lafayette, or whatever his goddamn name was."

LaVey. Tom was familiar with the name, had stumbled across plenty of websites about the occultist.

"I just thought it was another one of Frederick's phases, something else he would get over, once the novelty wore off, like when he started fishing over at Redbridge Lakes—that one only lasted a couple of weeks; cost him a fortune in equipment, too, and then it was all over as quick as it started—but it never did. The novelty never did wear off. He used to come home with library books, things that sent shivers up my spine, and he'd read them so fast, it was like he couldn't possibly learn enough." She cackled. "I daren't ask him why he needed to learn all that weird stuff. Why he wanted to know all about demons and angels. He was an Ice Cream Man, for crying out loud. It made no sense to me."

It was all falling into place. Frederick White had not only read the books he'd taken out from the library; he'd made them his life's work. He had somehow become immortal, the only caveat that he must return to the world of the living every seven years for a fresh soul to sustain him in his netherworld, until the next time...

Tom's legs were growing tired, and the stench of the place— thick with a fug from the old woman's chain-smoking habit— made him want to leave now that they had what they had come for. "Thank you, Laura," he said. "We won't take up any more of your time."

"So what happens now?" Laura stood, and Tom thought he heard every bone inside the woman's body creak and crack as she did so.

"We have to look into a few things," Wood said, wheeling himself steadily, cautiously, backwards out of the cluttered and filthy living-room. By the time he reached the hallway he looked exhausted, and Tom pitied the man, for he was no spring chicken himself.

Tom opened the door and pushed Wood out through it. They still had the overgrown front garden to work through, and once again Wood allowed Tom to do the hard work. Tom didn't care. Out here the air was fresh, at least until they reached the street and Tom lit up a cigarette of his own.

"You were right," Tom told Wood. "About the Ghuul thing."

"We don't know that for sure," Wood replied, breathlessly.

"You heard the widow," Tom said. "That sick sonofabitch was into all manner of weird shit. Hell, he probably learned everything he knew from a book just like the one you took delivery of today."

Wood, staring blankly at the road in front of him, blowing his nose—since when did he get that cold? —on a balled-up tissue he'd pulled from some secret compartment on his chair, said, "We can find out for sure."

"Find out for sure?" Tom repeated the words monotonously, autonomically.

Wood wheeled around to face Tom. "It's too late to do anything more this afternoon, and the library's shut tomorrow—Sunday, and all—but what if we could find out which books Frederick White took out? What he was in to?"

"Is there a way to do that?"

"Fucked if I know," Wood said, "but if anyone can tell us, Margaret Banks can."

"And what if there's some sort of privacy clause?"

"A what-now?"

"You know, like she can't dispense that kind of information?" Tom didn't know if there was—and if there was, whether it still counted after a person had been dead for thirty years—but it sounded like the kind of thing which could stand between them and the truth.

"Then I'll have to sweet-talk her," Wood said, grinning slightly. "She's got the hots for me. Did you know that?"

EIGHTEEN

OCTOBER 30TH, 2016,
ST. GEORGE'S HOSPITAL
TOOTING, LONDON

uke was thankful to be up and about. For three whole days he had been confined to a hospital bed, staring at the same four walls—and a tiny window through which he watched the doctors and they watched him right back—and although he was still hooked up to a drip, he could walk just fine, so long as he didn't rush.

As he left his tiny cubicle, and the incessant beeping machine which neither he nor the nurses apparently knew how to reset, he was accosted by one of the friendlier doctors making his rounds.

"You shouldn't be out of bed." And yet there was a slight smile upon Doctor Khan's face, as if it were a relief to witness a miracle at work.

"Don't give me that, doc," Luke said, also smiling. "I'm bored shitless in there. Didn't you guys think to install a TV? What am I paying my National Insurance for?"

Doctor Khan shrugged. "The food?"

"In that case," Luke said. "You owe me a rebate."

They went back and forth like that for several minutes. Doctor Khan was interested in how Luke was feeling today, and Luke told him that, apart from the agonising pain in his right side—cracked ribs will do that to a person—he felt good. It was a lie; he was in a world of pain, but he couldn't just lie here while the whole world crumbled around him. And besides, he had a visit to make.

And hopefully he wasn't too late.

"So, where are you thinking of going?" Doctor Khan asked. "Just getting a little exercise and a break from the lovely, albeit small, room we've provided you with?"

Small? That was an understatement. Luke had stayed in bigger sleeping-bags.

"Cafeteria," Luke said. "Just in case their food's better than the stuff you keep bringing me."

Doctor Khan nodded. "I can vouch for the lasagne," he said. "Just steer clear of the sausages."

Luke told him that he would, and for some reason that was one of the funniest things he had ever said out loud and they both laughed, at least until Luke was out of sight along the corridor leaving the doctor to finish his rounds.

It was a slow process, walking, trying not to slip over on the shiny tiled floor, but Luke was on a mission to find Ward D4. Karen had told him just yesterday that that was where they were keeping his friend, the boxer, for observations, and that she would take him down there when he was feeling a little better.

Well, I'm not feeling on top of the world, honey, he thought, *but I'm moving. Slowly, slowly catchy monkey...*

Today was Monday, and Luke knew Monday was discharge day for Marcus. He couldn't rely on the possibility that his friend would get the chance to visit him before disappearing again for thirty more years, and they needed to talk.

It was important.

Ward D4 was worse, even, than the gleaming, confined, chaotic shit-storm Hell Luke had been consigned to, starting with a receptionist whose entire personality was about as bare as the corridor walls through which he had just traipsed.

"Can I help you?" Clearly she could, but the tone of her voice suggested she didn't want to.

Luke stood in front of the glass, and he'd never felt more like a criminal in his entire life. "Erm, yeah, I believe my friend is on this ward. We were in a car accident together, and I wanted to catch him before he went home."

The receptionist's stoic expression said it all. "Visiting isn't until three this afternoon."

"I noticed that on the sign," Luke said, motioning to the framed printout attached to the glass. "But, like I said, I wanted to catch him before he was discharged. I'm a patient here..." Such a stupid thing to say! Of course he was a patient here. People didn't just walk around the streets wearing drab olive gowns and pushing drip-stands. She already knew he was a patient here, and seemingly didn't give two shits about it.

After several seconds, she relented with a sigh. "What's the name of the patient?"

Is this a quiz? Are we doing a fucking quiz now?

"It's Marcus Berry," Luke said, nervously laughing for some strange reason, which the receptionist clearly didn't appreciate. "My car hit his car, which is weird because we haven't seen each other in, like, thirty—"

The door to the left of the window began to buzz. "Just push the door," said the receptionist. "Bay 11."

Luke nodded his thanks before making his way through the door, dragging his drip-stand behind him. He wondered if she heard him mutter the word 'bitch' as he made his way along yet another corridor toward Bay 11. He hoped she did.

There were several differences between his ward and D4. It was a lot quieter here, for one; Luke saw only one nurse before he reached Bay 11, and there was a good chance she wasn't even a nurse at all, but a cleaner in disguise. Two, the patients down here were all waiting to go home, sitting fully dressed upon their made beds, waiting for discharge papers and prescriptions with their sad little bags packed next to them. Luke wished that were him right now.

The lights flickered overhead, blinking noisily off and on, and yet there was nothing supernatural about it. This was clearly just a thing down here on D4, something someone would eventually get around to fixing.

Maybe.

Luke arrived at Bay 11 and knocked before entering.

"Hey!" Marcus was one of the lucky few, the chosen ones, who were all packed and ready to leave. His bags sat on his bed and he stood waiting at the small window, even though the view offered only a glimpse of workmen and machinery installing yet another extension—or staff car-park—to the hospital. "I was going to come see you before I left. We need to talk."

So Marcus thought so, too.

"The Ice Cream Man?" Luke said, not quite a question.

Marcus nodded. "The Ice Cream Man."

"That's why you're down here, isn't it?" Luke already knew the answer. He stepped into the bay and allowed the door to slowly close on its hydraulic hinge. "You've seen him, too."

Marcus stepped away from the window, shaking his head and sighing. "I've seen a lot of things recently, things which have made me question my own sanity." He smiled, though it looked pained, more of a grimace. "I'm a boxer, you know? Maybe I've taken one too many punches to the temple, and now I'm a little confused in the brain."

"What does that make me?" Luke said. "I've been seeing this prick too, and I haven't been in a good fight since 1991."

Marcus paused for a moment, and then said, "Jack Bridge, on the football pitch at lunchtime."

Luke couldn't believe it. Even he had forgotten the name of the kid whose sole purpose in life was to bring him to his knees, humiliate him in front of the rest of the school. "Jack Bridge..." he said. "God, I haven't thought of that spotty little fucker in years."

"I remember that fight well," Marcus said, this time a genuine smile playing about his countenance. "You would have won if he hadn't got you in an arm-bar."

Luke rubbed at his shoulder, as if he still suffered the effects of said manoeuvre. When he realised what he was doing, and that Marcus was staring at him expectantly, he stopped massaging his shoulder and returned to the matter at hand. "Marcus, that... thing... tried to make me kill my own daughter."

"Karen told me," Marcus said. "After she left you yesterday, she and I had a little chat over the worst cup of piss tea I ever had the misfortune of being charged for."

"What else did she say?" Luke didn't know whether any of this mattered. That his wife would tell one of his best friends from childhood of his sudden murderous tendencies toward their daughter seemed a little strange.

"She told me she knew it wasn't you. That something had made you do it, because no matter how many times your daughter pesters you or disappoints you, there is no way in hell you would ever do anything to hurt her." He nodded. "That's when I knew He'd come to you, too."

Luke turned and slowly lowered himself down onto Marcus's hospital bed. Marcus moved around so that they were facing one another. "So, what are we expecting here?" Luke said. "I mean, if he's coming back, why now? After almost thirty years?"

Marcus shrugged. "Maybe it never left?" Referring to the Ice Cream Man as an IT seemed to make more sense than pronoun they had been using so far. That thing was not a man. "Maybe it's always been here, biding its time."

"Playing the long game?" Luke said. That was even more terrifying to him than believing the fucker had just shown up out of nowhere after so many years. To think it might have been hiding, waiting in the shadows, a vengeful wraith with nothing but time on its hands and a phantom truck in the garage. "And now it's coming back to Havering to play all over again."

"Seems so to me," Marcus said. "Only we're adults now. We can take this thing out."

Luke didn't know whether to laugh or cry. "I hate to break it to you, mate, but I've left my proton pack at home." It wasn't even funny, and neither of them laughed to prove it. "How would we even know where to start with this sonofabitch? What, do we just lurk around on Halloween, waiting for the sound of ice cream chimes—

Pop goes the weasel

—and then chase after him in our newly-mangled cars screaming in Latin at the top of our voices?"

That shouldn't have been funny, and yet it was. Marcus couldn't help himself. "You were always the cynical one, even when we were kids. Always telling us why something was a bad idea. *We can't swim in that, there might be piranhas in there.* Remember that one?"

Luke did remember that, remembered standing in front of the lake in nothing but his swim trunks while Marcus and Tom and Ryan goaded him in to going first. He never did get in that water, and from what he could recall, he managed to convince Tom it was a bad idea, too. "This is a little bit different to when we were kids," Luke said, for they could stand—or in his case sit—here all day remembering fun and not-so-fun times from their childhood, but it wasn't getting them anywhere. "If this thing is real, and we both agree it is, and that for some reason it's coming back, we need to figure out a way to stop it."

Marcus patted Luke's shoulder, and when Luke winced with pain he apologised before speaking. "That's the spirit, son," he said, more like a coach giving a pep talk to a bunch of amateur footballers than a guy about to go to war with an entity from another realm. "Now, this thing has made itself known to you, and it fucked up my last fight right in the middle of the ring, then we can be pretty sure Tom's had dealings with it, too."

Makes sense, Luke thought. Tom was their leader as kids; if anyone was going to get the brunt of the Ice Cream Man's wrath, it was him. "You think he's already on his way?"

"If Tom's anything like he was when we were kids, I'll bet he was the first one of us here." Marcus scratched his head. "We just need to find him, see what he knows—"

"Once again," Luke said, motioning to his incapacitated body, "I don't know whether you've noticed, but I'm in no fit shape to take on a supernatural force. And besides, they're not going to let me leave the hospital, not like this. Fuck knows how long I'm going to be here."

And therein lay their first problem. If they were going to beat this thing, Marcus would have to try to find Tom alone, and while they were separated, they were vulnerable, precisely what the Ice Cream Man wanted.

"If—when—I find Tom," Marcus said, "we'll come back here and take it from there."

"And what if He—IT—gets to us first?" Luke asked, knowing that the Ice Cream Man was growing in power, trying to attack them even now.

"Then we hit that fucker with everything we have," Marcus said. "And don't stop hitting until we knock it back to Hell."

NINETEEN

The library was quieter than the last time Tom had visited, just a few short days ago. A couple of students were browsing the non-fiction aisles, no doubt searching for psychology textbooks or huge volumes on astrobiology. A solitary old man sat at a computer in the media room; Tom wondered whether the old man was hiding something by facing the door, his computer screen not visible to librarians or browsers. Perhaps this was the only quiet time he had to search for porn, or maybe it was something more sinister even than that.

Once again, Wood had decided to use his wheelchair instead of the mobility scooter he had been zooming around on when Tom first met him in The Walnut Tree. It seemed to take more energy out of the ageing ex-copper, though he never complained, never once groaned or grumbled when his wheels snagged on something or dipped into a pothole or crack in the pavement.

"I don't see Margaret," Tom said, scanning the library stacks for signs of the librarian. "Don't tell me this is her day off."

"That woman doesn't take days off," Wood said. "She's a worker bee. Her first day off will be the same day she dies."

Or the one after, depending on whether she died the night before, Tom thought, but correcting Wood on such a trivial matter was ridiculous and so he kept it to himself.

Sure enough, they found Margaret Banks—the worker bee—pricing up donated books, which were not quite good enough to make the shelves of Redbridge Central Library, in an adjacent room to the Crime Fiction aisle. She was *tsk*ing and talking to herself as she went about her business, which seemed to primarily involve judging a book by its tattered cover before either slapping a 50p sticker on it or tossing it into the open black bag to her right.

As Tom and Wood approached the open door, she glanced up and then smiled. "Well, if it isn't Trevor Wood and his new favourite sidekick." She climbed to her feet, giving up on the task she was performing and discarding the remaining books in the refuse sack. "It seems not a day goes by when I don't see one of you or the other, but this is the first time I've seen you together." She arched her eyebrows, as if there might be something going which only she knew about.

"We'd stop coming if you didn't work here," Wood said. Tom had expected the charm offensive to come into play at some point, though not quite so soon.

"I'll bet you say that to all the librarians," Margaret said, reddening slightly.

I feel like the third wheel in some sick courting ritual, Tom thought, though he knew that only one of the superannuated people present were being genuine. "Margaret, the reason why we're back—yet again—is that we were wondering if there might, you know, be any way of looking into the books checked out by a deceased lender."

"A deceased lender!" Margaret said, mocking shock. "They'll give library cards to anyone these days." This might have been hilarious to her (and apparently it was) but to Tom it was simply wasting time, and not really answering his question. Wood, on the other hand, was laughing along with the librarian, making the most of his debonair ruse and hoping it was worth it in the end.

"I mean, books he took out just before he died?" Tom said, deflecting back to the question.

"I know, dear," Margaret said. "I'm just entertaining myself a little bit." She came out of the stockroom and walked purposefully through the aisles. Tom and Wood followed; for a moment, Tom wondered whether she had ignored the question and was off to perform some other menial task, but then as she walked, she began to talk. "You're asking if there is any way I have access to some sort of system that stores the names of all the books a particular lender has taken out over the years?"

"Exactly," Tom said, trying to keep up as they moved first through Information Technology and then Social Studies.

"There's a little thing called privacy," Margaret said. "We would never be able to store that kind of information on our system."

Wood sighed. *Fuck it!*

They arrived at the library's main counter, a huge island at the centre of the room, and Margaret slipped behind it and settled herself down at the ancient whirring computer that sat there. "However... we do keep a record of outstanding fines, though it's pretty clear a lot of these people are never coming back to pay up—"

"Will that let you know the title of the book for which the fine is owed?" Wood, Tom realised, had no idea how this worked, the same as he didn't. But if Frederick White had died before returning his books... maybe...

"What's the name of the lender?" Margaret's fingers hovered over the keyboard as she stared at the screen over her tops of her spectacles, which sat so far down her nose they were practically useless.

Wood cleared his throat. "Frederick White," he said.

The librarian typed slowly and deliberately, humming a tune Tom thought he recognised as she did so. We'll Meet Again by Vera Lynn, perhaps?

"I've got two Fred Whites," she said. "One from 132 Balfour Road, and another from 7, Burke Street—"

"It's that one!" Tom said, his heart racing inside his chest. He looked expectantly toward Wood, and Wood shook his head: *Don't get your hopes up, kid. Probably a book on botany...*

"Okay," Margaret said as an exhale. She pressed a few more keys and hit enter, and only then did she push her spectacles up so they would be of some use. Reading from the screen, she said, "Ah, this guy owes an outstanding fine of... hmm... almost eighty pounds. That can't be right—"

It is right! Tom thought. You take books out of the library in 1987 and don't return them, those fines are soon going to stack up.

"What were the names of the books, Margaret?" Wood asked, calmly.

A press of a button later, Margaret said, "Well, well, well. It seems Frederick White was into the same weird nonsense you're in to, Trevor." There was a hint of scorn in her voice. "That fine is the total for three books, the first of which is, I think, a history book. *Neo-Babylonian Empire* by J.C. Penworthy. The second book is called *Annunaki: Hidden Codes* by Colt Merry, and the third book is... well, you already know what the third book is..." She smiled at Wood; Wood did not smile back.

"How would we know what the third book is?" Wood asked.

"Because," Margaret said, after a quick click of her tongue and a roll of her eyes, "it was the book you ordered in, the one your friend here delivered to you."

"*Ghuul: The Children-Eater...*" Tom said, not a question.

"The one without an author byline," Margaret confirmed. "That book must be a bit older than I thought. I thought I recognised the name when you said it: Frederick White." To Wood, she said, "When you asked me to see if we had that book in, remember I checked on the system?"

"That's right, you did," Wood said.

"And it came up on the system as overdue from a mister Frederick White, which was why I said I'd order a new copy. And it came in for you, but the copy Frederick White took out of here in 1987 is still out there somewhere."

Tom turned to Wood and said, "We need to read that book."

"I thought you'd already started to," Wood replied.

"It's very... it's very wordy," Tom said. And it was. There were all manner of words in it Tom didn't understand. Sexagesimal? Heraclitean? Cuneiform? What did it all mean? Well, Tom had managed to get through the first chapter, and still he hadn't a clue.

"Of course it's wordy," Wood said, scathingly. "It's a book. What did you expect? Black-and-white pictures and a packet of crayons?" He must have realised that he was shouting, in a library, of all places, and took several deep breaths before continuing. "If we're going to stop this sonofabitch, we need to know everything about it. Bring the book back to mine this evening and we'll make a start—"

"Oh, you can start as soon as you like," said Margaret, cheerfully. "You'll never stop Him."

Tom and Wood turned to the counter, to where Margaret Banks sat smiling. "How do you mean?" Tom asked.

The librarian's smile turned altogether nastier, a grin, a sickeningly thin grin which seemed to stretch out the old lady's wrinkles so that she was almost smooth. "You can't stop Him. He's going to come, and He's going to make you suffer, and there's nothing you can do to stop *HIM YOU FUCKING CUNTS! YOU FUCKING CUUUUUUNNNNTS!*" And then she was up, leaping onto the counter as lithe as a cat. She hissed like a cat, too. Her face was contorted into an expression of pure hatred, and black drool began to seep from her impossibly wide maw.

"It's *HIM!*" Wood yelled, wheeling himself back, away from the counter, away from the crazed demon librarian tap-dancing upon it. "It's Ghuul!"

Tom, who had staggered backward as the librarian had jumped up onto the counter, could not speak. All he could do was watch as the transformation continued, as the old lady's spectacles fell from the creature's nose, and her skin turned black—as if someone was scorching her with an invisible blowtorch—as her eyes burned red.

"*FUCK YOU! FUCK YOU! FUCK YOU!*", IT/He/she spat in staccato rhythm. "*I'M COMING, AND I'M GOING TO RIP YOUR FUCKING HEARTS OUT! YOU AND YOUR FRIENDS!*"

Tom was knocked even further away by the power of the creature's voice. It was like being hit full-on in the face by a jet-engine. Even Wood was struggling to remain on four wheels as books and papers flew across the room. Shelves rattled and shook, threatening to fall over, creating a domino effect which would take years to clear up.

"*COMING!*" it said, and then it was moving across the counter, leaping over the archaic monitor, a stack of returned books, tendrils of black smoke whipping out behind it like a superhero's cape, screaming as it went.

Before Tom could even move, before Wood realised what was about to happen, and before anyone else in the library—were they the only ones left to witness this madness? Where was the porno-perv from the computer room? The students? —had a clue what was happening, the thing that was once Margaret Banks leapt up into the air, propelling itself so high, so far away from the counter that Tom couldn't watch what happened next.

He heard it, though.

A sickening thud, like meat being slapped down onto a butcher's counter, and then the broken and twisted bones of Margaret Banks as they settled into place for the final time.

Then... silence.

TWENTY

OCTOBER 30TH, 2016
BROMLEY, LONDON

Danielle stood, phone in hand, shaking nervously as she listened to everything her husband was telling her. Dead librarians, levitating ghouls, ancient books. She took it all in while her sister simply watched from across the room with her arms crossed and a telling smirk upon her face. Thank God the children were in bed. Danielle wouldn't want them to see this, to see what was about to happen.

A tear streaked down her face as she screeched into the phone. "*Stop!*" More calmly. "Tom, *please*, just stop!"

And still he persisted, trying to convince her that every word falling from his lips was true, and not just some terrible psychosis. His words were all garbled, jumbled together until they made almost no sense to her.

This was her husband, the man she loved—still loved? —but he was different now. Unstable. Insane. How could she possibly believe a word he was saying, when everything that came out of his mouth sounded like something out of a terrible horror movie? How could she help him, when he wouldn't help himself?

"Tom?" she interrupted once again. "Tom, I'm begging you, please. Call Doctor Kurian. He will help you, or at least point you in the direction of someone who might be able to." The last thing she wanted was for the love of her life, the man she had wanted to start a family with, locked up in some secure facility, but if that was what it took to make him realise that none of this was real, that there was help out there for him if only he looked for it, then so be it.

Rebecca had had enough, apparently, and left Danielle standing there, trying to talk some sense into her frantic husband, who was now chuntering on about Halloween, about how something—the same thing which kidnapped his best friend back in 1988—was going to come back, and come back stronger than ever. Danielle could take it no more.

She hung up the phone.

She cried.

After almost ten minutes, she dried her eyes and dialled the mobile number of the only person she thought could help. He answered on the third ring. "Hello, Doctor Kurian speaking, how may I help you?"

Danielle sighed with relief. She didn't think he would answer at this time of night. It was past eight; surely the good psychiatrist had better things to be getting on with than answering patient calls.

Seemingly not.

"Hi, yes, Doctor Kurian, it's Danielle Craven, here. Tom Craven's wife?"

For a moment there was only silence. Had Kurian forgotten who she was? Who Tom was? And then, "Ah, Mrs Craven! Is there a problem? Is Tom all right?"

Is Tom all right? Is Tom all right... erm, well, I've just had a conversation with him about ancient spirits and flying librarians, so no, I'd say he's far from all right.

"I think Tom's in trouble, Doctor," Danielle said, wishing all this madness would just go away, *and don't ever darken my doorstep again.*

"Trouble, Mrs Craven?" Kurian sounded calm. Of course he did; he was a psychiatrist. It was his job to remain collected while everyone around him lost their heads. It simply wouldn't do to have a psychiatrist on the edge. But still, Danielle resented that calmness; she wanted him to panic, like she was. She wanted Kurian to leap up, throw on his trousers, and rush out to the car. She wanted him to drive over to the house with orderlies and strap Tom to a gurney so that he would no longer be a danger to himself.

"More than just trouble," Danielle said. She told the doctor about how she was no longer living at home, how she had moved in with her sister—albeit temporarily—to allow Tom time to sort his life, and his head, out. The doctor told her that he already knew this from his prior meeting with Tom, and Danielle was relieved to hear that Tom had at least maintained the appointment. Lord knows she doubted he had. She told the doctor about how, over the past few days, Tom's phone calls have become increasingly nonsensical, that he was talking about Mesopotamia and things that go bump in the night. How he had somehow convinced a man in a wheelchair—a former police Sergeant, of all things—that the things he was seeing were real, and that now they knew how they could beat it, or at least where to start. While she told Kurian all of this, he *uhhm*ed and *ahh*ed and responded monosyllabically. Rebecca had returned to the room and, after pouring herself a large chardonnay, stood in the corner, frowning like a chastised child as she listened to the conversation.

"I'm worried he's going to do something stupid," Danielle said, her story finally told. "I'm worried for my husband, Doctor, but I'm terrified to go over there in case... in case..."

"Do not go over there, Mrs Craven," Kurian said. "If this is what I think it is, then your husband will need to ride it out for a while. Episodes like this—"

"Like *what*, Doctor Kurian?" Danielle needed to know. Needed to know what was wrong with her husband.

"I believe your husband has chronic hallucinatory psychosis, Mrs Craven." He sighed; Danielle took that as a bad sign. "Your husband is seeing things and hearing things which are very real to him. These are not things of flesh, of substance to *us*, but to Tom they are a tangible and material threat."

"So you're suggesting I leave him to his delusions?" It sounded so cruel, so inherently wrong. Across the room, Rebecca was nodding. At least she agreed with what the doctor was telling her.

"I will try to make contact with him," said Doctor Kurian. "If I can convince him to come and see me, we might be able to work out a course of treatment. You say he called you this evening?"

"Just now," Danielle said.

"Then he is retaining insight. In other words, he knows what he is doing. Believe me, I have seen far worse cases than this. If we can assess and treat your husband, Mrs Craven, there is no reason why we can't get this thing under control."

When Danielle hung up the phone less than a minute later, she was paralysed and unable to speak. Rebecca was saying things to her, but none of it was sticking; she might as well have been—might very well have been—talking in a completely different language.

Back on the sofa, Danielle trembled and sipped at a glass of red wine she didn't really want, but felt she needed. "It feels so wrong," she said. "Tom's sick, and there's nothing I can do to help make him better."

"You *are* helping," Rebecca said. "The rest is up to him."

That, Danielle thought, *is exactly what I'm afraid of.*

TWENTY-ONE

For almost two hours Wood had been silently reading the book. Even as Tom called his wife, Wood pored over the pages of GHUUL: THE CHILDREN-EATER as if he were trying to select a pair of slacks from a shopping catalogue. Occasionally he would stop to take a sip of brandy—a bottle they had picked up from Wood's as they stopped to collect the book—before delving right back in. He was nothing if not determined.

"Anything?" Tom was eager to know what Wood knew, and yet Wood seemed happy to be doing the legwork. When Wood found something relevant, Tom was certain he would be first to know about it, and yet he couldn't relax, paced back and forth across the room.

"Will you sit down?" Wood said without looking up from the book. "You're driving me crazy."

Crazy? Crazy was planning to bring down an ancient Babylonian evil. Crazy was watching a geriatric librarian leap into the air so high that most of her frail bones snapped on impact with the ground. Crazy was what Danielle thought *he* was—he could tell by the way she spoke to him on the phone, how she kept deflecting back to Doctor Kurian—and that only served to make him even crazier.

"Have a drink," Wood said, refilling his own glass. "It'll calm your nerves."

Tom had already considered it, but he didn't want to walk along that dark path tonight, not while that thing was out there, stirring up chaos and getting stronger by the second. "I need to keep my head clear," he told Wood.

"Suit yourself." Wood went back to the book, and didn't speak again for thirty minutes, but when he did it was with an excitement Tom had not heard from the man in days. "This is definitely our bogeyman!"

Tom, who had been smoking at the window—watching cats duel and neighbours drag their wheelie-bins to the ends of their drives—turned and said, "You sure?" He moved across the room, distinguishing his butt in the already over-spilling ashtray on the coffee table. "What does it say?"

Wood read over the paragraph he had just finished once again, perhaps for clarity. Once he was sure, he began to read from the page. Tom sat down in the armchair opposite and listened. "Ghuul endlessly consumes the souls of human children. His power grows alongside his collection; in other words, the more souls he has to feed upon, the more powerful he becomes."

"But he only has four," Tom said. Ryan, Cheryl, Harvey, and Rochelle, collected precisely seven years apart on the exact same night. If that was all it took to make the Ice Cream Man strong enough to possess people and drive them to suicide, he hated to think what the thing would be capable of in seven more years, or seven after that.

"In this incarnation he only has four," Wood said. "This thing is centuries-old. It has been picking up souls for thousands of years. Every seven years for as long as you can imagine."

Tom winced as if Wood's words had caused him actual pain. "That's a lot of kids."

"The book says that whomever summons Ghuul shall only lead him until the next."

"Lead him until the… what does that even mean?" Tom was confused, part of the reason why he hadn't been able to get into the book himself.

"It means that Ghuul is endless, infinite, at least the *demon* is. If someone were to summon Ghuul right now, this instant, Frederick White's evil soul would be forced out, expelled like a bad fart, go straight to Hell, do not pass go, do not collect two-hundred-pounds."

"But Ghuul would go on?" Tom asked. "Within its new host?"

Wood nodded; Tom didn't like where this was going.

"That's the gist of it."

"So how do we stop it?" Tom asked, the brandy on the coffee table calling to him once again. He managed—just—to ignore it. "I mean, there's got to be a way. There's a way to kill every-fucking-thing if you look hard enough."

Wood shook his head, flipped through the pages of the book. "If there is, I haven't got to that chapter yet. I'll keep looking, but you might want to get some rest. You'll be no good to anyone tired, and—"

A knock at the door startled both of them. Wood gave Tom a *were-you-expecting-anyone?* look. Tom shook his head. But maybe... just maybe...

"Danielle," Tom said. "It must be Danielle. She sounded concerned on the phone." He was already moving toward the hallway.

"Is she going to be okay with us..." Wood trailed off there. Tom knew how the rest of the sentence went. *Is she going to be okay with us doing all this weird shit in her house?*

Without stopping, Tom called back across his shoulder. "She knows about it." And while that was not the same as being okay with it, she would understand.

Tom didn't even check, didn't call out to make sure it was his wife standing there on the other side of the door. He simply turned the key, unlatched the chain, and pulled the door open, certain it would be her.

It was not.

"Hey, Tom?" said Marcus 'The Banger' Berry. "I'm not interrupting anything, am I?"

* * *

Tom couldn't believe it. He couldn't believe it so much that the brandy finally won, and he poured himself a large glass.

Marcus told Tom and Wood everything that had happened in the past week, how he had been attacked by the Ice Cream Man during his fight with Samuels Jr., and how Luke was over at St George's, slightly worse-for-wear. He explained how Luke had almost strangulated his own daughter, believing her to be that thing—the shadowy beast they had not seen since they were kids—and how the poor bastard had been taunted by the creature yet again, this time in the form of his mother's new live-in lover.

"Interesting," Wood said.

"I can't believe you're here," Tom said. God, it was so good to see Marcus. They had been so close as kids, inseparable, living in each other's pockets; latchkey kids, but that was okay back then. "I mean, I had a feeling this... this shit wasn't just happening to me, but I didn't think for one minute that you would actually come."

Marcus appeared to be slighted by that remark for a moment, but then he smiled, and Tom relaxed once again. "You didn't think I'd let you take on this sonofabitch on your own, did you?" he said. "I mean, no offence, but you were never the strongest out of us."

Tom would have argued if it weren't for the fact Marcus was telling the truth. Sure, he had been their self-appointed leader when they were twelve years old, but if it ever came to a fight— bullies, drunken tramps, older girls—Marcus was above him in the pecking order. Shit, even Luke was better at fighting than Tom. "And you made a living out of it," Tom said. "You know, I've watched every single one of your fights, some at least twice."

"You didn't happen to see that prick Samuels Jr. sucker-punch me while I was being attacked by that demon, did you?" He was still annoyed about that; Tom could hear the fury in Marcus's voice, no matter how hard he tried to stifle it.

Tom shook his head. "Missed that one. We've been a little busy, you know?" He motioned to Wood, who had returned to the book set out on the coffee table in front of him. He wasn't paying attention to Tom or Marcus, and Marcus surreptitiously mouthed, *Why's he here*? Of course, it had been Marcus's house they had all gathered at after Ryan was abducted, and it had been Wood who had interrogated them. A lot had changed since then; Marcus needed to be brought up to speed.

Tom mouthed back: *I'll explain later*. He didn't want to interrupt Wood while he was reading.

"So, how 'bout a glass of that brandy?" Marcus sat down; the armchair squeaked for mercy beneath him. He was a lot bigger than the last time Tom had watched him fight. Old age, he guessed. It was getting to all of them.

Without looking up, Wood said, "Help yourself, Banger." There was a certain affection to the term, and Marcus took it as such. Tom fetched a clean glass from the kitchen, and by the time he returned Marcus and Wood were laughing and talking about boxing.

"What'd I miss?" Tom poured Marcus a brandy and handed it to him.

"I was just telling The Banger here that he once cost me my trousers in a bet." Wood's cheeks were red from laughter, shiny. It was, Tom thought, good to see. After everything they had been through these past few days, a little humour and banter would do them the world of good.

"Your trousers?" Tom was intrigued; for a moment he had forgotten why they were all here.

So, Wood went through the story again, this time for Tom's benefit. How Wood had placed a bet with an old friend from the force that Marcus 'The Banger' Berry would knock out Reginald King within six rounds back in a 2008 championship fight. Tom remembered that fight well; King had made it all the way to the tenth before Marcus landed a great right hook on his glass jaw, putting him to sleep before he even hit the canvas. Wood had honoured the bet, removed his trousers, and wheeled himself through the city centre with nothing but a traffic cone to cover his modesty. "You should have seen the way people were looking at me!" Wood said, tears now streaming from his eyes. "But, you know, the great thing about being a cripple is that no one says shit. I could have smothered myself in chocolate sauce and sung the national anthem and still got looks of sympathy."

Now Tom was laughing hysterically, too. Hysterically because they were all terrified? Petrified of what was to come? What could come any moment? It didn't matter. They were laughing, and it was as if someone had turned a gauge to release the pressure. There they were, just three men, laughing out loud, tears streaming down their faces, and it felt good. It felt good because, just for a moment, there was no Ice Cream Man, no Ghuul, no Frederick fucking White. There was only there and then.

And then, as quickly as it all began, it was over with four words from Marcus.

"We're fucked, aren't we?"

The smile dropped from Tom's face, and Wood's wasn't far behind. "We're not fucked," Tom said. "We're together, and that's got to stand for something."

"We were together back then," Marcus said, nursing his brandy. "That didn't help us stop that thing from taking Ryan."

"That was different," Wood said. It was the first thing he'd uttered in over three minutes; that was how long they had laughed for. He was serious once again. Deadly serious.

"How was that different?" Marcus asked.

"We didn't know it was coming." Wood closed the book, seemingly satisfied with what he had gleaned from its pages for one evening. "Right?" He looked up; the question was aimed at Tom.

"Right," Tom said.

And then, "Right," added Marcus.

It wasn't much, but it was all they had.

TWENTY-TWO

G *huuuuuuul...*
Luke opened his eyes, expecting to see the dim incandescence of the Bay 11 light over his bed. It wasn't there. Instead, there was only darkness, but when Luke's sleepy-eyed vision cleared, he could make out tiny white pinpricks. Stars. That was when he realised he was outside. Outside and lying on his back, staring up.

"What the..." He pushed up onto his elbows, saw that he was lying in a field, a field with no borders, no fences, nothing but sodden grass all around him. He clambered to his feet, being careful not to slip on the muddy pasture beneath, which squelched noisily—as if it had recently rained hard and long. Staring down at his body, he saw that he was still dressed in his hospital gown, only now it was filthy, bloody, torn and shredded as if some long-clawed creature had been working on him as he slept.

Slept?

That was it. This was another dream, another vivid, fucked-up nightmare courtesy of everyone's favourite neighbourhood Ice Cream Man. Any minute now he would appear, hiss a few chilling sentences, make a couple of threats, and then Luke would awaken back at the hospital, where he would sit in his chair, reluctant to sleep again for the rest of the night, terrified and eager to get the fuck out of St. George's before it was too late.

Luke took one step forward, and then a second. His legs were just as tired, just as sore, as they were in the real world, but at least here—wherever 'here' was—he didn't have the inconvenience of a drip-stand. The grass was unkempt, hilly in places and dipped in others, and so pulling that cumbersome machine across the field didn't bear thinking about.

Just then, twenty feet in front of him, a spotlight came down, its source some invisible thing up in the sky. Luke started, for it was the last thing you'd expect to see in the middle of a field, dream or no dream. And there—oh! Of course! There she was again! —sitting on her knees in the pool of light, covered in mud and blood and wearing nothing to keep her warm, was Lydia.

"You're not her!" Luke yelled, his voice echoing around the field somehow. "You're not Lydia, you FUCK!"

The girl—his pumpkin, sweetie, princess, beautiful, darling—slowly lifted her head. Luke saw the grin first; black drool seeped from her mouth, hung from her chin like filthy cobwebs. He saw the dark pits where her eyes should have been next, and even though he knew this was just a nightmare, a construct designed to upset him, to break him down, he thought, That's what she'll look like. That's what Lydia will look like when he's done with her!

"No!" Luke screamed. "No, you can't have her!"

In a voice which was so plangent it caused every wet blade of grass in the field to vibrate, the thing sitting in the pool of light said, "Sssssshhhhhhh, Lucasssssss. It'ssss passsst her bedtiiiiiime..."

"You can't take her from me," Luke said, not realising he was moving forward until he almost slipped on the mud. "Choose somebody else, you fucker! Leave her out of this!" He was close enough to the thing wearing his daughter's skin to see that she was shivering. Wet and shivering when she should have been home in bed.

It's not *her*, you silly asshole!

It's not her!

"Then sssstop me..." hissed the creature. "Ssssstop me. Ssssaaaave her..."

Luke's right hand suddenly felt heavy, so heavy it almost unbalanced him, and when he looked down, he saw that he was *holding an axe.*

Ssssstop meeee...

"I'll stop you!" Luke said, and began to run toward the column of light and the target at its base. The creature's ungodly laugh seemed to come at him from all sides. Sulphur, vanilla, methane, cookie-dough, death, sprinkles; its breath swarmed around him like so many blowflies, waiting for him to 'Lie down and die already so we can crawl up inside you and go to work...'

Luke brought the axe up as he reached the edge of the light, and as he stepped into it, the creature dropped its head, accepting, ready to die? Ceding defeat? No.

The axe made an almost cartoonish WHOOSH! sound as it split the air, and then it stuck in the top of the creature's head— THUT! —and would go no further.

Luke was still screaming when the body (it's not her! It's not her! It's not her!) fell forward and blood began to puddle around it, staining the grass crimson. And when Luke looked— still sobbing and screaming and begging himself to wake up— he saw that the entire field was now blood red. A carpet of seeping flesh with him and the dead creature—

it's not her

—at its centre.

Then there came a clap, and another, and Luke turned just a moment too late, for the third clap came from behind, from the direction he had just been facing. This time when he turned, he came face-to-face with a slow-clapping Karen.

"Well done!" said his wife, only it wasn't Karen. It couldn't be. "You finally managed to kill our daughter. So proud of you. And here I was thinking you were nothing but a fuck-up, a complete waste of space. How wrong I was, huh?"

Razorblades filled Luke's throat. He couldn't speak—could barely breathe—and so he stood there, mouth flapping open and shut as if he were a creature not destined for dry land.

"On the bright side," Karen went on, "at least Christmas will be cheap this year. You were always saying how she didn't appreciate all that stuff we bought her, how she only used it once or twice and then, poof! Forgotten about. Think of all that

money we'll save! And we can finally move out of London! Yes! There's no need for us to stay here, now. It's not like we've got a daughter who needs a good school. We can pack up and move to the country, just like you always wanted. Good job, Daddy! Good job, indeed!"

Luke shut his eyes, prayed that when he opened them the demon-Karen would be gone and he would be back in his room at St. George's.

It's just a dream.

It's just a dream.

It's just a—

"I'M COMING, LUKE!" Luke opened his eyes as something wrapped around his throat and began to squeeze tight. The mouth next to his ear (sprinkles and acid and sorbet and gasoline and mallow and cancer) opened up wide and warm breath buffeted his face; the demon-Karen was right next to him now, lifting him up from the crimson grass with veritable ease. *"YOUR FRIENDSSS THINK THEY CAN SSSTOP ME, BUT THEY CAN'T…"*

Wake up, Luke. Wake up, Luke. Wake up, Luke.

"Your friend Ryan begged me to ssset him free," the demon-Karen hissed. Luke kicked and struggled, but it was no use; his feet were too far away from the creature, too far from the ground. *"You should have seen the tearsss. OH! Such tearsss as he pissed his pantsss and, for decadesss, pleaded with me to ssset him free."*

(jam and cordite and treacle and defecation and chocolate and gangrene and…)

"He still suffersss," whispered the creature. *"Still pleadsss and criesss and soilsss himself."*

Luke didn't know how much more of this he could take, but he knew that if he were to die here in the crimson field, he would never regain consciousness in his hospital room. He didn't know how he knew that. He just did. And the Ice Cream Man/Demon-Karen must have been able to read his mind, for the next words it whisper-hissed were:

"Oh, you aren't going to die here tonight, Luke. Where'sss the fun in that?" The creature's grip loosened from his throat,

and then he was on his knees, coughing and spluttering and gasping for air that never came.

And that was how he woke, only instead of the crimson grass—stained with the blood of his daughter—there was cold, hard tiles, and instead of his own hands wrapped around his neck it was an IV line. "Holy fuck!" he said, quickly unwrapping the line. "Holy FUCK!"

He climbed to his feet, using the bed to his left for support. Beyond the small window the ward was under night-staff operation. All was relatively quiet; Luke was surprised no one had heard him cursing.

Sitting down on the bed and pouring himself a glass of water from the clear jug on his bedside table, he managed to calm himself down. *I can't do this. I can't just lie in here while that fucker's out there.* And now there was a threat against his family, a clear message of intent.

The Ice Cream Man was going after his daughter.

Lydia.

That was how Luke would suffer, how his world would end without the Ice Cream Man so much as laying a finger upon him.

Luke pulled the IV from the back of his hand—it hurt like hell but bled very little—and began to dress.

He was getting out of St. George's tonight, or would at least die trying.

TWENTY-THREE

OCTOBER 31ST, 2016
HAVERING, LONDON

Luke didn't care what time it was, he hammered the front door as if he were trying to bust it off its hinges. "Mom! Dad! Open up!" Dad? His dad would not open up. It would be *Dave*, and *Dave* would be pissed off by the three a.m. wake-up call from his woman's psychologically damaged son. There would be a fight, despite Luke looking like he'd already been hit by a truck, and Dave would slam the door shut, leaving him to limp-roll down the drive, bleeding and whining and wishing he'd never bothered.

"Dave! Mom!" He hammered again three more times, and it was on the second thump that the door began to click from the inside. Luke took a step back, grabbed hold of his side—his ribs felt as if they were splintered and tearing at his insides like sharpened chicken bones—and took a deep, painful breath.

"Luke?" Dave was dressed in a yellow silk dressing-gown, the kind Roger Moore wore in *Live and Let Die*. "What the *fuck*... what happened to you. You look like shit?"

"Look, Dave, sorry to barge in like this. I know it's late, but I really need some help."

"You're right there, mate," Dave said, taking a step outside and pulling the door to behind him. "I don't know what this is about, but your mother's had a helluva bad night. She's got a really bad abscess, and she's taken a lot of painkillers just so she can get some sleep—"

"I don't need to speak to Mom," Luke said. "I need to borrow your car."

"What?"

"Your car, Dave," Luke said, motioning to the TR7 sitting on the driveway. "I have to get back to my wife and kid, tonight.

Something terrible is going to happen to them, and I—"

"What's going on, Luke?" Dave asked, arms folded across his chest, bald head glistening in the moonlight. Standing there in his dressing gown, he looked about half as intimidating as he had the first time they'd met.

"Please, Dave," Luke said. "I know you don't know me, and this is all a little fucked up, but you have to trust me, okay? I'll bring the car back first thing in the morning, I swear. Look?" He removed his watch—a not-inexpensive Larsson and Jennings Karen had gifted him last Christmas—and held it out for Dave to inspect. "Collateral. I promise, I won't put a scratch on her."

After quickly appraising the watch, Dave sighed. "Wait here." He went inside, and when he returned, he was holding a set of car keys. "She's a good runner," he said, "but if you park on a hill, make sure you leave her in gear. The handbrake doesn't work."

He handed the keys to Luke, but when Luke went to hand him the watch, he took a step back, shaking his head.

"What kind of an asshole do you think I am?"

"I don't," Luke said. He slipped the watch back onto his wrist and fastened it. "Thank you, Dave. First thing in the morning, I promise."

But Dave was already turning, yawning. He raised a hand (goodbye, Luke, now fuck off) and went back inside, easing the door shut behind him.

Luke ran for the car.

*　*　*

OCTOBER 31ST, 2016
LUTON, BEDFORDSHIRE

It never crossed Luke's mind that Karen would be angry with him; never once struck him, as he drove for almost an hour to the family home, that she would consider his sudden arrival an inconvenient intrusion, but that was precisely how it felt now, sitting in the living-room while she paced back and forth in front of the fire.

"So, let me get this straight, Luke," she said, her voice tremulous and full of sleep. "You discharged yourself from hospital—which, by the way, was a stupid thing to do in your condition—borrowed a car from a complete stranger, and then drove all this way because you thought Lydia and me were in trouble?"

Luke didn't care that she was annoyed with him, could even take the shrill of her voice without wincing, because he was back to protect them. "I didn't discharge myself," he said. Only because there was no one around to get the ball rolling, but he kept that part to himself. "And I don't expect you to understand, but—"

"I don't understand, Luke, because it doesn't make any sense." She glanced toward the living-room door, which sat ajar, and the next time she spoke it was softer quieter, so as not to wake Lydia. "This thing, this guy that took your friend when you were twelve-years-old, he's not going to come back for you, Luke. He's not going to take Lydia away, because he's all up here." She tapped the side of her head.

"Okay," Luke said. "So humour me. I know it's difficult to believe, but this thing is real, Karen. It's real, and it's coming back. Didn't Marcus tell you why he was down here? Why he was driving around Havering when I hit him?"

Karen shrugged. "Said something about scouting venues for a comeback tour. His father was doing the same in the north."

"Well, he was *lying*, Karen," Luke said, a sudden pain stabbing at his chest. Perhaps it *was* a bad idea to leave the hospital without letting anyone know. "Marcus was down here because that thing from when we were kids attacked him, it attacked him the same way it attacked me. I didn't see Lydia in bed that night; I saw the Ice Cream Man. It took over our daughter, because that's what it does. It gets to you through other people. I would never lay a finger on her, Karen, and you know that, but that night... I thought that sonofabitch was back... and I thought it was going to hurt her." He swallowed, but his mouth was absolutely dry and made a strange clicking sound as he talked. "Halloween, Karen. That's when it comes. Everything that happens now, everything that's already happened, is leading up to that, and the only way it can get to me is through Lydia."

Standing there, his wife looked like a stranger to him. Cold, distant, she could have been any woman from any town in the country. "I'm going back to bed, Luke," she said as an exhale. "Please, go back to the hospital. You should never have left in the first place, and you're no good to us in that state."

"I'm not leaving you—"

"That's exactly what you're going to do, Luke." She placed her hands on the sides of her head, as if she couldn't even believe this conversation was taking place. "If Lydia wakes up in the morning and you're still here, she's going to freak out, and I don't want that. I don't think *you* want that."

"But at the hospital?" Luke said. "You told me everything was going to be okay? That we could fix this and be a family again."

"And I *meant* it," Karen said, lowering her hands. "I meant it, Luke, but it's going to take a lot longer than a week, and I can't do this while you're not yourself."

"I *am* myself—"

"We're fine!" Karen snapped. "Lydia and me, we're fine, and we're going to be fine until you're better, but you have to go back to the hospital. You have to get right before we can have this conversation again."

Luke deflated; this was not how this was meant to go. He hadn't expected open arms from his wife, but the last thing he'd considered was that she didn't want him there at all, despite what he was telling her about the Ice Cream Man.

"So I should just *go*?" Luke shook his head, incredulous.

"Back to the hospital," Karen said. "Please, Luke, your daughter needs you. *I* need you, but we need you well, and not scared of things which are never going to happen."

Luke pushed himself up from the sofa, his busted ribs aching like never before. Inside he was screaming, but outside... outside he wished he could.

At least Karen had the decency to walk him to the door, to stand there nodding as he reversed out of the driveway: *That's it. Off you go, back to the hospital.*

But the hospital was the last place he would be going, for

today was Halloween and time was running out.

He had to find Marcus.

We don't stop hitting until we knock that sonofabitch back to Hell.

TWENTY-FOUR

OCTOBER 31ST, 2016
REDBRIDGE, LONDON

Wood was first up and making breakfast before the sun had even risen above the houses across the street. Tom found him in the kitchen, muttering something or other about sausages and bacon, and the lack thereof.

"Yeah, sorry about that," Tom said, motioning to the refrigerator. "Danielle does the shopping, and she's adamant that stuff puts you into an early grave."

"Some of us are banking on it," Wood grumbled. He was definitely not a morning person. "You might want to let Danielle in on a little secret, one I learned many years ago, when I still had working fucking legs and a will to live: Even pigs like bacon."

Tom set about making the coffee. "Only because they don't know where it comes from," he said.

"I doubt that would make a bit of difference," Wood said. "They eat their own shit, don't they? Pretty sure they know where that comes from."

There was a palpable tension in the air, an odd sense of apprehension as they went about compiling a half-decent breakfast. Tom knew better than to interfere, so other than handing Wood a box of eggs and a bag of bread, there wasn't much else he could do. He settled himself down at the table and stared anxiously out through the kitchen window.

"Something smells mmm-mmm, finger-licking good in here," Marcus said when he entered the kitchen five minutes later. "Is that an omelette? Mushroom and pepper? Oh, and toast and butter and all things gooooood. Damn, Sarge, it's like you read my mind."

For some bizarre reason, Marcus had started calling Wood 'Sarge', even though the old man had been out of the force for more than two decades, and they had never—*not once, nope, huhuh*—called him Sarge back when they were twelve. If they had, Wood would have stuffed them in the back of his Panda on general principle until they learned some manner.

"Just sit down, Banger, and try not to break the chair. Danielle does the shopping in this house, *apparently*, and I'm guessing it wouldn't take much to turn those Ikea stools to kindling," Wood said, wheeling himself back and forth between the kitchen counter and the table, each time carrying something new: toast, jam, plates, cutlery.

Marcus did as he was told. "So, what's the plan, boys?" he said. "We didn't really talk about it last night—my head still hurts—but do you think we're going to need to bust Luke out of the hospital? You know, like the A-Team used to do with Mad Murdoch at the start of every episode?"

Tom had been miles away, focussed upon a flock of pigeons alighting on the rooftops across the street. But when Marcus gave him a little nudge, he surprised even himself. "I don't know," he said. "Are we going to be putting Luke in danger by getting him out of that place? I mean, is he going to be able to run if he has to?"

"*I* can't run," Wood said, returning to the kitchen table with a steaming plate of eggs. "Does that make *me* a liability?" He was being facetious, and Tom knew better than to engage.

"I just think we'd be weakening ourselves as a group," Tom explained. "I'm not being an asshole; I just want to make it through the night in one piece. I love Luke as much as you—that guy went through it back in the day, and I made sure I was always there to pick him up—but do we really need someone slowing us down? You said it yourself, he was pretty bashed up."

Marcus, buttering a piece of toast, said, "I know, if *I* were him, I'd want you guys to come get me. That's all I'm saying." He crunched into the toast; crumbs fell to his plate. He began to push his thumb into the crumbs, and once he was satisfied, suck them from his thumb. It was something they would have done as children, but none of them had truly grown up, not really. It was easier to act that way now they were reunited. Who was going to tell them otherwise?

Maybe you're right, Tom thought. He hadn't looked at it from the other side, from Luke's point of view. The poor guy had come down here, just as they all had, to put an end to this maniac, and now he was lying helpless in some shitty hospital bed, waiting for it to all be over. That wasn't right.

It wasn't fair.

Tom was about to say as much when there came a knock at the door. All three of them turned in the direction of the noise, but none of them said a word. The caller—a man, gruff as if he'd smoked too many cigarettes and drunk too much bad vodka— was the first to speak, calling through the letterbox.

"Hello? I'm looking for Tom Craven? Answers to the names Tom, Tommy, Pin-dick, Warts, Piledriver, Anusol..." The list went on and on, but Tom was no longer listening. He stood from the kitchen table and rushed across the room, through the door and into the hallway, and unlocked the front door.

Looking tired and dishevelled, Luke Davis was a sight for sore eyes. His days' old stubble suggested he hadn't seen a razor for a while, and the bags beneath his eyes made him look more like fifty than his actual age, a decade younger.

Tom pulled Luke in for an embrace, ignoring his friend's pained hiss at first, and then, remembering that Luke should have been in hospital, he eased up "Good to see you, man."

"You have no idea," Luke said. Tom thought he detected fear in Luke's voice; fear and sadness. "Looks like I'm just in time for breakfast."

* * *

Tom, Marcus, and Wood listened as Luke explained what he had been through and the things he had seen. Of course, Marcus already knew some of Luke's story, but he sat silently and took it all in as if it were the first time.

Tom thought he had had it rough; losing Danielle (temporarily?), seeing Kurian change into Ghuul before his eyes, watching helplessly as Margaret Banks committed suicide in the most ridiculous of ways. But his experiences this past week were *nothing* compared to Luke's.

They ate eggs, drank coffee, and smoked cigarettes—all except for Marcus, who had never taken up that particular habit, and yet he didn't complain as the kitchen filled with a thick white fog—and for the first time in almost thirty years the gang were back together

(all except for Ryan)

and it felt good. It felt right, as if they had simply gone to bed back in '88 and woke up here, eating breakfast in Tom's smoky kitchen. Everything in-between was just filler.

Trust Wood to bring them all back down to earth. "Boys, I know this is a fun day for you all. You haven't seen each other since you pulled each other's puds in the woods, I get it, but we need to focus. That thing is coming back tonight—"

"Or today," Marcus said. "Who knows *what* it's capable of."

Tom shook his head. "No, it only comes at night," he said. He didn't know how he knew that; he just did.

Wood seemed to agree, for he was nodding. "Tom's right. Ghuul is a demon of the night. Whatever it's going to do, it will do it after dark."

"Wait a minute," Luke said, pouring himself a third cup of coffee. He looked like he needed it. "*Ghuul*? I've heard that name in my nightmares. What does it mean?"

There wasn't time for Luke to read the book, so Tom motioned for Wood to give Luke the concise version.

"That's its name," Wood said. "It's a demon, a devourer of children—their souls at least. Every seven years it returns to our realm for nourishment."

"By nourishment," Luke said, "you mean a kid?"

Wood nodded. "It abducts a child, transports it back to its own netherworld, feeds upon its soul." As Wood explained, Luke grimaced. Was he picturing Ryan in that situation? Tom was, and it was almost too much to bear.

"But why an Ice Cream Man?" Luke asked.

Tom lit a cigarette and walked across the room, where he opened a window. It was getting a little too smoky in there, even for him. "Also a long story," Tom told Luke. "But the guy who summoned Ghuul was an Ice Cream Man."

"Kinda convenient," Luke said. "I mean, you're an ancient

eater of children, just passing the time away in your own little nether-netherworld, and then boom! You're summoned by a guy doing the only job in the world where it's perfectly fine to chat up kids. I'll bet its fucking eyes lit up when it realised how lucky it was."

"Just the way it goes," Wood said, waving a hand dismissively through the air. "It could have been a welder, a window-cleaner, a cop... it wouldn't make a difference. All Ghuul needs is a willing host, and there were none more willing than Frederick White. Just so happened he had a little evil in him already."

"And now he has a lot," Marcus said. "And we're up Shit Creek without a paddle until we know where and when it's going to appear."

Luke cleared his throat. "I think it's going after my daughter," he said. "The last two dreams I've had were about her, and it seemed to thrive on the fact I almost killed her myself. I tried to convince my wife, Karen, I was telling the truth, but I guess phantom ice cream men stories aren't as scary as they used to be."

"How sure are you?" Wood grunted.

"Pretty sure," Luke replied. "It knows how much she means to me, that I would give my own life for hers if I could. And since I'm the only one of us who has a kid..." He trailed off, perhaps unsure if he had offended any of his friends.

Marcus turned to face Tom. "He's right."

"Then what? We park up outside Luke's house and hope for the best?" Tom didn't like the sound of that; talk about putting all your eggs in one basket. The Ice Cream Man was not limited by geography. Harvey Poulson had been snatched outside a supermarket in Brighton, Rochelle Chambers from her bedroom in Glasgow. The odds on it showing up at an exact place at an exact time were miniscule.

"We can't speculate on where and when it's going to appear," Wood said. He wheeled himself away from the table. "It's too much of a gamble. When tonight comes, all we can do is wait. We'll hear it before we see it, and then we go after it."

"Hate to break it to you," Tom said, "but we don't have a car between us."

"I've got a TR7," Luke said, "but even if we could all fit in it, which we can't, it's not mine. I'm supposed to be dropping it back this morning. In fact, I'm already late." He glanced toward the clock: 08:25AM.

Look at us, Tom thought. *Going into battle against an ancient force and not one of us a set of wheels to keep up with a phantom ice cream truck.* "We could rent something," Tom suggested. "Something quick and big enough for the four of us."

"Three," Luke said, and when all eyes fell upon him, he explained. "I can't leave it to chance. If that thing goes after Lydia, I'm going to be there to protect her. I need her to know her father loves her very much, would never do anything to hurt her, and I couldn't live with myself if... if that fucker got her because I was an hour away on some wild goose chase."

"We need you," Marcus said. They were all thinking it, but Marcus was the one who voiced it. "Luke, we'll be stronger with you. I don't know, but I think that thing was trying to prevent this, to stop us all from gathering here. That's why it's been making life hell for us all. It's been trying to drive a wedge between us. It knows what frightens us and it's been using our fears against us, but now we're all here... I don't know, man. I'm just not scared anymore. I'm pissed. I'm ready to kick this thing's fucking head off, but I'm not scared."

"I hear you," Luke said, "but Lydia—"

"What if we could somehow convince her to come here?" It was a hypothetical 'what if', but Tom knew they could come up with something between them.

"There's no way," Luke said. "There's nothing here for her, or for Karen..." He paused, extinguished his umpteenth cigarette, and began to slowly nod. "There might be something, but it's a long-shot, and I doubt Karen will go for it."

"Willing to give it a go?" Tom said.

Luke nodded. "If it keeps her safe tonight, I'm willing to do whatever it takes."

* * *

Tom shivered as Luke steered the TR7 onto the driveway of

his mother's house. Being back in Havering was like returning to the scene of some brutal murder-suicide; it was just a location, a place on a map, but the things that had happened there made it haunting. Tom would have felt more at ease driving into Chernobyl with the windows down.

Luke slowed the car and pulled the handbrake. When it came off in his hand, and he glanced down at it as if it were a banana, Tom erupted with laughter.

"Tell me, how big is this Dave geezer again?" Tom couldn't help himself. And besides, it was a much-needed respite from the misery that had filled the car on the drive over.

Luke dropped the broken handbrake into the foot-well and pushed the car into first gear to prevent it from rolling back down the drive and out onto the main road. "It was already knackered," Luke said. "I forgot. I'll tell him I'll pay for it."

"I wouldn't," Tom said. "The guy's boinking your mom. I'd say a broken handbrake makes you about even."

They climbed out of the TR7 and approached the house. Their respective breaths crystalized in front of their faces; it was a cold, dismal morning, but at least it wasn't raining.

It wasn't the bald giant who answered the door—much to Luke's apparent relief—but Luke's mother, Anne. Tom hadn't seen her for decades, but he could see that the years hadn't been kind to her. She looked ill, as if she might be afflicted with something terminal. Her hair was huge on her head; an eighties perm which had somehow got away from her. Tom wouldn't have recognised her if he'd past her in the street. And she didn't seem to recognise Tom, either, which was fine by him.

After handing his mother the keys to Dave's beloved TR7—now with 100 per cent more snapped handbrake—Luke explained what he wanted of his mother, and she seemed to brighten at the thought.

"Here?" she said. "Tonight?"

"I'm thinking it would be good for you to see her again, you know? She's eight years old and you were right. What happened between us is in the past. There's no reason Lydia should miss out because a bunch of grown-ups can't act civilly."

And it was as easy as that. Luke's mother, looking younger

and happier than when she'd answered the door a few moments ago, invited both he and Tom in for coffee, but Luke told her they didn't have time. "Lots of planning to do," he told her. "Maybe put on a bit of a spread, Mom? Lydia really likes Halloween. It'll be nice for her to spend it with her grandma."

They called a cab from the house and waited out front for it to arrive, during which time Luke put a call through to Karen. Tom didn't envy his friend. He would call his own wife before tonight, but right now he was in the zone. He couldn't allow anything to knock him off-kilter.

It sounded to Tom as if Karen was giving Luke a hard time on the phone; Luke explained—or at least *attempted* to—why he had not returned to the hospital. *Feeling much better*, was one of the reasons he gave. *Waste of time* was another. All the time he spoke he held onto his ribs as if he was afraid they might fall out. Tom could see his friend was not 'feeling much better' at all; he was simply making do, the same way they all were.

"*Tonight*, Karen. My mother really wants to see her. Will you do that? For *me*?" Tom heard her screeching madly on the other end of the line, and then Luke cut her off with, "Dad's not even going to *be* there. Remember, they're divorcing. It'll just be you, Lydia, and my mother."

Not enough to swing it, Tom thought, and then contemplated knocking the door once again and telling Luke's mother, *Sorry, change of plan. Can't see your granddaughter tonight. Whoopsie.*

"I know, Karen. Don't you think I... please, just do this one thing for me. I promise I'll go back to the hospital. Whatever it takes." A few seconds later, Luke gave Tom the thumbs up. "Okay, yeah, around six. She'll be really happy to hear that." Another thumbs-up. "And when you're here, don't open the door to anyone, not even Trick or Treaters... *nothing*'s going on, Karen, I just want you to be safe... okay, tell Lydia... well tell her Daddy loves her so much."

The cab arrived just as Luke finished saying his goodbyes. They were halfway back to Redbridge when Luke said, "I hope we're doing the right thing."

That, Tom thought, was such a strange thing to say. The

right thing? As opposed to what? Doing nothing? "I guess we'll find out tonight," Tom said.

Neither of them spoke for the remainder of the journey.

* * *

When they arrived back at Tom's, Wood and Marcus were outside giving their car for the evening—a Range Rover Sport—a once over.

"Couldn't you have got anything bigger?" Tom said, sardonically. The vehicle was huge, a mechanical elephant, and though it wasn't what Tom had had in mind, Wood assured him it would do the job.

"Nought to sixty in seven seconds," Wood said. "She'll reach one-thirty, easy."

Tom looked at Marcus, who held his hands out. "I *told* him it was overkill," he said. "I said, 'we're gonna be chasing an ice cream truck, not Lewis Hamilton. You can't argue with him."

Apart from its obvious excessiveness, Tom found the vehicle to be perfect. It must have cost Wood a week's pension to hire, maybe even more. It was just another sign that Wood was incredibly serious about ending this tonight. No expense spared.

Tom made his excuses and went into the house, where he called Danielle. She answered after the eighth ring, just as Tom had been about to cancel the call. "Hey." She sounded out of breath.

"Hey," Tom replied. "Just thought I'd check in, make sure those boys aren't bullying you too much." He lit a cigarette and sat down at the kitchen table. Wood had tidied up after breakfast, but the myriad smells—toast, eggs, coffee—remained.

"They're hard work, but nothing I can't handle," Danielle said. There was an awkward pause, the sound of something crunching underfoot, more panting. "We're actually out at the moment, Tom. Jayden wanted to pick his own pumpkin for tonight, so we decided to head out to a PYO farm."

"Leaving it a bit late," Tom said. "I'd be surprised if there are any left."

"Well, we'll see when we get there, though to be honest I think you're right. I just didn't want to be the one to tell Jayden."

Quieter now, so that her nephew didn't hear. "Let him find out for himself."

Danielle wanted to know what Tom had planned for the day, and Tom told her he would be taking it easy. She said he should expect a call from Doctor Kurian, who was a little concerned about him and his erratic behaviour, and Tom told her that there was nothing to worry about, that everything was fine—*he* was fine—and he wouldn't be doing anything silly.

"So, the whole thing..." She trailed off, but Tom knew what she was getting at. She wanted reassurance that he wasn't losing his mind, that he didn't actually believe some demonic Ice Cream Man was going to pierce the thin veil between their respective worlds tonight and steal another child.

"Just bad memories and even worse dreams," Tom said. "I'm thinking about taking a little time off work, you know? Take better care of myself, and to hell with Michael & Michael for the time being." He wasn't lying; he had been considering a few months off, only now that he had verbalised it, he wanted— *needed*—it even more.

"If you think it'll help," Danielle said. "I'm sure Kurian will write you a note."

"I'm sure he will, and if he doesn't, next time I see him I'm going to steal his pen. Steal his pen and defecate on his desk."

Danielle erupted with laughter. Breathy laughter which was like music to Tom's ears. He hadn't heard his wife laugh in... well, a long time. He had almost forgotten what it sounded like. He knew, then, that he would do whatever it took to get her back, for he couldn't survive without her, couldn't make it through another week without seeing her or waking up to find her wrapped around him in bed.

"I promise," Tom said, "everything is going to be okay, Dani. I know you can't see it right now—and that's understandable; I've been selfish, and a dick—but we're going to be together again. Once all this is over... once I've got my head sorted..."

"I know," she said. "And you're not a dick, Tom. I wouldn't be with you if you were. You just need to... you just need to get some treatment, okay? It's nothing to be ashamed of, and I'll be with you every step of the way, if you want me to be."

Tom told her he would like that, he would like that very much, despite knowing that there was nothing wrong with his head, with his mental stability. He was as sharp as a tack, and this thing was very much real. Since Danielle was never going to believe in it, however, he knew he had no choice but to play along, just like Nicholson did in One Flew Over the Cuckoo's Nest. Anything for a quiet life.

"Guess what?" she said.

"What?"

"There *are* some pumpkins left. Can you believe that?" Then she was shouting, calling after Jayden, who must have gone off a-running, excited at the prospect of picking his own pumpkin. "I have to go, Tom," she said. "Better make sure he doesn't pick a rotten one."

"I love you," Tom said. It felt like the last chance he would ever have to tell her, and maybe it was. "I love you, and I'm going to make everything right between us, you have my word."

"I love you too, Tom," Danielle said.

Then she hung up.

TWENTY-FIVE

OCTOBER 31ST, 2016, REDBRIDGE, LONDON

Night seemed to fall quicker than ever before. Darkness descended upon Redbridge, and with it came a chill. Tom, Luke, Marcus, and Wood piled into the 4x4, with Wood's wheelchair folding away in the spacious boot. It had taken Tom and Luke to lift Wood across into the back seat, while Marcus held the door as wide as he could. By the time the former copper was loaded up, Tom was sweating sheets. Ten minutes later, he would be shivering again.

"So, how are we going to do this?" Luke said as he climbed into the passenger seat. Marcus was happy sitting in the back with Wood. *'Me and Sarge, sitting in a tree'* was how he put it. "We just going to drive around, listening out for Pop Goes the Weasel, and hope for the best?"

Tom pushed the button which electrically took his window down. "You got any better ideas?"

"I think we should head to Havering," Wood said. "That's where this all started, that's where it's going to end."

Tom didn't know how Wood could be so sure, but there was a certain poetry to what he was suggesting. *A perfect circle*, he thought. *And thanks for all the nightmares...*

Turning the key, Tom listened as the engine started. It wasn't a noisy car—not idling, anyway—but he would have to keep the window down in order to listen out for the discordant chimes of the phantom ice cream truck. Marcus would complain about how the chill was hitting him right in the face less than five minutes after pulling off, but Tom new they couldn't risk it. They had one shot at this, one chance to bring this fucker down.

"Into the abyss," Luke said as Tom pulled the 4x4 away from the kerb.

"Amen," Tom added.

"I think I need the toilet," Marcus said.

"Shut up, Banger," Wood groaned.

* * *

OCTOBER 31ˢᵀ, 2016
BROMLEY, LONDON

It wasn't the greatest carved pumpkin in the history of Halloween, but Jayden seemed pleased with himself, and Danielle had managed to escape with only minor cuts to her fingers, so the night was off to a good start. In the background, an album Rebecca had put on—*The Best of Halloween,* or *Now! Halloween,* some such compilation—was already starting to grate. There were only so many times you could listen to The Monster Mash without wanting to punch the next Trick or Treater to knock the door.

Justice, Joel, and Oscar were bobbing for apples at the kitchen table. Oscar wasn't doing too well, since he hated water in his eyes, and was already begging for his brothers to play a different game. "Stop whining and get your head in the bucket," Justice said. "Joel and me have already managed to get our five-a-day."

Oscar cried. Oscar threw a tantrum. And then Oscar went to bed. Halloween didn't mean anything to Oscar, and Danielle was honestly surprised Rebecca's youngest had stayed up this late, since he hadn't a clue what was going on.

"So, remind me," Danielle said, settling herself down at the kitchen table with a small glass of wine. It didn't feel right drinking, knowing that Tom was going through hell trying to quit. But one little glass wouldn't hurt. "Who are you two supposed to be?"

Justice was painted green from the neck up and the wrists down. Other than that, he was pretty much the same old Justice. "I'm the Hulk," he said. "You know? Avengers?" He said it as if he were talking to a simpleton.

"I know The Avengers," Danielle said, bobbing her tongue

out at Justice. "John Steed, Emma Peel, British intelligence, black umbrellas—"

"What the hell are you talking about?" Joel said.

Danielle couldn't help herself; she burst out laughing. "I'm just winding you up," she said. "I get it: The Hulk, Iron Man, Captain Armenia—"

"It's Captain *America*!" Justice said. To Joel he said, "She knows what she's saying. Don't take any notice of her."

Joel nodded before bobbing for an apple. When he came back up, mouth empty and gasping for air, Danielle said, "So your brother's the Hulk? Who are you?"

"I'm *Aquaman*," Joel said.

"Oh!" Danielle said. "Does Aquaman wear an orange tee-shirt and green marigolds?"

"Don't listen to her," Justice reminded his younger brother. "She's just jealous because Halloween is like dress-down Friday for her."

"Smart-aleck," Danielle said. "Where did you hear that?"

Justice grinned. His front two teeth at the top were missing, and it made his smirk even more mischievous. "Jayden told me to say it. Only he told me to say it to Mom, not you, but Mom wouldn't have taken it as a joke."

"Good call," Danielle said. Then she realised something; she hadn't seen Jayden for almost five whole minutes. She was so used to him always being there, hanging on her every word and defending her to the hilt, that she had just assumed he was in the room, silently watching, perhaps jealous she was giving the time of day to her other nephews.

But he wasn't in the kitchen, and when Rebecca walked in a moment later—dressed as a black cat, replete with eyeliner whiskers and lipstick-pink nose—Danielle said, "Is Jayden upstairs?"

Rebecca frowned. "I didn't see him. Is that music loud enough, do you think? I'm trying to piss of the neighbours." She was already slurring her words; Danielle could see it was going to be a long night.

"Music's fine," Danielle said, standing from the kitchen table. *Maybe even turn it off, yeah?* she thought but didn't say.

This wasn't her house, and these weren't her children (not that she would ever find out what that was like) and so it was best to keep her opinions to herself.

"I'm going to check on Jayden," Danielle said. She stood from the table and walked toward the hallway. When she reached it, she discovered that the door was open; not fully, but enough for a chill to seep through the crack.

Jayden was still outside. But surely it didn't take that long to find the perfect spot for a pumpkin. Unless he was admiring it, or perhaps he'd got chatting to a group of Trick or Treaters, friends from school. Either way, it was time to come in now. Outside it was cold, and the last thing Rebecca needed was to have Jayden off school, sick.

Danielle pulled open the door and...

She saw the pumpkin first, or what had once been a delicately carved pumpkin. Now it was reduced to mush, an orange mulch whose candle had gone out. It was right there on the path; Justice and Joel's pumpkins still glowed either side of it.

Lost. Danielle felt suddenly lost, and so she called out to her nephew. "Jayden? Jayden, are you out here?" She looked toward the end of the path; the rust-eaten gate swung gently back and forth on squeaky hinges.

And then she heard it. A sound so surreal at this time of night—this time of year—that her brain struggled to comprehend it.

Pop Goes the Weasel.

Ice cream van chimes, terribly out of tune, repeated themselves over and over, and now Danielle was running toward the gate, her heart racing within her. "Jayden! Jayden!" But no matter how many times she called out his name, her nephew did not appear, for he wasn't hiding in the front garden, wasn't playing silly buggers for the sake of one good scare.

Danielle knew where he was, and yet she still refused to believe it.

Refused until she reached the gate, spilled out onto the dimly lit street just in time to see the yellow-and-white ice cream truck go whizzing past, its driver nothing more than a dark shape behind the wheel. A dark shaped with blood-red eyes.

She screamed.

From somewhere inside the truck, Jayden Lebbon screamed back.

* * *

OCTOBER 31ST, 2016
HAVERING, LONDON

The Trick or Treaters were out in force in and around Havering, despite the chill in the air and the frost on the ground. Gangs of kids—some accompanied by grown-ups, others simply out to create mischief, something you can't do with a responsible adult watching your every move—walked the streets. Many were dressed as their favourite superheroes, something which Tom didn't quite understand. Halloween was meant to be about ghosts, about spirits and the dead and things that make your hair stand on end; it was not an excuse to throw on last summer's Spiderman costume and hope no one noticed.

Under advisement from Luke, Tom drove past Luke's mother's house, just to make sure everything 'looked okay'. And it looked more than okay. Carved pumpkins peppered the driveway. Dave's TR7 now wore a ghostly sheet of its own, but perhaps that had more to do with its recent broken handbrake than the fact it was Halloween.

"Happy?" Tom asked Luke as he pulled away from the kerb.

Luke nodded. "I feel like I should be in there, you know? Protecting Lydia, making sure that son-of-a-whore can't get anywhere near her." He sighed, lit a cigarette and dangled his arm out of the window so that the smoke didn't offend Marcus in the back seat.

"You're protecting her just fine," Tom said as he reached the end of the street and took a right. They had enough fuel to drive around Havering all night long, and that's what they would do, if it came down to it. Tom almost wished the truck would appear now so that they could get it over with. He had considered the possibility that it wouldn't show at all, that a child in some other part of the country, hundreds of miles away from where they now patrolled, was already on its way to Ghuul's netherworld. A feeling of helplessness washed over Tom, but it was a feeling which he quickly dispelled. There was no time for weakness tonight.

They had to be strong.

They had to be ready.

And when it came right down to it, they had to be mentally prepared.

"This is going to be one long-ass night," Marcus said from the back seat. "Does anyone else feel a bit strange, cruising the streets while all these kids are out here? I mean, I know we're not doing anything wrong, but I'm pretty sure there's a register for people like us."

Ignoring his comment completely, Wood said, "How's your father doing, Banger? He still collecting money for people more powerful than him?"

Tom looked in the rear-view mirror, saw Marcus smile before answering. "You do realise my dad's an old man now. Almost as old as you, Sarge. He hasn't done anything illegal for at least three years, and I don't know how illegal it is to eat a grape from a supermarket display without paying first."

Wood sucked in air through his teeth. "I'd say six-to-twelve in the Scrubs. It all depends on whether the supermarket wants to testify."

Laughing, Marcus said, "Things have changed since you were on the force, Sarge. Everyone knows it's community service for grape theft nowadays."

"This country's too soft by half," Wood said, and then he and Marcus were both laughing. Another surreal moment in a long line of them, Tom thought.

Just then, Tom's mobile started to ring; Rossini's William Tell Overture filled the car. Tom fumbled around in his jeans pocket, managed to pincer the phone and pull it free before the call rang off. He answered it, slowed the car to twenty as he spoke. "Hey, babe. Everything okay?"

Danielle was hysterical. Screaming down the line at him and uncontrollably crying. It took Tom a while to realise she wasn't yelling at him about something he had or hadn't done. "Babe, Dani, please try to calm down. What is it? What's happened?"

Everyone else in the car watched Tom as he tried to placate his seemingly panic-stricken wife. Tom slowed the car even further before pulling over completely. Danielle's frenetic voice filled the car. Tom's heart was now racing. And then she said three words which seemed to grip his heart and squeeze it tight.

Ice

Cream

Man

"Just stay there and call the police!" Tom said, shouting now. "We're on our way."

Danielle began to say something else— *"We're on our way? who are you with? —*but Tom didn't let her finish the question. He cancelled the call and passed the phone to Luke. "I don't fucking believe it!" Tom said, hammering the steering-wheel with both hands. "I didn't see it coming. We thought it was going after Lydia, but it never was. It never was!" He slammed his foot down on the accelerator and sped away from the kerb. The 4x4's tyres squealed beneath them.

"What is it?" Wood asked, leaning forward. "What's going on, Tom?"

"It got Danielle's nephew," Tom said. "It got Jayden. Fuck!" He took the next corner without braking; a trio of witches, pound-store plastic buckets swinging from their arms, stopped and glared at the speeding Range Rover with open mouths.

"How far?" Marcus asked.

"Forty-five minutes with no traffic," Tom said through gritted teeth. "It's Bromley. Just past Greenhill Nursing Home."

"Shit!" Luke said. "By the time we get there it'll be long gone."

Tom grunted agitatedly. Luke was right; there was no way they'd catch up to the Ice Cream Man if he was all the way over in Bromley. They had never stood a chance. All this time it had been throwing them off with nightmares, appearing to them in visions with threats and revealing to them their true fears. Misdirection. All of it.

The feeling of helplessness returned as Tom screeched around another corner, only this time there was no pushing it down, no light at the end of the tunnel. Ghuul had won, had destroyed another family, a family he and Danielle were a part of.

"Stop the car!" Wood said, so suddenly that Tom almost *crashed* the car.

"Why? What are you—"

"Just pull over!" Wood said, tapping the back of Tom's seat with his hand.

"We don't have time for—"

"Just do it!"

Tom reluctantly slammed his foot down on the brake, and the Range Rover skated to a halt. He was about to ask Wood what the hell was going on when he heard it for himself. Distant, but getting closer. Perhaps an estate away, maybe closer.

Pop Goes the Weasel.

"I don't... that can't be..." Luke looked astounded. "It has to be a different one. There's no way it could have got all the way over here from Bromley, not—"

"It's *him*," Wood said. "This isn't just any old ice cream truck we're talking about. It doesn't even exist, not really. It's simply a door to its netherworld."

Tom took his foot off the brake, hit the accelerator, and the 4x4 worked its way back up to thirty-forty-fifty...

"It's coming for *Lydia* now," Luke said. "Shit, it's trying to take more than one. It's coming for Lydia."

"That's not going to happen," Tom said, following the inharmonious chimes through the night. "It has to be stopped."

We're going to be the ones to stop it, Tom thought. *Or die trying.*

*   *   *

Karen had to give it to Anne, she had certainly pulled out all the stops. The table was laden with party food, far too much for just one little girl. Lydia didn't eat a great deal at the best of times, and so there would almost certainly be lots left at the end of the night. Meanwhile, Karen was trying to shake off the uncomfortable feeling which had swamped her since arriving. It was so strange, being here.

Without Luke.

Almost as if they were imposing upon a complete stranger.

Lydia was having no such trouble. Sitting on the sofa next to her grandmother, she looked happier than she had in months, which only added to Karen's guilt. She had tried to prevent this, tried to keep her daughter from having a relationship with Luke's mother all over a silly dispute. They had all been selfish, too stubborn to see what they were doing, how unfair it was to Lydia.

Dave, Anne's new boyfriend, stood at the dining-room table filling a paper plate with goodies. Karen wasn't too sure about him, but he seemed nice enough, and he'd been good with Lydia so far, making her laugh with ridiculous magic tricks and daft jokes. Karen knew that Luke would never like the man, but that was just Luke.

"You're such a clever girl!" Anne said, clapping her hands excitedly together as Lydia finished reciting her seven-times-table. "I'll bet you're going to be a scientist when you're older."

"Actually," Lydia said in that precocious way she had fine-tuned over the past year, "I'm going to be a dog-walker."

Karen smiled. "We talked about that, honey," she said. "I don't think you'll ever make enough money to live in London by walking other people's dogs."

"I think you'll make a wonderful dog-walker," Anne said, running her fingers through Lydia's hair. "But your mother's right. That's something you do as a hobby. If you really concentrate at school, you can be anything you want to be. Aim for the stars, sweetie."

Dave, with a mouthful of scotch egg, returned from the table and collapsed into an armchair. A sausage roll slipped off his paper plate, but he didn't hesitate in picking it up from his lap and pushing that into his mouth also. After a few seconds of noisy chewing, he said, "Your husband owes me a new handbrake."

"Excuse me?" Karen must have misheard. How can anyone owe anyone a handbrake?

"Not now, Dave," Anne said, shooting daggers at her boyfriend. It seemed to do the trick; Dave sucked the pineapple and cheese from a stick and nodded.

After an awkward silence which seemed to stretch on forever, Lydia said, "Daddy's not here tonight because he's in Mommy's bad books." Just like that, and without any inflection whatsoever. She might as well have been a robot.

"Is that so?" Anne said. "Well, I'm sure your father is very sorry for what he's done to upset Mommy." She cast inquisitive eyes toward Karen ("*What's going on?*") but Karen was in no mood to go into it, especially not with Luke's mother, who would defend her son's behaviour, no matter what he'd done.

"Mommy says Daddy's getting help, but I don't know who is going to help him. Daddy doesn't like help from anyone."

"Well, sometimes," Anne said, in that patronising voice grown-ups use when talking to children about something they have no right to be discussing, "even the strongest people need help. Even your father."

"Not Daddy," Lydia said, shaking her head adamantly.

Anne sighed, gave up on the argument. "Go and get some food, darling," she said. "And when you come back, I want you to tell me all about your favourite lessons at school."

Lydia bounced from the sofa and marched toward the table, with its feast of sweet and savoury, and as she went, Anne turned her attention to Karen.

"Is everything okay?" Anne said, her face lopsided with faux concern. "At home, with Luke?"

So, this is how it ends, Karen thought. With a punch to her mother-in-law's nose. This was how her marriage finally reached its climax, not with a whimper but with a geriatric assault. And to think that, up until last week, both she and Luke would have both taken a shot, should the opportunity have ever presented itself. Something had changed, though, and now here she was with Lydia in tow, playing nice with the in-law(s) because it's what Luke wanted.

"Everything's fine," Karen said as an exhale. "Luke's just having a few issues, that's all. We're getting through it. Lydia must have just heard us arguing, that's all." Oh, and your son tried to kill her, but we're not talking about that, not unless you try to bolster his good character.

"He's off his tits, that one," Dave said, wiping grease from his mouth with the back of his hand.

"Dave!" Anne said. "And don't use your hand. There are napkins on the table, you animal."

Dave growled playfully, and Anne burst into hysterics. Karen imagined she was in some terrible nightmare from which she would soon awaken. This was all too much. Too much and too soon. She wanted to scoop Lydia up into her arms and run out into the night, call a cab from somewhere further down the street.

"Do you hear that, Mommy?" Lydia said. Her plate was overfilled with cupcakes and biscuits. A solitary chicken leg balanced precariously on the edge of the plate, Lydia's way of saying, *Look! I'm being healthy!*

"Hear what, honey?" Karen couldn't hear anything, at least not at first.

"Is that... sounds like an ice cream truck," Anne said.

"Don't be silly, Anne," Dave said, making his way back to the table for seconds. "In October? He's wasting his time if it is."

Karen's heart began to race, for this couldn't be happening. A coincidence, that's all it was. An ice cream truck on Halloween? It was bound to happen sooner or later.

As it drew closer, its chimes fluctuating up and down some hellish musical scale that was like nothing she had ever heard before, Karen identified the tune, and then she knew it was no coincidence.

She stood, pulled Lydia up into her arms. Lydia's plate tipped, fell in slow-motion to the carpet. Cakes and biscuits broke and crumbled and bounced underneath the sofa, where they would remain until Anne next vacuumed.

"No," Karen said, staring toward the drawn curtains as if she expected the truck to come barrelling through the front of the house.

"Don't worry about it," Anne said, pushing herself to her feet. Weary bones cracked. "I'll get the dustpan and brush."

A screech of tyres out front.

The chimes grew louder
(half a pound of tuppeny rice, half a pound of treacle)
and time froze as Karen realised that something terrible was about to happen.

*   *   *

The ice cream truck turned onto Blackmore Street, its tuneless music echoing around the estate like some hurricane warning siren. Its driver, tendrils of black smoke gripping the wheel, could almost taste the little girl, couldn't wait to add her to its collection. Twenty-eight years was a long time to wait, but now the moment had finally arrived.

It was time to make those bastards suffer.

Two streets to go.

The Ice Cream Man/Ghuul/Frederick White licked its lips, for tonight it would feast upon the tastiest souls it had ever captured.

*   *   *

"Please don't let it be too late... please, please, please..." Luke was a wreck in the passenger seat, rocking back and forth, head between hands: *how could we have been so stupid? How could we have let this happen yet again.*

"We're gonna make it, Luke," Marcus said. Just words—meaningless—but Tom was glad someone other than Luke had said something.

"Take a left here!" Luke yelled. "And then second right. Fuck! Fuck! Fuck!"

Tom did as Luke said, for a lot had changed since they were children. New roads had been added, new housing blocks built, islands where there hadn't used to be islands, and Luke knew the area better than anyone right about now.

Soon they were on the street Tom and Luke had visited earlier that day in order to return Dave's cherished TR7, only now it looked different.

Eerie.

There were no Trick or Treaters here, just flickering

pumpkins and unlit houses. Tom focussed on the road ahead, tried to block out Luke's anxious shuffling in the seat next to him.

"There!" Wood called from the rear.

Tom had already spotted it. The yellow-and-white ice cream truck approaching from the other end of the street. "Motherfucker!" Tom said.

"This is not going to end well," Marcus said, bracing himself for impact.

Fifty yards...

Twenty...

There was no way Tom was going to move. To hell with the 4x4; this was a matter of life and death. Jayden Lebbon's life. Lydi Davis's life. "Hold tight!" Tom cried.

A second later, there came the sound of twisted metal, of screeching and crunching. The last thing Tom thought before the 4x4 flipped onto its roof was:

Gotcha.

TWENTY-SIX

om pulled himself free of the overturned Range Rover, pain coursing through his entire body, but it was a pain he would have to deal with, *could* deal with. Luke was already out, doubled over and gasping for breath on the pavement. He had a cut to the head, but nothing more.

"Shit, Tom," Marcus said as he dragged himself free of the wreckage and climbed to his feet. Other than a bloody shoulder, he seemed to be in good condition; not good enough to go twelve rounds with Samuels Jr., Tom thought, but not bad given the circumstances.

Between them, they managed to pull Wood out of the car. Marcus pulled the wheelchair out through the smashed rear window and quickly unfolded it. "Get him on this," he said, snapping the wheelchair into place.

Wood grunted and groaned as they carried him across to his wheelchair, but he was conscious. They were lucky. All four of them extremely lucky. Tom had never been involved in a car crash before, and it wasn't something he'd do again, given the choice.

At the edge of the road, a hundred metres away, the ice cream truck was also on its roof. Smoke drifted up from its exposed undercarriage; even from where he stood, Tom could hear its serpentine hiss. "I'll be damned."

Just then, someone called out Luke's name, and when Tom turned, he saw a woman and a little girl running towards Luke. The little girl—Lydia—looked happy. Happy to see her father again. Happy he hadn't just died right in front of her grandmother's house. The woman, on the other hand, looked terrified. Confused and terrified.

Luke pulled his daughter into a tight hug, whispered something into her ear, and put her back down again. "Take her back inside, Karen," he said to the woman. "And lock the doors, okay? This isn't over—"

"What the hell is going on, Luke?" the woman cried.

"I'll explain later. Please, just take Lydia and get in the house."

Reluctantly, and after providing Luke with an angry stare, the woman snatched Lydia up from the pavement and run-walked back to the house. Tom wondered whether they were cursed. All of them cursed by what had happened to them back in '88, and what was happening to them again tonight. Cursed to live their entire lives with people who simply wouldn't—couldn't—understand that what was happening was real.

"Come on," Tom said as he moved slowly, cautiously, along the road towards the overturned truck. Luke was right there with him and, bringing up the rear, Marcus pushed Wood's wheelchair.

"Second worst Halloween ever," Marcus said.

"You're still alive, ain't ya?" Wood grumbled. "Quit your yapping."

Tom was pleased to hear it; Wood had had him worried for a moment back there.

The rear of the truck was buckled; once it had read MIND THE CHILDREN, but now the decal said MID E CHIDRN. "Jayden?" Tom called out. "Jayden, are you in there?"

No reply.

"He's in there," Wood said. "And not."

"What does that even *mean*?" Luke said as he circled the truck. "That fucker's not here. Gone. Fuck!"

"It's in there, too," Wood said, motioning to the rear doors. "Get the doors open, quickly."

It didn't take much effort; the doors were practically falling off already. There was a groan as the buckled metal swung open, and then Tom saw it. They all did.

Inside, the truck was not a truck at all. It was a hole, a tunnel, a pathway to another world. Pitch black and swimming with stars, the strange effect was terrifying and mesmerising and tangibly impossible. It hurt to look at, and Tom blinked away the pain, but how could you not look at something so beautiful, so strangely captivating?

"Just when I thought this shit couldn't get any weirder," Marcus said.

"It's the doorway to its realm," Wood said, and it should have sounded ridiculous but didn't. "It's where it takes the children, where it resides for seven years at a time before..."

"Are you saying Jayden is in there?" Tom said. "That thing has him in there?"

Wood nodded, sighed sadly. "We're going to have to go in after it. If we don't bring that boy back tonight, his soul will be lost forever. Just like Ryan's, just like those other children."

"Sure," Marcus said. "We'll step into the whirling vortex of nightmares and stars. I don't see how that could possibly go wrong."

Tom, once again hypnotised by the strange portal inside the truck, wiped blood from his lips. "This is what it's all been leading up to," he said, trance-like. "It ends tonight."

Luke nodded, patted Tom on the shoulder. It was such a small gesture, and yet its implications were massive. Luke was saying, *I'm with you, buddy. Every step of the way.*

"Well?" Wood said. "Are we going to stay out here all night, shivering and bleeding like stuck pigs, or are we going to finish that sonofabitch once and for all?" He motioned to the back of the truck.

After you.

"Watch each other's backs in there," Tom said. "We have no idea what we're going in to, but we're on its turf, now. It will be strong, stronger than ever before."

"As pep-talks go," Marcus said, "yours needs a little work."

Tom nodded.

Tom shook each of their hands.

Tom stepped first into the back of the van and was swallowed up by the starry black portal before he'd even had a chance to take a breath.

* * *

OCTOBER 31ST, 2016
SOMEWHERE, NOWHERE

Despair. Wretchedness. Self-loathing. Hate. Tom had never felt such emotions so powerfully; he thought his head might implode under the weight of anguish.

This is what it feeds on, Tom thought. *This is how it survives here in the place, this world between worlds.*

At first there was only darkness—a blank space in reality, as if the Creator had simply forgotten to put something here—but then shapes began to appear. Spines, the vertebrae of fallen creatures, needles and thorns taller than buildings, trees limned by some distant red moon, human limbs as fronds and trunks of flesh. This place—whatever it was, and wherever it was—was Purgatory.

This was Hell.

And here, Ghuul was in charge.

Tom turned to discover his friends had followed him through, were standing there with equally dumfounded expressions upon their faces as they tried to comprehend their surroundings. Marcus tried to say something, but there was no sound. Here, it seemed, there was no cause to speak. Marcus pointed to his mouth, shocked that nothing would emerge, but Tom simply nodded. He understood.

Behind, the star-speckled vortex continued to whirl. It was their door out of here, their link back to reality. To get lost here was tantamount to death.

Somewhere, off in the distance, a child screamed. Not all voices were silenced in Ghuul's netherworld, it seemed. Jayden's cries echoed around them as if they were standing in some sort of underwater cave.

Tom turned, and now that his eyes had adjusted to their new surroundings, he could see a pathway lined with fiery crosses. Symbolism, perhaps? Or just the place-markers for each soul Ghuul had devoured over time? There were so many of them, Tom hoped it was not the latter.

They walked for what seemed like hours. Bones crunched beneath their feet, beneath the wheels of Wood's wheelchair, like forest twigs. Ash drifted through the air, carried along on a wind hot enough to bake bread. Sweat poured from Tom's face, soaked his clothes as he moved inexorably through the netherworld in search of Jayden. Every now and again the boy cried out, and each time his voice seemed to come at them from a different direction.

Even here, the Ice Cream Man/Ghuul/Frederick White liked to play games.

The first body they came across was an emaciated glitter-cat; a young girl dressed for Halloween, only now she looked more like something you would find at the edge of a road during a missing persons search. Her eyes were wide, her mouth even wider. The drawn-on whiskers had faded but were still visible.

Cheryl Mitchell, Tom thought, and when he turned to Wood and saw a tear roll down the old man's cheek, he knew he was right.

They left that gaunt little girl lying there, for she was beyond saving, had been here far too long.

Jayden screamed again, this time from their right. Tom altered their course and began to ascend a mountain made of smooth red rocks which were hot beneath their feet. Wood struggled initially, but Marcus was once again behind him, forcing him up the incline using his shoulders, his legs, his entire body. No one was getting left behind here. No one.

It was at the top of the mountain they found Ryan Fielding, his black-and-white stripy tee-shirt stained with muck and blood. When Tom saw him, nailed to an upside-down cross like some sort of inverted Jesus, he dropped to his knees as sobs wracked his entire body. Luke had turned away, perhaps afraid that this was one more thing that would return to haunt him in his dreams.

Though Ryan was dead, had been dead for many years judging by the state of decomposition, in this place his soul remained, trapped, lost.

Marcus placed a hand on Tom's shoulder and Tom climbed to his feet. Gravity was different here; it took a lot of effort for Tom to stand, and even then he felt too heavy, as if he was being pulled down, held to this infernal terrain too firmly. It was as if the land feared they would escape and was doing everything it could to keep them here.

"*Foolsss!*" came the sibilant cry which had taunted them for most of their lives. Tom turned, saw the black shape rising over the edge of the red mountain. Thick dark shoots danced around the hovering creature like so many snakes. And up and up it went, its blood-red eyes regarding each of them individually as if it were trying to decide which order to finish them off in. "*My world,*" Ghuul said. "*You ssshouldn't be here!*"

Ah, rules, rules, rules, Tom thought. Even ancient Babylonian demons liked things ship-shape and above board, it seemed.

For a moment, Tom forgot that he was voiceless. *Where the fuck is Jayden Lebbon?* It was only when he spoke and nothing came out that he remembered.

"*The boy,*" hissed Ghuul, "*isss prepared to die for me. Are you?*"

So the fucker could hear Tom's voice, even if they could not. "You can't have him!" Tom yelled as loudly as he could. "You can't have anyone!"

Ghuul drifted down to the rocks, trailing its smoky tendrils over them. Its eyes never left Tom. "*You ssshould know by now,*" it said, "*that I am forever. I am forever becaussse they sssummon me. Before the Ice Cream Man there were othersss. Hundredsss of othersss, and there will be more.*" Its sudden lunge for Tom caught him off guard. The creature had him by the throat, was lifting him up from the rocks. If it wanted to, Tom thought, it could squeeze and kill me right now.

Then why didn't it?

Below, Marcus and Luke were silently shouting. Tom looked down and saw them, and he couldn't help feeling that this was the last time he would *ever* see them. Wood was not protesting like his friends were; the ex-copper was fumbling about beneath his wheelchair.

"*I will exissst for asssss long asss your world does. Perhapsss longer.*"

Tom could barely breathe, and yet he could taste Ghuul's putrid stink. Go to Hell! He thought, and Ghuul must have heard him, for it answered.

"*Hell? Hell isss for the cursssed. I am not cursssed, Tom*

Craven. I merely am." Then, it glanced down at the three men still with their feet firmly on the ground. One of them—Wood—was calling up to it, was holding something in his hand. Tom couldn't hear what Wood was saying, but Ghuul certainly could. It began to descend, interested, it seemed, in the object Wood now held aloft.

What the hell are you doing, Wood? Tom thought. *It's going to kill you! It's going to kill us all!*

Then Tom was falling, and from a great height, too. As he impacted the earth, his legs buckled beneath him like strands of uncooked spaghetti. A sharp pain rushed all the way up from the base of his spine to the top of his neck, and he thought, just for a moment, that he would be paralysed, that it was better to die here now, because the thought of spending the rest of his life in a wheelchair, just like Wood, was too much to take.

But he wasn't paralysed. He was hurt, but he could move, and when he rolled onto his knees, he saw Ghuul standing in front of Wood holding the object Wood had just been waving around.

"*Isss thisss sssupposssed to make me sssad?*" said Ghuul. "*A picture of a child?*"

Tom stood. *You wily old dog*, he thought. Wood had taken the picture from Burke Street, the one featuring an unsmiling Isobel White. How long had he had that on his person? Had that been his plan all along? To present the framed photograph to Ghuul and hope that, deep within it, Frederick White reacted?

"*You sssentimental humaaansss,*" Ghuul said, staring down at the picture, a little girl frozen in time. "*Sssooo predictable with...*"

With?

The smoky figure's tendrils began to writhe, licking at the air like jet-black flames. Something was happening. Tom moved around to where Luke and Marcus stood watching, terror etched across both of their faces.

"*Sssssssgggghhhh...*" Ghuul tried to look away from the picture, but something was pulling it back.

Frederick White?

Wood screamed something toward the frantic creature, and

the creature responded with a savage roar, but Wood did not look frightened. Wood looked angry. Wood looked as if he might suddenly get up from the wheelchair which he had lived in for the past few years and punch the demon right in the kisser. Wood screamed again, and now the creature rose up into the air, its talons reaching down to the rocks but not quite making it. There was a rumble off in the distance; this realm's equivalent of thunder, Tom thought. And then Ghuul howled as a white slice appeared down its front.

A bright light shot out of the creature's torn abdomen; the slice widened as more and more light spilled out into the realm, and still it held onto the photograph, the object which seemed to be causing it all this pain, suffering, damage.

Tom shielded his eyes, and his friends did the same. At the centre of the light, the shadow-demon, Ghuul, screamed and writhed. Parts of it fell away, dissipated—or eaten by the light?

Then there was an almighty blast, followed by a shockwave strong enough to knock them off their feet. When Tom opened his eyes, he saw, sitting there on the boiling-hot rocks, a man. Just a man. A man sobbing and staring down at the face of his daughter.

Frederick White.

The Ice Cream Man.

"I never wanted this," he said, running a hand over the now-cracked glass of the picture frame. "It took over. I never wanted any of this."

He was already aging, visibly changing before them. His eyes bagged, his jowls sagged, and his mouth puckered until it was barely visible. Tom felt something like pity for the man, but it didn't last.

And neither did Frederick White.

The Ice Cream Man's bones began to appear through his parchment skin, which yellowed with jaundice as his eyes clouded over with cataracts. No longer able to support his rapidly decreasing form, Frederick White fell back like a marionette whose strings had been cut. His skull cracked, though nothing but dust spilled out. His hair curled, fell out, blew away with the hot wind.

In the distance, another rumble of netherworld thunder.

Frederick White became dust, and then he too was gone, carried off to forever circulate this world. Only the photograph remained.

Tom couldn't be sure, but Isobel White seemed to be smiling now. Just a little. Perhaps not.

More thunder. Everything was dark again, and that was when the ground beneath their feet began to shake.

The end of this world, Tom thought. *And we're going to be stuck here when it goes.*

Tom rushed across to Wood and grabbed onto the wheelchair handles. Marcus and Luke began to clamber down the small mountain, being careful not to slip on the dusty red rocks. Another tremor sent rubble cascading down. Tom traversed the mountain as best he could without getting himself or Wood killed. Ten minutes later, breathless and aching, they reached the base.

Thunder.

A scream.

Tom snapped his head across and saw Jayden Lebbon tied to a tree. No, not tied. The tree was holding him in place with its many arms. Ghuul had brought the child here to the mountain, then left him at its base while it did battle.

Go! Tom shoved the wheelchair over to Marcus, and after a slight pause, Marcus understood what Tom wanted from him. *Head for the portal. Don't look back.*

Already running toward his bound nephew, Tom struggled to remain on his feet. The ground beneath was crumbling away; the sky above tearing in half. They were running out of time. The realm was going to collapse, whether they were in it or not.

When Jayden Lebbon saw Tom approaching, he frowned, mouthed *Uncle Tom?* Of course it was strange; not too long ago, the poor kid had been miles away, enjoying Halloween with his mother and Aunty Danielle. And now he was here, in some fucked up place, with his uncle.

Without pause, Tom began to peel the fingers
(talons)
away from Jayden's shoulders, arms, legs. Every time he

managed to unhook one, another latched onto the boy somewhere else. Tom cursed, grabbed onto Jayden's hands and placed a foot against the base of the flesh-tree. He pushed as hard as he could with his foot and pulled as hard as he could with his hands. Jayden's mouth fell wide open in a silent scream of pain, but Tom didn't stop.

He had to get the boy free, or they would die here in the netherworld.

The hand fronds began to snap off. Claws tore for purchase on the boy, but Jayden was moving away from the tree, momentum carrying him forward into Tom's arms.

No sooner had the final hand broken off than Tom was pulling Jayden away from the tree, leaping over crumbling red rocks and rushing for the starry portal. Overhead, all Hell was breaking loose. The sky was falling in on itself; Tom didn't know which would come first, the destruction of the earth or the scorching of the sky. He just knew he didn't want to be there when either happened.

Huge rocks began to roll down the red mountain as it came apart. Tom dragged Jayden away and out of the basin, lest they get trapped there, or worse, crushed to death by boulders which might not exist in a few minutes' time.

Tom could see the gateway and its myriad dancing stars, and relief washed over him. They were going to make it. They were going to make it.

We're going to make it.

Six feet from the vortex, with the whole world decomposing behind them, Tom leapt forwards and took Jayden with him.

Pop goes the weasel, Tom thought as a huge hot blast hit him in the back and shot him forwards into the gateway.

TWENTY-SEVEN

OCTOBER 31ST, 2016
HAVERING, LONDON

"Tom? Tom, are you okay?"

Tom opened his eyes and bolted upright. It took a few moments for him to realise where he was—sitting in the middle of a frosty street and surrounded by people, some he knew, others he didn't—and it took another moment still before he realised that he was naked from the waist up. "Wha... where's my coat? My tee-shirt?"

"It was on fire," Luke said as he helped Tom to his feet. "We had to get it off you. You were going to go up in flames."

Tom turned around. Over beside the overturned 4x4, Jayden Lebbon was being comforted by Karen Davis. He looked in good shape, considering what he'd just been through. His own jacket had been removed, but at least someone had had the decency to throw a sheet over the boy, who was shivering from the cold, or shock, or both.

There was a deafening squeal which seemed to come from everywhere all at once. Tom spun just in time to see the ice cream truck begin to fold in on itself. Metal twisted, rubber melted, wires fizzed and cut out as the truck slowly self-destructed.

"What's happening to it?" Marcus said, wheeling Wood forwards so that they were all in a line. Luke, Tom, Marcus, and Wood.

"It's going," Tom said. "It doesn't belong here."

White orbs drifted up from the concertinaing vehicle, slowly at first and then much quicker. Tom knew what they were, but he waited for Wood to confirm it.

"Souls," Wood said, lighting a cigarette and exhaling a plume of smoke into the night.

"I'll be fucking damned," Marcus said, watching the orbs as

they flew into the sky.

Ryan, Rochelle, Cheryl, Harvey, all freed from that Purgatory. Tom had already forgotten what Ryan had looked like in that place. Something about an upside-down cross?

The truck was almost gone by now, no bigger than a football, and still it whittled away to nothing, rattling around on the ground like a child's tin robot. The whole thing had taken less than a minute. Tom was suddenly aware of the approaching sirens.

"Karen," Luke said to his wife. "Take the boy inside. Get him something to eat, a glass of water. Introduce him to Lydia."

Karen looked as if she might protest, but then Tom said, "Please, Karen," and she sighed, pulled Jayden toward the house. The onlookers, many of them neighbours of Luke's mother, began to head back to their respective houses. No one was going to believe them, that they had just witnessed the death of an ice cream truck, that four men—one in a wheelchair— and a young boy had come through its doors a moment before it imploded, spat out onto the street like flavourless chewing gum.

"What are we going to tell the police?" Luke said. He sounded tired.

Wood began to wheel himself toward the overturned 4x4. "We tell them we had a bit of an accident," he said. "It's frosty as shit out here, and Tom here lost control of the wheel, hit the kerb, and over we went. Coulda happened to anyone."

It was believable, Tom thought. Far more believable than the truth. "I'll take one for the team," he said. "Leave it to me; I'll talk to the cops."

No one argued with that.

A young group of Trick or Treaters came dancing along the street, trying to scare one another and laughing maniacally, a result of too much sugar. A witch, a Batman, two vampires and a clown, and when they saw the capsized Range Rover they gasped in horror.

"Are you all okay?" the clown asked. "Had an accident?"

It was a stupid question, but kids will be kids. Tom smiled. Flashing blue lights appeared at the end of the street, drove slowly toward the wreck and the men standing around it.

"We're fine, kid," Tom said to the clown. "Happy Halloween."

"Happy Halloween," the kids said in unison before skipping away, their treat buckets swinging from their hands.

As the police approached, Marcus said, "This is going to be a long ass night."

Yeah, Tom thought. *Yeah it is.*

THE END

1ST JULY 2016 – 2ND SEPTEMBER 2016

ABOUT THE AUTHOR

Adam Millard is the author of twenty-two novels, thirteen novellas, and more than two hundred short stories, which can be found in various collections and anthologies. Probably best known for his post-apocalyptic fiction, Adam also writes fantasy/horror for children and Bizarro fiction for several publishers, who enjoy his tales of flesh-eating clown-beetles and rabies-infected derrieres so much that they keep printing them. His "Dead" series has recently been the filling in a Stephen King/Bram Stoker sandwich on Amazon's bestsellers chart. Adam is a regular columnist for UK horror website, *This Is Horror*.

ALSO FROM
BLOODSHOT BOOKS

THE SPECIMEN (THE RIDERS SAGA #1)

From a crater lake on an island off the coast of Bronze Age Estonia...

To a crippled Viking warrior's conquest of England ...

To the bloody temple of an Aztec god of death and resurrection...

Their presence has shaped our world. They are the Riders.

One month ago, an urban explorer was drawn to an abandoned asylum in the mountains of northern Massachusetts. There he discovered a large specimen jar, containing something organic, unnatural and possibly alive.

Now, he and a group of unsuspecting individuals have discovered one of history's most horrific secrets. Whether they want to or not, they are caught in the middle of a millennia-old war and the latest battle is about to begin.

Available in paperback or Kindle on Amazon.com
http://amzn.to/1peMAjz

WELCOME TO THE BLACK
MOUNTAIN CAMP FOR BOYS!

Summer,1989. It is a time for splashing in the lake and exploring the wilderness, for nine teenagers to bond together and create friendships that could last the rest of their lives.

But among this group there is a young man with a secret-a secret that, in this time and place, is unthinkable to his peers.

When the others discover the truth, it will change each of them forever. They will all have blood on their hands.

ODD MAN OUT is a heart-wrenching tale of bullies and bigotry, a story that explores what happens when good people don't stand up for what's right. It is a tale of how far we have come . . . and how far we still have left to go.

Available in paperback or Kindle on Amazon.com

http://bit.ly/OddManKindle

I KNOW WHAT YOU HAVE HEARD ABOUT ME

You say that I am a madman. You say that I am dangerous. You say that I am the one who has been abducting women, slaughtering them, and burying their corpses all around this city for years. You are wrong, because only part of that statement is true...

I AM NOT A KILLER

I know that you probably won't believe me. Not now. Not after all that has happened, but I need to tell my side of the story. You need to know how this all began. You need to hear about the birds, but most of all, you need to understand...

I AM NOT THE BOULEVARD MONSTER

Available in paperback or Kindle on Amazon.com

http://bit.ly/B0ulevard

A TERRIFYING HAUNTING

This is the place where the harrowed ghosts of a dozen generations whisper in the shadows of their ancestral home, where one family's dreams of a new beginning turned into a nightmare that ended in tragedy.

A CURSED BLOODLINE

This is the place where a line of witches bound themselves—in blood—to a primeval entity. Here, nightmare and reality meet beneath frozen skies, and even time and space fall under the power of the demonic being that rules this remote northern wood.

A CHANCE ENCOUNTER

This is the place where the path of a tormented survivor meets that of an unknowing innocent. Past and present collide, and secrets long buried crawl back into the pallid light of day as the shadow of the Beast falls over them both. But even the bloodiest dreams of that demonic being may pale in comparison to what lies buried within the human heart.

This is the place where evil dwells... **ABODE**

Available in paperback or Kindle on Amazon.com

http://bit.ly/Ab0de

ON THE HORIZON FROM
BLOODSHOT BOOKS
2019-20*

Dead Sea Chronicles – Tim Curran

The Hag Witch of Tripp Creek – Somer Canon

Behemoth – H.P. Newquist

Dead in the U.S.A. – David Price

Somewhere South of Midnight – Stephen Laws

Blood Mother: A Novel of Terror – Pete Kahle

Not Your Average Monster – World Tour

The Abomination (The Riders Saga #2) – Pete Kahle

The Horsemen (The Riders Saga #3) – Pete Kahle

* other titles to be added when confirmed

BLOODSHOT BOOKS

READ UNTIL YOU BLEED